D0438594

KRISTINE NAESS

Only Human

Translated from the Norwegian by Seán Kinsella

Harvill *Secker*
LONDON

1 3 5 7 9 10 8 6 4 2

Harvill Secker, an imprint of Vintage,
20 Vauxhall Bridge Road,
London SW1V 2SA

Harvill Secker is part of the Penguin Random House group of companies
whose addresses can be found at global.penguinrandomhouse.com

First published by Harvill Secker in 2017
First published with the title *Bare et menneske* in Norway by Forlaget Oktober in 2014

A CIP catalogue record for this book is available from the British Library

penguin.co.uk/vintage

ISBN 9781910701805

This book was published with the financial assistance of NORLA

Typset in 10.6/16 pt Charter ITC Std by Jouve (UK), Milton Keynes
Printed and bound in Great Britain by Clays Ltd, St Ives PLC

Only Human

I

I switch on the TV, listening to it as I walk out onto the veranda and down the stone steps into the garden. The press conference is being shown. Hearing the noises from it through the open window seems to divide everything into two streams of sound: one fast flowing, choppy with bright light, belonging to the TV, and the other. Out here. Which is slow-moving, ponderous and indefinable. Midges and mosquitoes buzz about my face, my shoes sink a little in the moss that has supplanted the grass in the more shaded areas around the house. On the news they are saying there have not been any new developments. I step into the sunshine to feel the warmth. Rainwater from last night's showers has accumulated along the folds of the tarpaulin protecting the firewood. It might get wet. Every time it rains I think about covering the woodpile with strips of corrugated iron instead. But I never get around to it.

A white plastic chair stands at the gable wall of the house. There is green mould spreading up the legs, and two of them have sunk into the soft earth, leaving me slightly lopsided when I sit, but the chair has to stand in this spot, precisely where the sunlight breaks through the foliage. The stool on which I usually place the radio is made from wood and has begun to rot because of its soaking up the damp. Small snails cling to it.

The plastic feels warm against my back as I sit down. I have my mug with me. In the mornings I fill it up with tea or coffee, in the evenings usually red wine. The peony, gooseberry bushes and plum tree are still doing well among the scrub and weeds. Strips of sunlight rest upon all the green, upon the bracken and the moss growing where previously there was a lawn. Now and again, a damp smell from the wall of the house hits me, possibly the foundations have absorbed moisture, that would explain the musty odour in the cellar. I am sensitive to smells. When down in the cellar you can see the sunlight through the spiderweb over the window, dead flies, the four legs of the chair outside, white, flaked plastic.

They were in the garden just before six this morning. I was not afraid.

No, I was not afraid, and maybe that was a bad sign, I thought and rolled onto my back to hear better, I have become listless, irresolute, could not care less about things. That was the customary accompanying self-analysis, I would usually admonish myself for that too, even at the same time as I was indulging in it, filled with self-contempt. This inner nagging, always there. At the same time I listened to what was going on outside, tried to identify the noises. Could it be animals? A badger or cat, perhaps the roe deer I sometimes saw making their way through the garden early in the morning. But the rustling of the tarpaulins covering Dad's junk seemed too purposeful, and it could only have been footsteps I heard going across the grass. When the sound of men's voices reached me, I got up and opened the window. The casement stay struck the window ledge as I was fitting the hole over the peg. A man wearing an orange reflective vest came out from behind the garage and said something to another man standing in the yard. They both looked up at the window. The logo of the Red Cross was visible on their vests.

We're searching for someone.

The one who spoke was about my age, with short hair, greying at the temples, and glasses, an academic sort I thought, but evidently an out-of-doors type too. He was tall and well built, healthy, agile-looking. I felt something stir in my chest, before remembering how it was too late for that, men, sex, all that stuff. I had spent my sexual prime on individuals with serious faults and shortcomings. Individuals with low self-esteem, not unlike myself, as I was only too well aware.

The men neither smiled nor apologised for the intrusion into my garden. They knew what they were doing, and how it took precedence over other considerations. It was all to do with dignity and respect. They had undertaken an important duty to society. They were searching for a person. I did not dare to ask whom, did not want to appear nosy. Sensation-seeking. I was above that kind of thing. I missed out on a lot because of it, had done my whole life.

I withdrew from the window, made my way downstairs and went online. Sure enough, the newspapers already carried stories of a missing person. A twelve-year-old girl had disappeared from her home in Slemdal in Oslo.

The photograph must have been taken in the early hours, at daybreak. The tarmac was wet, the leaves on the trees still dark, the street lamps glowing orange. It was on this road, they believed, that she had been walking at two o'clock the previous afternoon, and since then nobody had seen her. I recognised it immediately as Skådalsveien, and suddenly felt my body drain, my thoughts grasping at the words on the screen. Like believing yourself hidden, only to be seen, incredulous, the blanket being torn away. I was panic-stricken, and the anxiety took its usual form, a chaos of black and white dots in my vision. Alertness.

Skådalsveien branches off from Gulleråsveien, continues uphill, past my house and straight on to the lower side of Vettakollen railway station, where it intersects Skogryggveien, before swinging uphill to Skådalen station. On the far side of the railway tracks, a little way up the slope, a forest path leads off to the left, past Mindedammen pond, and carries on into Nordmarka, the huge forested region north of Oslo, while Vettaliveien continues towards the top. This is where the Montessori school is situated. On the other side of the school playground, Huldreveien runs down to Vettakollen station and Skogryggveien. Skådalsveien joins this road again a little further down and the ring is closed, unless you walk up the steep slope between the blocks of flats behind the station and end up in the woods.

So that was where she had taken her dog for a walk. On the residential streets, close to the woods the whole time, and my heart pounded, because it could not have been anyone else but Emilie, the Emilie I knew, Emilie with the poodle, my Emilie. Yes, my heart pounded madly, the blood beating in my chest, throbbing at my temples and by my collarbone, it was fear that could easily be mistaken for anticipation. This was happening, finally something was happening.

A child. I should have guessed. Their faces would not

have borne those expressions had it been a senile escapee from the nursing home, because old people run away, it is not uncommon, they stumble and fall in confusion, end up out at night, exposed to the elements, freeze to death.

The rescue services had not searched gardens when Agnieszka Andresen was killed the summer before last, nor did they use helicopters. Now two of them hung high above the rooftops. Perhaps they never got as far as organising a search from the air, seeing how a rambler came across Agnieszka's dead body less than twenty-four hours after she was reported missing. Up by Mindedammen pond, in the thicket. It was a warm, quiet summer afternoon, midges swarmed in the sunlight, the forest smelled of pine and evergreen needles.

She had been beaten with both blunt and sharp objects. Perhaps with rocks, a club or cudgel, and something resembling a pickaxe. The newspapers and online media published drawings of possible murder weapons, and I was not the only one to associate these with the medieval, due no doubt to these illustrations, which left you with the sense that we were dealing with something from a different era. A monk made an appearance on TV, talking about how he could not go out in his cowl any longer. He had, of course, always attracted attention when wearing it, he said, but this was different. Children were terrified, and grown men ran after him in the street, demanding to know both his name and his details. He had been interviewed by the police and they had searched his flat and storage space in the cellar of his building. Everyone who knew him described it as absolutely ridiculous. Two tabloids, *Dagbladet* and *VG*, featured lengthy interviews with his brothers from the monastery, his family and his friends, many of whom were well known. In the comments sections beneath articles and in editorials there was debate about how the enormous media focus on the case had given rise to a certain level of hysteria and whether or not this was healthy. Jesus, this was the way things had become. All the talk and talk and talk made me feel as though my head would explode, and yet I followed the story closely, gorged myself upon it, but in an almost absent-minded way, with indifference, yes, that was the way I had become. The newspapers piled up on the table, the TV had been on, the radio too, as well as the PC.

I listened to an in-depth interview with the monk on the radio. The journalist asked what made a young man choose an existence behind monastery walls, rejecting the chance of a family, children and an ordinary love life.

Love is not ordinary, he had replied, not enough.

I did not know whether he meant there was not enough of it, or if love was not enough, as in a person's life, and if that was the case, I thought, not enough for what or for whom? Because what is greater than love, what could be? Something extra, something that unfolds, and then unfolds anew, and so on, a blossom within a blossom?

You could say, he said, that I have turned away from loving one in order to love everybody. I have such great yearning. So I seek expansion, constant expansion.

I can remember being frightened of men in coats when I was little, at least when it was dark outside and I had to pass one on my way home, in the autumn gloom or on winter evenings. He might open his coat and trap me. He might be naked underneath, with a huge willy sticking right out.

When I was around eight years old, a flasher used to turn up on the streets from time to time, he would open his coat and expose himself, or at least that is what I remember. I also recalled an aunt, laughing, opening her coat and jumping out in front of me in the living room and saying boo. Perhaps there was no flasher, just a prank. Or perhaps I remembered both a flasher and a prank? It can be hard to know the difference. If what you think you see is what you actually see. I was even more scared if a man had both his hands in his coat pockets, or walked slowly. If I could see he had his hands in front of him, in the pockets, over his crotch. When I thought about it, I was sure that on several occasions I had seen men on the road touching themselves under their coats. I did not believe it, but even so it happened. They touched themselves while looking into my eyes and walked slowly past. Why did they do that?

No one knows exactly what happened to Agnieszka Andresen, the police would not go public with all the details and neither the perpetrator nor the murder weapons were found. Agnieszka was fifty-two years old when she was killed, living on benefits and a moderate alcoholic, but described as kind and unassuming. She had no husband, but she had a dog, as well as a crowd she hung out with, they would meet at a bar in Kampen.

Middle-aged old bag, was my first thought, and I found myself filled with contempt, something flabby and ageing that had a knife put to its throat and was suddenly thrashing about, full of life.

Where did that disdain come from? Because it often came, an abhorrence of people I did not know, a furious urge to destroy, to crush and obliterate. Or I might hear the most terrible stories without feeling anything at all. A person was killed, raped, blown up – you don't say. Then I would just think about something else. About the weather. About myself. My children. Cold. Selective.

But when they found Agnieszka Andresen's dog, all those callous thoughts of mine melted away. It had been strung up in a tree. A black, flat-coated retriever. Its stomach had been slashed open, and it was hanging helplessly from its hind legs; stretched out like that it was as long as a person. That made me cry, and made the police revise their theory of the murder being an alcohol-related incident.

I had stood at the window watching the police cars that time too. They drove back and forth on the road outside. An ambulance arrived, but without sirens. I turned on the TV, sat up all night following the story. They showed footage of the crime scene, the walking trail, the neighbourhood I had never really settled into. Was angry with. All those unfriendly, rich cows who lived around, in their perfect make-up. I had caught a glimpse of my own house on the screen. The residents were outside on the street talking to one another. Some of them had given interviews on camera, and they kept showing them on a loop, the same clips over and over again of the neighbours' nosy faces. Horrible to think it happened so close by, they said, and we could not understand what she was doing up at Mindedammen pond. Why would she take her dog for a walk up around here when she lived on the other side of town? Those who knew her said she never went far from home. Mostly down to the bar in Kampen, but she did not take the dog with her then. She walked it close to the block of flats where she lived, or took it for longer walks in the woods, from Steinbruvannet lake and further into Østmarka, the forested area east of the city. So how could she have known about the trail in Skådalen? She was not even Norwegian. Polish, married to a Norwegian, then divorced. Agnieszka did not like dogs at all, her weeping mother in Warsaw had revealed. An entire TV crew had made the trip there to talk to her: 'It was *his* dog, Olaf's dog.' Olaf was the husband. He knew nothing about it, he said on the phone from Spain, while the TV displayed a blurry photograph of a plump man playing golf in the sunshine. It's just awful, he said. And the dog, here he was on the verge of tears, Agnieszka loved that dog, he had not had the heart to take it with him when they divorced. He had given it to her, he said. She had taken it in, the mother said, because Olaf 'wanted to kill it'. Agnieszka was dutiful and kind, she said, 'of course she was not drinking'. I wouldn't have said she drank more than anyone else drinks, said Olaf, she didn't drink any more than him in any case, it was rather, look, he met someone else, you know. A bit more perky.

They did not find the killer. I thought about that now, while the search parties walked through the woods towards the forest lakes of Bånntjern and Sognsvann, went over gardens, outhouses and paths in the neighbourhood with a fine-tooth comb. Maybe he has been here all the time, I thought, maybe he lives nearby, has a face I know or a gait I recognise because I usually see him at the shop, on the train or on the road.

Yes, it might be down to pure chance, because sometimes you are lucky and other times not. If you cannot be with the one you love, then love the one you are with, all food is good food, and so on.

Maybe things were looking up for Agnieszka at the time, and she was thinking about doing something with her life, trying new things. At any rate, she had begun going to the library to read the newspapers every morning, and that, her best friend had said, was something new. Maybe it had been a sunny day and she had been dazzled by the light on the newspaper spread out on the table in front of her. As she lifted her head and looked around for a chair in the shade, she caught sight of the librarian filling up the nearest display shelf with newspapers and brochures. The sunlight shone on the librarian's bronze-coloured hair, it was so beautiful. Agnieszka felt the impulse to take a look through the adult-education catalogue she saw in the librarian's hand. Maybe she could enrol for something, she thought, a sewing course, for instance, she'd had that in the back of her mind for a long time, to learn how to make her own clothes. Sometimes at night she would dream about patterns and colour combinations, in fabrics she had never seen the like of in real life, they would hang in an open window, diaphanous in the sunlight. In the dream, she only had to run her fingers over them, and they turned into outfits and dresses, garments she had never imagined could exist, and the body they adorned was her own, Agnieszka's own face, *ethereal*, she dreamt.

Is it free? she asked, pointing at the catalogue, yes, nodded the librarian, everything here is free. Agnieszka got up and stood by the display shelf, feeling the warmth of the sun on her back as she browsed through what lay there. Between the local newspaper and a stack of events calendars lay maps of hiking routes and walking trails, and Agnieszka picked out a map for each part of Oslomarka, the forested and hilly areas surrounding the city: south, east, north and west. On the way home, she felt buoyed, her thoughts flowed freely and she hit upon the idea of familiarising herself with new places, of taking the dog for a walk in areas she had never been, she was looking forward to it already.

Maybe that was how it was. When the police released information about the investigation it emerged that they had found several such maps open on her kitchen table, and it was as though she had made a packed lunch before leaving: there was a roll of greaseproof paper on the worktop, a bottle of squash out, as well as crumbs on the breadboard.

This, I thought, or similar circumstances, must have been the reason she wound up on the Skådalsløypa trail, on a warm, summer afternoon, the kind of day that drives lonely, disturbed people onto the streets, out of hot, stuffy, dusty rooms where the pressure is only increasing and who knows what is building up. Is it frustrated desire, despair, anger, sorrow, just a mush of emotions without a name, which your mind does not have room for, and is released at some given moment? An explosion of white that could perhaps be called hate, or aggression, or nothing, it is nothing, a cacophony of atoms, snow.

I pictured how he might have looked that day on the trail, wearing a baseball cap, dressed in a green army jacket and carrying a rucksack. Inside it, his home-made weapons, both blunt and sharp, in case the opportunity should arise. Perhaps he had not so much thought in words, as been led by emotions, by the fantasy of striking out, of using all his strength, of injuring, killing someone, these were the types of images he had in his head, bloody, crunching, filled with screams, but he did not so much think about it as picture it, just felt he should take the weapons, *on the off chance*. Take them with him, along with the bottles of beer and the shiny hipflask. Then he sat there, partially hidden by some bushes, on dry, warm pine needles, and drank, while looking at the dark pond. The trees blocked the sunlight, but now and again the brownish-black water captured a ray of light, making visible the insects hovering above the surface of the water.

When the sun was going down, and the air was getting chilly, he began making his way home, but the alcohol had unsettled his mind, his eyes kept playing tricks on him. He thought he saw people and animals where there were only trunks, and stumps, of trees and large stones. The wind caused the branches to move, he turned to look and trod off the trail, a twig struck him across the face, it stung, making him angry, and just then a black dog appeared. Agnieszka followed close behind, giving a start and coming to a sudden halt as a man stepped out in front of her, short of breath with a dark look in his eyes, but by then it was too late to run.

I would have been the one more likely to encounter him, after all, I usually took walks along Skådalsløypa. But not Emilie, she was barely ten years old at that time and had yet to get a dog. Whereas now she was out all the time, walking that little poodle. I thought she kept to the road but maybe not, maybe she had gone into the woods, had the misfortune to run into him on the way to Bånntjern lake or up towards the summit at Vettakolltoppen. Or had he picked Emilie out long ago, eyed her as she passed him on the road, stood outside her school taking note of what time she finished on which day, watched her walk home with her friends after the last class, tailing them? Did he know when she was in the house on her own? Did he hang back, waiting for her to come out with the dog on a lead, yes, could it have been that guy maybe, that bloody stalker type, was he the one who had grabbed her somewhere in the woods? The guy with the red baseball cap. He was the one I was picturing. Not so strange, his albino-like appearance made him stand out. His eyes were light blue, eyebrows almost white, his hair too, but it was usually shaved, only stubble and pimples on the back of his neck visible below the edge of his hat. I guessed he was about my age, or a little younger, in his mid-forties. He usually looked over my garden fence when passing, walking slowly by with heavy steps. Must be a psychiatric patient, I thought, on medication, that would explain the plodding, and the bloated, puffy face. All the same, he looked fit and seemed alert to some extent. You could see he had strong thigh and calf muscles beneath his clothes, and his jacket sat tightly around his upper arms. Initially, I was nervous every time I saw him, did not like that aggressive stare, but after a while I got used to it. He could hardly be dangerous, could he, if he was free to walk around, in full view, and nobody seemed overly concerned?

He had a dog for a while, a Rottweiler. I do not remember exactly when he stopped turning up with it, but it was not long after we moved in, after Balder died. Georg was fourteen and Tuva had just turned nineteen. They sat on the floor together at the vet's, both heartbroken, Balder, feeble, lying over their legs. His kidneys had failed, there was nothing that could be done, the vet said. Balder snuggled his muzzle under the sleeve of Tuva's jacket, was unable to stir, but beat his tail a couple of times upon hearing his name. The vet crouched down beside us. He's had a long life, he said, there's not many people have their dog for fifteen years. We watched as he inserted the cannula into one of the front paws and opened it to allow the flow. Clear fluid ran through the tube and into Balder's circulatory system, his body quickly grew heavier, then he twitched a few times and a little of the fluid ran from his nostrils. He's gone now, the vet said. Georg buried his face into the curly, poodle hair and sobbed, Tuva got to her knees and stroked the dog's head frantically, called his name, shouted it, but his eyes did not see, his tail did not wag, Balder was gone and Tuva howled. I took off the dog collar for the last time, sniffed it, smelled the scent of Balder and hoped I had red wine at home. As we walked across the square in front of the School of Veterinary Science, I became aware of a strong feeling of nausea at the sight of the empty collar in my hand. Was it really necessary for me to take it home? The kids were furious when I tried to put both the lead and the collar into a green plastic bin mounted on a post, and Tuva said that if I didn't get a boyfriend soon then I would end up completely emotionally stunted, yeah, if I wasn't already, that is.

The man in the baseball cap often passed by my gate, up to several times a day on occasion. Back when he had the Rottweiler it did not seem so odd, he is just walking his dog, I thought, and has his fixed routes. Still, it was a bit strange, him stopping right outside and staring at the house, it made me uneasy. The dog would sniff and then pee, not on the gatepost, but on the gate itself. It was also peculiar how he let the dog defecate, making no attempt to hide it. Once I was even out in the garden when it happened. The dog squatted down and released the contents of its stomach exactly where the gate would swing out as I opened it, but the man showed no sign of removing it. Why I did not say anything, I do not know, instead I hurried into the house. My heart was pounding and I kept a good bit back from the kitchen window so he would not see I was watching him. When he left, I took a plastic bag, walked out, climbed over the fence, put my hand in the bag and picked up the poo, turned the bag inside out, tied it and threw it in the rubbish bin. I was afraid. I do not remember what I was thinking, how I explained the incident to myself, but I know what I saw, I mean, when I think about it now it is blindingly obvious that I reacted the way a dog would upon encountering an aggressive member of their species. They register the creeping gait and the rigid tail from a good distance off, hear the low growling, turn their head away to placate the other, and walk in an arc around it. The man, not the dog, was the aggressive one in this case. I wonder what happened to that dog. It used to wag its bobtail affectionately and stick its thick snout in between the bars of the gate if I was in the garden. I pretended not to see it and never went over to them. It was due to that hostile, barefaced gawping, I cannot stand people staring like that, getting too close and never letting up. This generally took place in the shop. He would suddenly be standing there, in his baseball cap and tracksuit bottoms, either grey ones or a pair of black ones with stripes down the sides, carrying a shopping basket full of bottles of beer.

Still, it did not necessarily mean he was dangerous. Granted, he was not a pleasant sight, but you get used to unpleasantness too. Besides, he was not the only one. There was local authority housing in the area, in Slemdal, and a number of people living there could behave in an alarming manner. The woman with the wheelie bag and the sunglasses, for example. She was also in the habit of staring. To be fair, I could not see her eyes behind the black sunglasses she wore, but she would stop in front of me and stand mumbling continuously in my direction, disjointed half-sentences. Although the words were recognisable, and obscene, you cunt, you cunt, she could suddenly exclaim. I wondered if there was something wrong with me, my body language, my eyes, if she read something in them that gave her cause to despise me, to allow herself to say whatever it might be. Oh, but I was used to it. Not just around here, not just those two, but constantly, especially in town, always someone getting in my face, begging, being brazen, angry. I wanted to vomit when I caught the odour of filth, piss and unwashed bodies, I hated it and thought what is it with me, what *is* it, why do I attract all the borderline cases, the decrepit, the dotty or half mad? Or did I have no more of a magnetic attraction to them than other people did, and the crazy treated us all the same, as frightened idiots?

The helicopters hung above us until dusk. I turned off the TV at midnight and lay down on the sofa to sleep. The forest at night. Face down in the heather.

2

OSLO, THE FIFTH OF JUNE 1939. She is writing to him. In the account book. The columns of numbers abruptly broken by furious handwriting. Confounded heat! The claw-foot table stands in the centre of the dining room. There she sits. Around her the heavy furniture, the sunshine. Outside, the veranda, then the garden, the birch trees, and the tall pine trees that screen the neighbours' house. The boy is on the lawn. It is nice not to have him indoors. He stands facing the copse. She writes: *You must understand! My nerves cannot take this strain!* The boy starts making his way into the trees, probably going over to the Heyerdahls' to play. But Mrs Esther Heyerdahl and her friends, they are not her cup of tea. When she has been over there, they speak to her as though she is slow on the uptake. They do not think she knows anything, whether it be about politics or modern child-rearing, she can sense it, in the air. Just because Esther has an education in mental hygiene she thinks she is above everyone, but no education in the world helps if you are foolish. And no matter if she is a psychologist or not, Esther is foolish. She and Alice agree completely on that.

Thank God for Alice, she would never have managed without her. You're my only friend, she often says, you must never leave me. Nonsense, Cessi, Alice says, laughing, you know plenty of people. Yes, but none of them are like you,

Cessi says, no, and they're certainly not like you either, she replies, after all, you're not exactly normal, and then they would both laugh. But Alice knows what she means. They are best friends, for life. Not so strange perhaps, since they have always known one another, the same way Mama has always known Alice's mother. Speaking of which, Mama could give Mrs Heyerdahl and those gossiping geese a good run for their money herself. There is nobody like Mama, and the boy adores her. But he stays away from his own mother. It is mean, he is mean. It is not her fault at any rate. The boy has a difficult nature. She is not able to cope. You're of a delicate disposition, Mama says, you can't help that.

It feels as though someone is watching her. A malicious eye upon every single wall in the house. In the sky outside. She is not good enough. But after all a child should not be allowed to scream so that they get their way. It makes her want to scream herself. She is livid, livid, out into the garden with him, bloody child. She writes to Hartvig: *You are simply too dreary to be a man, you are weak, it is unmanly. Why should I keep house for you? You are never at home. I hate you!*

Sunshine behind the curtains. The room is much too bright, she will not get back to sleep again. Hartvig is snoring. Lying on his back thinking no doubt he is well within his rights to do so. A quarter to six according to the alarm clock, but it is already far too hot. A heatwave, while she wants rain, it would better suit her frame of mind.

She cannot manage anything. She has to organise everything on her own. Even though it is Hartvig who will soon get up with the boy, she is the one who ought to do it, feels it is her responsibility. The burden of responsibility is on her shoulders, and she just does not have the energy. This big house. She does not even know if she likes Hartvig. He is so slow and boring. She hears Margit beginning to prepare breakfast down in the kitchen. The boy turns from side to side in his bed, soon to wake up. The sun disappears, the light in the room changes, now we are in shadow, she thinks, picturing a planet in outer space, and that from it she is able to look down at herself in bed, she feels a pull, grows dizzy and experiences a falling sensation even though she is lying flat out on the mattress. When she was a child she thought feeling dizzy was lovely, but now she finds it unpleasant.

The boy does not call out for her but for Hartvig. He takes a little time to react, first turning over on his side, breaking wind twice and sighing, before he throws the duvet aside. The smell of fart makes her queasy and she turns her back, cannot face talking to him.

We mustn't wake Mummy, she hears the boy say from the nursery, he prefers his father and she is only too pleased, for the moment at least, as she is so dreading getting up. Their voices grow weaker as they make their way to the bathroom and close the door behind them. A rushing sound in the pipes as the taps are turned on. Hartvig helping the boy wash. Then the door to the hall opens, and Hartvig calls out to Margit. Indolent Margit. She is the one who helps Finn get dressed. She hears them laughing and chatting in the nursery before going downstairs and all is quiet again. Very well, so she was cross with him again yesterday. But if he only understood how impossible he can be. Constantly doing things he is not supposed to, climbing up on the worktop, standing on it with his shoes on, pulling things out of drawers and cupboards, turning switches on and off, spilling water, and when he does not get his way, he howls. Very well, so she howled back at him, took hold of his arms and shook him, tugged him by the hair a little too. Then he was quiet, but afterwards he would not speak to her, and went out to Margit who was doing something in the garden, and a good thing too. What is wrong with that boy, she said to Hartvig, he is not as he should be, she cannot deal with him, but generally it is impossible to tell what Hartvig thinks. He chuckles while she is speaking, but what about? Then all this about Finn being a boy, how she needs to remember that boys are more boisterous. But does he actually think that or is it just codswallop?

She turns over onto her back, makes to get up, but sinks back down. Is she going to have to drag herself around, force herself through every single chore? She must cover a few miles each day just moving around the house. Running up and down the stairs, four storeys from cellar to loft. The tall pine trees outside make the living room so dark, yes, there are shady, sad nooks all over the ground floor. But Hartvig will not cut back the trees, he likes them, he says.

She feels grubby, it's disgusting everywhere, she does not feel like doing anything. But a cigarette. When things are quiet. Once Hartvig has left, and the boy is in the garden, the weather is nice after all. She really does not know why she allows that story from November to trouble her now, so long afterwards. It is probably down to the scene that took place yesterday. That she did not manage to control her temper then either. Still, it does not happen as often as Hartvig makes out. She is only human. There is no sense in dredging up something that happened months ago. Besides, she had her reasons for doing what she did, even if she cannot quite remember what they were. It all started because the boy was to accompany her into town to pick up her wristwatch at the clockmaker's. Margit was ill and could not look after him and, true to form, she had also forgotten to leave out clean clothes for him. Cessi had to look for some, while at the same time the boy was making such a commotion over something or other. Then she lost her patience. After all, they had a tram to catch. She had jabbed him in the chest, had she not, again and again, out of the living room, get out, impossible child, you can't be in the house, you changeling, had she not shouted things like that? Yes, you changeling, she shouted. The hearth, the boy tripping and crying. They had both cried, but what good was that?

The stove had gone out and the house was cold, nevertheless, she grabbed her coat and ran out to catch the tram. Down at Honnørbryggen pier, the sea was black and gaping. Always a bitter wind there, along the jetties out towards the headland at Vippetangen. She walked and walked. She had forgotten her purse, so the wristwatch stayed where it was.

There was no way out, of course. Nothing fixes itself. She had to pay, and she had nothing to pay with, only dark sea. That child was difficult though, he was the one who made her feel this way, angry and unhappy. Damn him.

The stove had not lit itself, the house was empty and just as cold when she got home. There was food out in the kitchen and the boy had made a mess, but he was nowhere to be seen. By the time she found him it was getting dark. He was sitting in the outhouse with Hartvig's torch turned on beside him, without a coat and white in the face. It was obvious he had tried to make something, tools and short lengths of plank lay on the floor. The saw was there too, and the sheath knife. Oh no, oh no, what had she allowed to happen? Her tongue tingled and the pulse at her collarbone throbbed, it was as if the boy was dead and she had come too late, he was dead and it was her fault, everything seemed to teeter on an edge, her head pounded, wave upon wave of warm pain beating against her temples. But nothing has happened, she told herself, it is not that bad. All the same, she went back out when the boy had fallen asleep, threw away everything he had cut and sawn up, and hung the tools back on the wall. She double-checked to make sure they were all in the right place. Hartvig must not notice anything.

She tried talking to him but got no response. He would not make eye contact, would not answer her, and his hand lay limp in hers as she led him inside. She gave him hot chocolate at the kitchen table and told him he looked like his uncle, my brother, she said. That was something she said to him at happier moments, but it was also meant in reproach, because he was *not* his uncle and all the times he was impossible it was doubly obvious, for how could he let down his own mother in such a way, by bearing a resemblance to her beloved brother, and yet be different?

But Christmas came soon after, and it went well. As though nothing bad had happened. Perhaps the boy had already forgotten the whole thing. Hartvig stood in the kitchen, his coat open and a layer of wet snow on his shoulders. He had one hand on the Christmas tree he had bought, the stem of it resting on the black-and-white checked floor, gloves on so as not to prick himself. The room was chilly, she was airing out the steam from the roast and outside it was dark and snowy.

They laughed about something, she could not recall what. The boy ran from room to room, stopping now and again to hug her, filled with anticipation. The apron was tight and her hips were a little too round for her liking, but she was not tired and Mama was spending Christmas with them. Thank God for Mama.

There is a Persian rug in the doctor's office that looks like the one in the living room at home.

It is of course her nerves. Dr Vold tells her as much when she asks him for a diagnosis, something definite. Her nerves would certainly appear to be the cause. She needs to take it easy. He says other things as well, but what sticks in her mind as the single most pertinent is: in future she must avoid these distressing episodes. She must get up out of the mire, she tells herself.

She tells Hartvig that they need to send the boy away for a while. He seems perplexed, is reluctant. Shouldn't she manage to mind her own child? he says. Looking after the boy does fall under her remit and in point of fact was the very reason for her being at home instead of earning a living. Then she snaps. She pounds her chest, slaps her face with both hands, tears at her hair and throws things at him. The whole of this big house. The maid. The garden. That demanding boy. Her health. Her nerves. Doesn't he understand anything? She's weak. She screams and sobs. Smashes things. But fine, she cries, the boy stays but you have to stop working so much. Home at five o'clock. No more twelve-hour work days.

He gives in then, naturally.

*

She groans about having a headache when Hartvig and the boy come in to say goodbye. That will make them realise how mean they are being. This is certainly not something she wishes for, but something that has to be done. Her body is crying out for rest. It is impossible to make Hartvig understand that, even though she has explained it over and over. So she resorts to having a headache. He cannot object to that. She is confined to bed and has terrible head pain, she cannot look after a child. Moreover, a demanding child. Even Hartvig can appreciate that. All the same, she has to choose her words carefully when speaking to him. She does not quite know why, but she can sense it, him watching her. It could happen suddenly: his not wanting to have anything to do with her any more.

The boy is so excited, he can hardly bring himself to sit still on the edge of the bed while she cries and kisses him. She comforts herself with the thought that it will be a delight for him to take the train, regardless of everything else. Together with his father. He loves trains and begs Hartvig every single Sunday to take a walk down to the station to look at the locomotives. Yes, the train journey will be simply splendid. And at the children's home he will get lots of fresh air and have friends to play with. People to keep him out of mischief, that will not do him any harm. Truth be told, he is mollycoddled. Mama does not agree but the children's home comes on the highest recommendations. They have not told him yet, after all, he does not know what a children's home is. Like visiting Aunt Marthe, Hartvig now attempts to explain, but with that the boy thinks he is going to Marthe's to help out with the animals. The sheep and the hens and the cat, he says. Hartvig leaves it at that, he is *not* terribly fond of crying or emotional to-dos. She can almost hear him: '*There's damn near nothing but scenes in this house.*' Her scenes, mind you. He wants peace and quiet. Decorum. Well, in that case he should not have married her. Now he can attend to the boy, then he will get some peace.

3

My childhood memories are as clear to me as the things I perceive around me: the grain of the wood in the kitchen table, the pen, the paper, the yellow gerbera in the green glass vase, the cup of lukewarm tea, the dark shadows of the trees outside the window, the wind blowing. I am thinking about Plato's allegory of the cave. It was difficult to understand his reasoning when I was young and studying philosophy at university. Now my thoughts flow easily. The allegory comes and goes. The shadow of 'the good' on the wall and the prisoners in chains who did not know of anything else but that. And yet the shadow itself was the very proof that 'the good' existed. The One. The starting point. These were the kinds of thoughts you could have before thoughts became relative: that you could not get behind the origin. There was a limit. It is not like that any more. Now our thoughts lead us all over the place and nowhere at all.

I picture the room in the attic. It must be a particular day that I recall. The restless shadows on the wall, not possible to see if they were cast by people. Had we visitors? *Your birthday.* I understood all the words but not what they meant. I heard them talking about the strong sun, about *down-in-the-harbour* and *the fleet.* About *Nortraship* and *the war* and *the torpedoing.* My only brother, Granny said. Daddy was named after him, his Uncle Finn who was torpedoed. Oh, he was one of a kind, all right. And there were shadows from branches, but no tree outside, not that I could see. Granny lit up a cigarette, and said *fuck* to Daddy, *fuck, Finn*. She liked to be teased. When she laughed in anger she was not angry. But excited.

The playhouse was in the garden. It was delivered on a lorry. But what did I know about the relation of numbers to time, I was only four years old. Sandalled feet went up the steps. They were made from old, tarred tram sleepers. Soles skidded on sand grains. There was sand on the bench too. The bench was the cooker. A yellow plastic cup and a red mug. The pine tree seen through the window quite different from the pine tree seen when outside. It was smaller seen from outside, when you saw it together with everything else that existed around it. The walls were smooth. The playhouse smelled of shadow and sand.

There were nettles behind the big house. Thin blades of grass tickled my legs. I got a cold bum when I sat on the stone steps at the kitchen door. It was always in the shade. Moss grew on the foundation wall alongside the steps. The door faced the spruce hedge. A little path ran beside the hedge down to the garage. Well-trodden, compacted sand. Stones sticking up here and there. Feldspar. The garage door was often open. Daddy lay under the car. Then he was not under the car any more but standing and showing me different tools. Adjustable spanner. Saw. Screwdriver. Pliers. The grown-ups smiled almost all the time. I did not understand every word they said but they were happy. It was me who made them happy but I did not know that then. They called to me from the window, asking if I was hungry. Asking if I would not like to take the spade and spread what little snow was left by the gate under the hedge. There was another girl there, 'a little companion', as Granny put it. Granny came to see us, visited the house that had once been hers. She had lived in America and I pretended there was an American city under the hedge. The grown-ups walked back and forth on the gravel, and the car drove out of the garage. Someone was expected. Several men came, and emptied manure onto the grass beside the yard. The heap lay there in sunshine and rain. Another day they burned grass and leaves. The gravel crunched beneath their feet, I heard the tram through the smell of smoke. It was a nice garden to be out in, with a potato bed, berry bushes and lawns. A small wood connected the garden to the neighbouring gardens. Tall pine trees, roots, pine cones and needles, I played in there.

Later on, we did not live in the house. That was because of Mum and Dad's divorce. We had to move. I do not remember why, but I do remember successive flats, stairwells, lawns and washing lines between the blocks of flats, with wet sheets that were lovely to put your face against. One morning I entered the kitchen and noticed the gleam of the knives beside the breakfast plates and saucers. The dazzling light was of more interest to me than the loss of the house and the happy grown-ups. That is how children are. They take advantage of every lonely moment to play by themselves and in their games the world is recreated. It can be wonderful or less than wonderful. Enthralling, but empty, or dark, dense and boundless. This was in the early seventies, but I distinctly remember the linoleum flooring was from the fifties, and slippery. And so the days, the years and decades pass.

Mum and Dad are friends again now, even live under the same roof sometimes, other times not. Thinking back, it is clear to me that I understood very little of their quarrels, why they had them, I do not remember a word of them. Children really do not understand an awful lot of what grown-ups are doing. How childish they are. No matter, the time around the divorce was not all that bad. But then family does not count for everything in a child's life, almost but not everything, ninety per cent perhaps? The rest is genes and other kids. Little shits. At least at my school, but I cannot face thinking about that any more.

It is as if the fear in my body has already informed me, even though my mind is dull and distant, slumped in rumination: it is Emilie who is missing. They have released her name and a photograph. It must have been taken recently, on one of those hot days last week, because she is only wearing a T-shirt, and I think it must have been in the afternoon, when the sun is low and the light is golden. She is sitting on a wicker chair, against what looks like the wall of a house, on a veranda, with the poodle on her lap. Her eyes appear bluer than usual against the yellow wall, the whites of them shining, and her skin is a little red, sunburned perhaps, her freckles prominent where shadows fall on her face, cast by a tree, a softly defined pattern of leaves and swaying boughs. Her hair is strawberry blonde and up in a ponytail, which is coming loose. Her smile is broad and open and whoever is holding the camera may have said something at the moment the picture was taken, something that made her happy, because she is looking right at the lens, brimming with laughter.

*

A wasp crawls over a congealed tea stain on the kitchen table. I place my hand over it, cupping it first, so that the wasp buzzes and flies around inside as if in a cave, smacking into walls. Then I gradually press my palm down. It stings me at the bottom of my middle finger. I open my hand. A red circle appears and starts to swell. It hurts. I pluck out the black stinger. The wasp is not moving any more. I lift my head and look outside. The windows are streaked with a film of pollen and other dirt. There is a magpie on the fence. The post van arrives and the bird takes off. I go out, walking down the driveway. It is muggy and moist, rain on the way. The postman sees me and smiles. We usually say hello to each another. He even waves to me if he passes me on the road when I am returning from the shops in Slemdal. He is probably keeping an eye out for Emilie too. Driving slower than usual, looking in the gardens, feeling he could catch sight of her at any moment. A foot behind a bush. Something pink protruding from behind a woodpile, from between some trees.

If I am out in the garden when Emilie is passing by, I usually go over to the fence. I pet the little grey poodle and we talk about animals, especially dogs. She is going to join the Society for the Prevention of Cruelty to Animals, she has already decided that, and wants to be a vet if her marks in maths are good enough. Because she loves animals and hates to see them suffer. When she grows up she is going to buy a big house where animals that have had a hard time can live. She is going to look after them. There may be so much work with the animals that she will not be able to get married and have children, she tells me, but if it turns out she does have children, she thinks they will enjoy growing up in a house like that, because animals and children like each other, love each other in fact.

Emilie often looks down at the mobile in her hand while walking along, in her lopsided pink Uggs, which she wears all year round. The dog scurries from one side of the road to the other. She lets the lead out too far, I always think when I see her, what will happen if a car comes, if the dog suddenly pulls, makes for the other side of the road and the car does not stop?

I can clearly picture Emilie's pale, delicate scalp showing through her centre parting, can imagine how it feels to hold that soft, smooth ponytail, pointed at the end, a brush of hair gently prickling the palm of my hand. She always wears the same piece of silver jewellery around her neck: a symbol combining an anchor, a heart and a cross. I had a similar trinket when I was at primary school. A charm. That was what we called them, the little silver figures we wanted as birthday presents, and hung on bracelets. The best was if you had figures no one else had, or at least the same as everyone else had, and everybody had hearts, anchors and crosses. Granny had given me my bracelet, and lots of charms too, I had forgotten that, but I remember now: a cat and a dog, a horseshoe, a four-leaf clover, a unicorn, my star sign, several angels and hearts. We talked about charms on the telephone, about how many different types there were, how new ones were always coming out, and I told her which of these I wanted most. Granny's voice was cheerful, they are nice, she said, very pretty. Sometimes I received several in the same box from her, and not just at Christmas or on birthdays, I had a large collection in the end, but do not know where they are any longer.

Once I bent down and carefully lifted the trinket from the hollow of Emilie's neck with my index finger. I wanted to examine it properly, to see if it was the same as mine. The warm, distinctive scent that children have hit me, a combination of hair, soap and something dry, sweet, but perhaps it was as much the absence of smell that I noticed, because children lack that pervasive odour of hormones and private parts.

That's lovely, I said, I had one just like it. Yes, Emilie said, standing completely still while I examined it, Mummy gave it to me. She said she'd been keeping it for me her whole life. You know that it means faith, hope and charity, don't you?

A woman in her thirties pushes a buggy up the hill and passes behind the postman. I often see her. I have considered exchanging a few words with her on occasion. I have also been thirty years of age with small children. But she does not seem the type to be interested in others. She is so thin that you might suspect she had an eating disorder, and always wears expensive brands, at least according to Tuva, who knows about that kind of thing. A caricature, Tuva says, a posh, west-side bitch. Her eyebrows are plucked, make-up evenly applied, face closed. She is unlikely to be thinking about Emilie. Perhaps about herself. Thinking about things she wants. Furniture to get. Clothes to buy. Trips to take. Or she is thinking about what she can eat and what she cannot eat. Things like that. You should never judge a book by its cover, I am aware of that, but still, she is a fucking cow. I don't know why you let yourself get worked up, Tuva says, you don't even know her. Because Tuva does not know that I am always on the run from my inner self and external things provide a welcome break, in the nature of other people, and Sod's law. *Release.* How nice it would be to disappear into the world. It is different for Tuva, she knows so many people, has no need to compensate with either eating disorders or escape, for Tuva nothing is too small to talk about, and she talks to everyone, leans forward over tables, shop counters, information desks, she connects with people. I miss having her around, the sound of her determined footsteps through the rooms, the doors flying open and closing, her face appearing in the doorway: Hi Mum, what's going on?

I open the gate. I have no shoes on and only a thin cotton skirt covering my legs. The temperature is in the high twenties and there is not a breath of wind. There are two newspapers and an earwig inside the post box. It begins to rain, a warm, light shower that increases in strength throughout the afternoon. I stand by the worktop and drink red wine while listening to the radio and looking at the gravel in the driveway, which has become wet, dark and glistening.

I am nothing but love to the children. Yet I continue to exist for myself.

I hear a rumbling in my stomach and take the crispbread packet from the cupboard, count out five and put cheese on all of them. They taste dry and boring on their own, but together with wine and a few slices of apple they are something else entirely. I do not know if I am eating in order to drink the wine, or drinking the wine so I can manage to eat.

My teeth are sore, or rather my gums I should say, they must be inflamed. I have to ring the dentist, but do not like using the phone any more, not since having a mobile. It makes it hard to concentrate, people calling while I am on the train, while I am walking along busy streets or am in the shower. I jot down messages and appointments on scraps of paper that I leave wherever I was when the phone rang, because it rings when I least expect it, when I have gone to bed, when I am on the toilet, and still I answer it, I have to when somebody wants me for something, it vibrates in my body, in my brain. Landlines are different, they can ring and ring in empty rooms without anyone hearing, or managing to reach them in time, and thus not bothering to try, but I do not have a landline, because I do not know how long I will be able to live in the house. As long as you want, Dad says, because it is his childhood home, but how long is that? Besides, I'm in two minds. I am not sure if I want anything at all, neither want nor do not want. When life drifts on and disappears all the same. Sooner or later memories break down, Dad's, mine, the children's, and then the house will fall into the void, out into the open. Whether it is knocked down or not. They may well tear it down soon. Dad and his sisters. There are lots of eventualities you cannot foresee. What did Granny and Granddad want with this house, to play at being grown-ups?

Yesterday I was sitting watching TV in the dark when Beate rang. A sudden blue glow on the coffee table, followed right after by the buzz and vibration of the telephone against the tabletop. I liked that. Two screens glowing for me, and I thought: What is it that goes wrong the whole time, between people?

Family life destroys everything.

And that is how you become a person.

I invited Beate for tea. Not that I needed to. She comes around quite a bit, just as often as Tuva and Georg. I make her food too. I do everything I once longed to do. Prepare tomato soup from scratch. Refrain from upkeep of the house, just clean here and there. Watch TV at all hours. Sleep when I feel like it. That's the freedom of getting on in years and being divorced, I tell Beate.

I have a fair idea why she comes to visit, but I do not like to think about it, I do not actually want to know any intimate details about Beate's life, her secret dreams and ambitions. I just want her there in front of me, young, fair-haired and pretty. I am hardly somebody who ought to be admired, I think, quite the contrary, but I cannot deny her, I have to play my role to the full. I am the adult. I am that other. Not her mother, not a relation, I am the alternative. In addition to being an author, something off the beaten track. Oh, if she only knew how it was to negotiate those meandering paths on the outskirts. But she does not. To Beate I am her mother's exotic friend. I was once her best friend, but now Anita does not want anything to do with me. She is so busy. With what I do not know, but I do not fit into it in any case. She is in a place where the future is open, whether illusory or not. There are things happening in Anita's life all the time. Over at the university. She has a career there to devote herself to. Colleagues, money and purchasing power go along with that. She buys clothes and other beautiful items, trips and experiences, she is thriving. And me, what am I doing? I do not quite know, I wander in the shadows, and if there is one thing Anita does not want, it is shadows. Darkness and loss. I can understand that. But then neither is she exposed to the power of thoughts, those distinct thoughts, unforeseen, unexpected ones that elevate you. Stirring something great, penetrating, opening impression after impression and making the world a different place, for a while at least.

But suppose she does concern herself with the big questions too, imagine she does have everything, and I am just someone who has lost out?

I have baked lemon cakes and a kringle for Beate's visit. The cakes are resting on the green glass platter, sunlight flickering here and there on the worktop, which has not been oiled for a long time, and the wood has absorbed some stains. Why does it bring tears to my eyes? Because it is beautiful, and beautiful things do one good, and good things are painful.

I think too much.

Good things are dangerous. They bring shame.

Good things always slip away.

First the thoughts are here, then they are not.

Beate is standing in the middle of the kitchen with a bag of Twist chocolates in one hand and a new handbag in the other, or an old one rather, bought in a second-hand shop, with a catch that could surely be described as – I cannot think of the word, the image is hazy. That is surely – no. That closes securely. No, that was not what I meant. It's retro, Beate says, and that helps, because I know what *retro* means, it comes from the French *retriever,* to get or fetch back again, recover, or as it says in the dictionary: *Retriever, breed of dog used for retrieving game.* But fetch what: handbags, letters, boxes of old photographs and account books, merely things others have left behind, and after all what did they know about us? I have lots of stuff like that, old stuff: letters, post office delivery notes about parcels filled with goodies on their way, postal orders, and several folders with summaries of assets and division of inheritance. Mahogany, crystal and jewellery. Easy chairs and a painting.

The catch must be a hundred years old, and as Beate tightens the strap and sticks the prong of the buckle through, something happens in my head, I see visions and hear voices: *Mama*. Women fill the room (is it a church service?) wearing heavy, clammy dresses, there is powder and dust in the air, unfamiliar smells (naphthalene, camphor, sweat?). When I die I will take these images with me to the grave. The women's feet are freezing and the sweat within the dresses makes them even chillier. How are they supposed to regulate their hormones? Their bodies are perched, out of balance, but at least they can sit idle for a while, rest, half-asleep, gazing listlessly at the untreated wood on the back of the pew in front.

Is my life a result of this, an imbalance, a skewed relationship between wealth and earnings, work and rest, gender and longing?

My thoughts are out of control, I cannot steer the visions, I am a novel without a plot. Because an intrigue implies something definite, but I cannot manage to find the words for what that is. Just *know* it. And I am supposed to be some kind of writer? Is there something wrong with me, I wonder, growing frightened, am I sick, suffering the onset of dementia?

Do you think I'm very absent-minded, I ask Beate, but Beate's mind is filled with thoughts of men. It must be, after all she is only twenty and has not had a boyfriend yet. Not that I know of anyhow. Beate in tight-fitting, faded jeans and thick mascara. Do men scare her, or does she scare them? And how is that I, a middle-aged woman, cannot formulate an answer to this question: Is it normal for young women to be frightened of men? All my experiences and memories suddenly flutter, come loose, blow away, and rush off, I am sat here and I know nothing. And this 'am sat'. I have never used that before. Do I not always say 'am sitting'? I AM SITTING HERE AND I DO NOT KNOW. Christ above. It is like one of the songs they play at the gym: *Fuck you. Fuck you-ou-ou*. That's how it goes. One random word says it all. That is as close as I get at the moment. But Lily Allen has a tune – *fuck you-ou-ou* – I do not, I only have an isolated word or two. That means it is probably not Alzheimer's after all, because at least then there are other words, instead of saying 'knickers' you come out with 'glasses', and instead of 'man' you say 'cry', and that makes for a different jigsaw puzzle, but the overall picture makes no sense, it is chaotic. It is rather *the password* that I lack, the key, the tune. A plot presupposes at least one connection. A causal connection.

I put on Leonard Cohen, it is for Beate's sake, *I have to give her something with love*, but I do not know if Beate understands what I want her to hear in the line where he says, if it's the person's will, he won't speak anymore, he will still his voice, as before.

I know what he means but I cannot say it, it would sound ridiculous, not just to Beate but to anyone, to try and explain an intuitive understanding with exalted, religious concepts. Besides, what is the point in consoling someone who is not sad?

Beate is not unhappy, as well as which my son could not possibly seem frightening to girls. Granted, Georg is himself young, just turned nineteen, but I cannot picture him ever becoming a man it was dangerous to fall in love with. I still maintain that everything is different for the young, for Beate, Georg and Tuva. They are not aware, nor should they be aware, of how things can go the wrong way, how a girl can practically invite a man to cause her pain. Penetration entails that. What is it about that, or the absence of it? That accounts for so many unhappy moments. It is beyond the reckoning of time, but that is hardly a sensible answer. It can be just as pleasurable as painful, but you do not know when it is going to be one or the other, you do not know why, and sometimes it can be both simultaneously. Is it perhaps a break in the narrative, in the personal storyline? Before it begins again, and moves in another direction?

I am not supposed to be able to explain everything.

I cannot.

Gender values change.

I hardly know anything.

These circumstances begin anew every day.

I am not lonely, not in the physical sense. Actually, yes, of course, particularly in the physical sense. The body is always alone. But seen from the outside. No. A mother is not lonely.

On occasion, I go to Halvorsen's bakery with Mum and Dad, it is a compromise, because Dad would rather not spend money on cafés or restaurants. But Halvorsen's is different. Granny would always take him there when he was small and buy him a millefeuille. Pity you can't eat two slices, he says, lifting the plate and licking it clean, but they're so bloody expensive. Mum looks another way. So eat two, you can afford it, she says. But the second one doesn't taste as good, he replies, you mustn't have too much of something. Nor too little, Mum mumbles, and asks for a top-up of her coffee.

Or nothing at all, I think. Nor the opposite of not getting: being pushed away.

I speak to old friends on the telephone sometimes. The mobile vibrates and lights up, and I do have a social life of sorts. Sometimes we meet up and drink wine. Knut calls me up every now and again as well, to talk about the children. He does not visit of course. That would not be on, him being my ex-husband. That is how he speaks, that is one of his stock phrases: *That kind of thing is just not on.* Actually, did he not die? It feels like that at times, and I grieve. I sometimes ask Tuva as well: Is he alive? Oh yeah, absolutely, she will reply, in such a way that I gather he is very much in evidence. With his obstinacy, no doubt. But he loves the children.

I would love to hold his hand, tell him loneliness drove us apart, but that it was not our fault. It was all God's fault. Thoughts like that make me well up. Everything could have been so good, could it not? Love, no bed of roses? Then I remember. The irritation and everything just building up: anger, furious anger, the subsequent cold stand-off and finally nothing at all. He was so tight-fisted and so demanding. He was a drain on me, a huge drain and I was so empty.

You should get him a dog, I tell Tuva. It might be good for him. Mum, she says, laughing. You're the one who needs a dog.

4

She can hear the tram coming down the hill, tell exactly where it is by the sound and adjust her tempo accordingly, how long she takes to button her coat, how quickly she walks. The gate has to be lifted slightly as she opens it, so as not to scrape the ground.

The sense of liberation at leaving the house, of turning the right way, downhill towards the station, of stepping onto the tram and heading into town, where there is life. Even though she is only going to Dr Vold. As well as running a few errands perhaps, if she is up to it. She must not manage to do too much though, that would only make Hartvig suspicious.

The doctor seems to be sitting far away from her. She is nearly falling asleep in her chair, this happens every time: she enters, sits down on the opposite side of the desk, and suddenly experiences a floating sensation, like when she dozes in bed with the curtains drawn in the afternoons. She also feels extremely tired. She tells him that the boy has been in the country and is soon coming home.

She says she has heard that children should not be too dependent on their mothers. Dr Vold seems neither to agree nor to disagree. Perhaps not, he says, probably unwise, generally speaking.

He is terribly difficult.

My nerves can't take it.

He won't behave as I want him to.

She says things like this and feels like crying. Imagine she could accompany the doctor home, was invited to dinner, was placed at the middle of the table with the doctor and his wife at each end, looking at her amicably, nodding when she spoke, thinking her charming and fascinating to converse with. Dr Vold would then see that she was funny, spirited and kind. Because she *is* kind.

Her eyes drift around the room while the doctor is speaking, asking her questions that she answers, about what time she is going to bed, if she is devoting enough of her day to diversions, eating regularly. She notices a green brooch on the Persian rug, enamel and shiny, slightly bent, with two tulip leaves on it.

There is a long, brown leather couch in Dr Vold's office. He has never asked her to lie down upon it. Perhaps she is not sick enough. She wonders what his wife is like. Beautiful, of course, and slender. Is it her brooch on the carpet? Has she been to visit, has she lain here, on the floor, her clothes in disarray with his hand on its way up under her skirt? She has only seen him once without that white coat, she had been the last patient of the day, perhaps he was hot and tired, was thinking about getting home and had readied himself to leave as soon as their appointment was finished. His trousers were tight across his bottom. Narrow hips and long legs. Strong hands with hair creeping further up under his shirt cuffs. He is manly. Yes indeed, she could imagine what they get up to. Even professors have appetites. Yes, is he in fact a professor? See, she does not know. Dr Vold is a respected neurologist, Hartvig says. He was the one who suggested him of course. One does not contact a GP for an illness of this character, he said, as though he knew something about it. A doctor cures illnesses, she had replied, not characters. That was well said.

She does not quite know what is wrong with her, she says. Tiredness, headaches, dizziness. As well as which she is irascible. Hartvig cannot cope with that. He is weary of her neuroses, he says. Yes, him, who scarcely knows what a neurosis is. She is the one who is weary, weary beyond words. But I am not mad, really, she said to Dr Vold during her first consultation, and they both laughed, no, nobody thought that, he assured her.

It grows quiet. Dr Vold apologises for the noise of the traffic outside and closes the window. She asks for a glass of water. His secretary brings it in. The doctor shifts in his chair, causing the material on his shirt front to crease. She knows that he was born in the same year as her. Just think, she is thirty-seven years old. She will be forty before long. Now *that* is old. But Dr Vold's skin is smooth and his hair is dark. Sometimes, on entering his office, she experiences a certain sensation in her stomach, not unlike delight. The two of them could just as well be sitting flirting in a restaurant, he could be admiring her, her looks, how witty she is. Not in reality of course, she does not fit in with the likes of him. A doctor. Besides, most of the time she considers him as being around the same age as her father. That mean man. There is a large portrait on the wall by the door, not of Dr Vold, but of a well-known senior consultant. Or is he the director of a hospital? She could not remember what Hartvig had said, he told her after they had been there the first time, when he had accompanied her. Why had he done that actually? Had she asked him? She could not remember that either.

How is it that some people can do anything and know almost everything, are they born that way, are they some sort of miracle? The consultant in the painting looks quite normal, a man of mature years, of ordinary appearance. Ordinary people are the worst thing she knows of. His doctor's coat is only buttoned over his stomach, a blue waistcoat visible beneath. He is holding his pocket watch in his hand, part of the watch chain hanging down between his fingers. She does not think he looks mean.

It is different with Dr Vold. Does he think there is something seriously wrong with her?

It is first and foremost *a feeling* that arises when she attempts to discern the nature of her sickness. A feeling of everything being terrible, unbearable. She is wicked, the world is wicked. Everyone is mean and nasty, even Mama. Even though there is nobody who dislikes Mama, she is so *lovable.* So how could her daughter turn out like this? She knows they think she is difficult. Hartvig and his family, her parents-in-law, sister-in-law, all those cousins, uncles and aunts, ugh, there are so many of them. An artistic temperament, Mama says, in her defence. That just makes Cessi angry. But I'm not an artist, she screams, I'm nothing. Nothing but mean and horrible, I know that's what you all really think. And that upsets Mama, so she goes out in the garden to Finn, while Hartvig laughs. Not out loud, but you can see it in his face. What did I tell you, his expression says, what did I tell you. Outwardly pleased.

Moreover, there's her *hysterics.* She gets in such a state of excitability, Hartvig says, and if he is irate enough he accuses her of putting on an act, of feigning more than feeling genuine despair. But that is not true. It just flares up, cannot be controlled, she really can do nothing for it. Because Hartvig is like a wall. Cold and immovable even when he is worked up. That lack of response. Impossible to budge him. He is wilful and obstinate as well. The way he sees it, if something has been decided upon then that is that, and everything must be thought through thoroughly all over again if anything crops up requiring a change of plan. But with Hartvig things rarely change. She is simply helpless.

The room will not stop moving, the air turning grainy when she notices Dr Vold looking at her. Is this the only possibility of any form of contact between them? Images race through her mind, the wind in the trees, over the small forest lake, through the boy's hair. She would rather be sitting on the tartan blanket by Mindedammen now, watching him swim. She does love the boy, in spite of everything. But where would Dr Vold fit in this scene? This is becoming too difficult. These troublesome images, they often overpower her. They are like photographs, only sharper, and in colour. As though she is there, almost there. But they are taking place in her head. The visions: hospital beds. A bedpan. Deaconesses. Light blue bonnets, light blue tablets. The trees in the forest.

The tram passes by outside. He asks what she is thinking about and she replies that she wishes he was an older gentleman, she likes old men. There are so many tiny dots in her vision that she can hardly make him out, she should not have said that, because now he asks if she and Hartvig have sexual intercourse. It is as though they are actually sitting in that restaurant she pictured earlier and she has had one drink too many. Her laughter is high-pitched and excessive because the question is so impertinent, because she was not prepared for anything like that, and does not know what to answer. So she shakes her head. It does happen of course, Hartvig will come to her and she is, as he quite rightly points out, his wife. But she does not feel any actual desire to be intimate with Hartvig.

Once in a while, she says to Dr Vold, naturally, I have conjugal duties, as all married women do.

Dr Vold leans forward in the chair, his elbows on the desk, holding the fountain pen between his hands as he absent-mindedly screws the top on and off, and asks:

Do you find yourself masturbating on occasion?

Well, I mean really, she replies, turning her head away. She does not even want to think about it, that sort of thing does not belong in here. The room fades completely to grey, she can vaguely make out the windows, as bright patches far away.

Dr Vold asks why she wishes he was old, and this time she just tells it like it is, that with age comes experience. That was probably a very stupid thing to say, because now he no doubt thinks she means experience of women, so she hurries to add that, moreover, older men no longer dwell on erotic matters. Now it is getting impossible. Dr Vold is by no means an elderly man, now he must think that she thinks that *he* harbours such thoughts about her, or even worse, he will assume that *she* entertains such thoughts about him, which she certainly does not. Or rather, she does, but that has nothing to do with *this*, with sitting here in his office.

A man must win his wife over and over again, he then says.

She feels intense warmth in the pit of her stomach. Perhaps he finds her attractive, he looks at her and would like to have what only Hartvig is entitled to. The purely erotic. Besides, it is true.

Hartvig is a practical man, she says, but she knows that is not the right word either, it is something else.

Ah, so he's good with his hands, Dr Vold says, that's a fine attribute.

But Hartvig is by no means skilled in that way, she is, she can both sew and do carpentry. It is more that he is so level-headed. In everything, she says. And quick to reason, but slow when it comes to action.

He's perhaps extremely rational?

Yes, that is the word. She nods. But it is not.

He can have such a cold look in his eyes, she says. No, I mean ironic. He looks at me as if looking down from a mountaintop.

Or is it the opposite? Suddenly she is unsure. She can become terribly annoyed when he is too kind and lays his hand upon her, her body becomes too hot, she cannot breathe.

No, I don't know, she says, I really don't know.

Dr Vold leans back, folds his arms across his chest and nods at something, although she does not know what. He then looks at the clock on the wall and says that their time is up for the day, and she can schedule a new appointment with his secretary, a fortnight should be suitable.

She gets to her feet, takes one step and picks up the brooch. Holding it in her hand, she can see it resembles one of Mama's, the shiny green enamel.

Someone seems to have lost this.

The doctor thanks her, but barely raises his head, the consultation is finished, he sits making notes in her journal, now she is merely another patient, one of many who come and go, she wants to cry again, does nothing matter?

She could sew an outfit to match that brooch. She usually listens to the wireless when she sews. It is a recent acquisition, a gift from Hartvig. To offer you some diversion in your spare time, he said, by which he meant a number of things, she understood that. That he had a guilty conscience for being away so much, but would not admit it. Moreover, that he was of the opinion she could do more work than she does. Giving her a radio was a way of saying that. She is not stupid. He does not consider sewing actual work. Not even when she had made him an entire suit had he appreciated the amount of work involved. After all, she was able to sew, so she should just get on with it, there was no more to it. That was the way Hartvig thought. But it was kind of him, to get her a radio. The Heyerdahls do not have one yet.

It is comforting to listen to the weather forecast, they often broadcast it. She has heard some lectures too, about the home and child-rearing, but that put her so out of sorts, irritable. As if she was not already aware of the mistakes she made. These know-it-alls, Brinchman and Mrs Grude Koht or whatever their names were. She does do one thing right, the boy gets good food and plenty of sleep, wears proper clothing and footwear and gets lots of fresh air in their lovely garden. What they said about not subjecting children to distressing scenes was more difficult. But she knows there are worse things, oh yes, she herself is living proof of that. A sudden and uncontrollable temper. Life is wicked. Oh dear, no, she would rather listen to the music they play, that seems to send waves of gladness over her, as it were, that is a feeling of happiness, she thinks. And then cigarettes, they are like chocolates, she cannot just have as many as she likes. She has to wait at least an hour between each one and the next. At times, she can have both Freia chocolate and her cigarettes out on the table. Smoking is even more enjoyable when you suck on a piece of cooking chocolate at the same time, as well as take a few sips of coffee. No matter if it is lukewarm. She probably drinks at least eight or nine cups a day. The sight of the cigarette packet also makes her happy. She tried out her new brand as soon as they began to advertise it. It was the picture on the packet that attracted her, those clean, deep colours, blue and green, besides, it was new and did not look like any other type she had seen before. She looked at the billboards up at Majorstua and Nationaltheatret stations, and took pleasure in the knowledge that she had just such a packet in her handbag, that she was a part of what was happening, and for once it was something beautiful. Blue Master. She liked the sight of the blue horse rearing up. Oh, she has such a yearning for beauty, she really does. As sensitive people often do.

Moreover, smoking helps keep her slim.

She goes into the wardrobe on occasion. She is really good at sewing, everyone says so. She slides the clothes on their hangers, takes out dresses, suits and blouses she has made. She is slender at times, no one can say otherwise. She has lovely outfits, and dainty feet.

5

Beate really likes her suntanned skin. She has rolled up her shirtsleeves, the white material accentuates her colour. Her arms are thin, which is nice, but she would rather not have hair on them, although it's fair and not that thick. She does not dare shave, because then it grows longer, darker and thicker, Selma told her so in second year at school, that you must never *shave* hair, that just makes it worse. Nor does she want to wax them, she has heard it is really sore, and makes your skin red and bumpy. Besides, now in the summertime, the golden hairs look quite nice against the brown of her skin. Actually, Beate considers, she has, in a way, model's arms, and is struck by a sense of summer nights, Mediterranean heat, a dark ocean, something cinematic, something she has not experienced or even been close to experiencing. It sweeps over her, followed by a craving she wants to escape from, a disgusting feeling. Like after masturbating.

Beate walks about, her body an unattainable fantasy for most. Beate is in fact beautiful. She and her body are of course inseparable, yet all the same she is not certain that her body is *her.* She does not think this in so many words. Beauty is not such a boon as you might be inclined to believe.

Beate looks in the mirror hanging in the hallway of the functional apartment where she lives. The room is painted white, and the strong light from the energy-saving light bulb in the ceiling makes everything cast sharp shadows. When she moves, the shadows lengthen. The white shirt reaches midway down her thighs, she is wearing her tight faded jeans beneath, nothing is wrong, she is tanned enough, slim enough, pretty enough, the clothes are right, she is pleased and applies deep pink lip gloss.

Outside, light rain is falling, Beate opens her jacket, the wind blows warm against her throat, small droplets land on her shirt and face. She plugs the earphones into her iPhone, puts on some music and walks out onto Skovveien.

The music makes Beate happy, it pounds within her. The pavement is wet but the air is warm, she smiles at passing men and their hungry looks, walking past on nimble feet, *gazelle,* she thinks, *graceful, sexy,* her nipples chafe against the shirt material and her sandalled feet are moist.

She is looking forward to the lecture. It is strange: a professor stands there speaking in front of a whiteboard. Sometimes searching for words and clicking a little back and forth on her laptop, perhaps pulling down the projection screen to show them a PowerPoint presentation with keywords, graphs and charts. In a way it is pretty boring, while at the same time Beate gets the feeling of something unfamiliar taking root within her, she begins to picture things. Other countries, other times, strange faces. But it requires strenuous, almost unbearable, effort. She feels that somebody wants something from her, it is an exacting, unchecked demand. A hand that wants to drag her in. Further and further in. Into serious matters. Like when she is at Bea Britt's. It is a relief to go for coffee in the canteen with the others afterwards.

Sometimes she does not attend the lectures. Today she is going to two: *Evil in the history of ideas* and *What is a childhood?* Oh, Beate is so looking forward to it, she cannot get enough of what the lecturer says, everything ignites her interest, clusters images: forests, flames and crucifixions, cries towards the night sky, asylums, hospitals, institutions, muddy farmyards, the beating of child labourers and pauper apprentices, the tiptoe of feet in the drawing rooms of the bourgeoisie, the caning of a hand, china cups, factories and mines. If she had spoken of these things with Bea Britt, she would immediately start talking about the children, with tears in her eyes, the small, defenceless children, alone and vulnerable, how could they feel loved in such circumstances? Beate thinks she herself must be lacking in some essential emotion, because she does not think about the children, she just wants to be there, struggle and decry, speak to the people, move them to protest, go forth together. With a man by her side. A strong man. A handsome one.

She knows several boys, who like her and shift uneasily when she sits down beside them. Ones who are into music, activist sorts, farm boys, different types. Who smile and whisper things to her, tilt their heads to look at what she is writing in her notebook. Or who just stare straight ahead, stiff with shyness. Diligent students with considerable knowledge, who would gladly include her in their earnest ways and their Sunday hikes, their frozen pizzas and some treat in the form of going to see a film and having a beer, but just one, because they do not squander their money. Sometimes she wishes she was like them, but not so often, because their ascetic way of life rubs off on their way of thinking, making everything so boring and she wants something different, she likes intensity, heated discussions, visions, venturing grandiose analyses, your own. But no matter, they are boys, they are receptive and she likes them, Beate has always liked boys. Girls do not like each other in that way. At least they do not like Beate. She is too pretty. Beate knows the kind of things they think about her, and not only think but say. Badmouthing Beate is a subject all of its own. She is stuck-up, they say, *smug*, thinks she is pretty and perfect. Or at least that was what it was like in secondary school, now she is not completely sure. There are so many girls at the university here in Blindern. A lot of them are pretty. A lot of them are clever *and* pretty and slim, all in one.

Erik is different from the other boys. Good-looking, of course, and neither shy nor serious, on the contrary, he is pushy, jokes and flirts, dares to stick his neck out, asks questions during the lectures and has strong opinions. Fortunately there are always lots of people about when she has talked to him, around a table in the canteen, outside the door to the lecture hall, she does not know how it would go if it were only the two of them. Cringe, so embarrassing.

She wonders how things would be if she stopped being perfect and pretty. Suppose she goes through a change and is suddenly completely different, ordinary, or ugly, gets loads of spots, puts on weight, what would she do then? Die? She is not quite sure where things are going from here either in, like, the future. That seems so blank, yet filled at the same time, confused and disorderly, and when she ponders it, she always ends up thinking about love and sex, no matter what.

She has only had sex once and that was during all the end-of-school partying, she regrets that, it was horrible. All the same, she wants so much to experience it again, only in a different way, the next time will be completely different, and she just does not know how she is going to manage to wait, you cannot want something so badly without it happening, it must be right around the corner, maybe already under way.

She can picture it. Being naked with a man. Him saying: *I didn't know you were so beautiful.* Sometimes these images are all she sees, she fantasises about being plunged into a mad love affair, and cannot manage to concentrate on anything else, it can last for hours. She knows, therefore, what it is to love, to be loved, that is how it is. But afterwards, when she is walking on the street, looking around her, it is gone, empty. She sees only trees, houses, lawns, roadways, cars, people, nothing.

She buys a chocolate bar, but regrets it as soon as she has eaten it, it is only empty calories, her blood sugar will soon fall and she will be starving by teatime, because now she cannot eat lunch. It is either-or, chocolate or an open sandwich, otherwise she will put on weight. Now the whole day is out of balance, she is on the verge of tears.

She had planned to walk the whole way to the campus at Blindern, across Majorstua, past the students' union and between the university science labs, but there is not enough time, so she takes the tram and gets off in Majorstua to take the underground. Skipping the lecture had not occurred to her, but she begins to consider it while waiting on the platform. If the train to Holmenkollen comes first, she thinks, I will go up to Bea Britt. The Holmenkollen train does not come first, but she waits for it all the same. She wants to go to Bea Britt's place. The missing girl, Emilie, has something to do with it. She feels a kind of tension in her body the entire time, the girl is the first thing she thinks of when she wakes up, and she checks the online newspapers on her iPhone before getting out of bed. It is a serious matter, something gruesome has happened, something out of the ordinary, everyone is following it, Beate is not the only one checking the Net more often than usual and turning on the TV to watch the evening news, anxious to hear the latest.

She can study at Bea Britt's. She has done it before. Sitting at her kitchen table. Bea Britt does things around the house then. More often than not in the living room, the door ajar, and Beate can see her sitting on the sofa with her eyes closed, or sometimes listening to music or watching TV. She can go out to the garden, be gone for a while and return with something in her hands. Flowers, maybe, or tomatoes, plums and apples if it is autumn. Now and again she will work at the kitchen bench even though Beate is reading in the same room. Cut vegetables, cook, bake. Sigh, stop what she is doing and look out the window. Make a comment if someone passes by on the quiet road. There's the man in the baseball cap, she will say, he's at the gate gawking again. Beate will go over and stand beside her. It is not the first time she has seen him, Bea Britt has pointed him out before. A loner, Beate says, or, actually he seems a little backward, I think, retarded. Always wearing that cap, and just standing there, even though he must know we can see him.

No, Bea Britt will then say, he's not retarded, it's something else.

A nutter then, Beate says, returning to her books. There is a limit for how strange a person can be, she thinks, feeling suddenly irritated. Bea Britt always has to make a problem out of things, nothing is allowed to just be normal.

Sometimes she will see Bea Britt write something in a notebook, but only on rare occasions. Seldom, considering she is a writer. What does she think about? She looks as though she is pondering something so intently, her features darkened.

Whatever she is reading has a different effect on her when she reads it at Bea Britt's. It takes on a darker cast she does not understand. It might be due to Bea Britt taking everything she says so seriously. She listens and responds as though they are talking about profound, inescapable truths, things you have to take in, yes, almost take on and suffer for. If Beate brings up something about the plight of some children in the seventeenth century, the events seem to grow and somehow meld with the kitchen, they are face to face with them, with all the terrible things which befell them, and life outside, here and now in Slemdal, hardly exists. It is as though Bea Britt has everything within her the entire time. The whole world in her body and the more that comes the more she is filled. It cannot be good. But all the same, it is as if Beate needs to be in proximity with it. Even though what is written in her books assumes unfathomable depths at Bea Britt's kitchen table, threatening to drag her down into the darkness. She needs it. For everything written to have physical meaning. The thought of having sex fades when she is here.

It is dark and raining outside. Beate lies down on the sofa. Bea Britt has taken some berries from the freezer and is making redcurrant jelly at the worktop, the radio is on but the volume is low. It must be a repeat of *BluesAsylet*, because she can hear the voice of presenter Knut Borge between songs. Bea Britt's sofa is soft and deep. Beate places a cushion under her head to avoid feeling as though she is sinking down into all the softness. Through the window, she sees the branches of the huge birch tree swaying in the wind. The street lamps are on, their light reflected in the raindrops on the pane.

Beate dozes, but now and again the music on the radio pulls her back up to the surface, the tones seem so powerful out of context, then she nods off again, but she is not aware of doing so before she wakes to hear Bea Britt crying in the kitchen. Beate sits up and coughs, places her feet heavily on the floor and coughs once more before going out to the kitchen. Perhaps they have found that girl, has there been some news on the radio she did not catch? But Bea Britt is not crying any longer and neither does she say anything about the Emilie case.

Do you know that girl who's gone missing? Beate asks.

No, Bea Britt replies. She's just a girl I usually see walking by with her dog. That's why it feels so close, more real somehow, when I know who she is.

Beate thinks about how she is never going to walk around here on her own again, not at night-time at any rate.

She sits down on the antique day bed with all the cushions. On the table between them stands a basket of freshly baked buns, a bowl of redcurrant jelly, butter and tea. A pair of three-branched candlestick holders with lit candles, reminiscent of a picture of the apostles, Beate thinks, something to do with Jesus and Italy and the Last Supper, a painting she has seen, maybe in one of Mum's art books.

Why were you crying? Beate asks. Bea Britt shakes her head a few times and does not answer.

The radio is still on but the sound is down. Jazz is playing now. Listen, says Bea Britt. She stands and turns up the volume. Beate thinks Bea Britt was crying because she does not have a man. She looks happier now. It is probably down to the music, maybe helped by the wine, which Bea Britt does not think Beate knows she drinks from her mug. Bea Britt sits back down.

Have you got a boyfriend? she asks.

I don't know, Beate answers. As though she is already together with Erik.

Bea Britt has blown out the candles and turned on the ceiling light. Beate gathers up her books. She is cold and longs for home.

I'm going to head back to my place and take a shower, she says.

Okay, says Bea Britt. You can always shower here. Or have a bath, she says, smiling. She knows that Beate likes a relaxing soak. But Beate needs to tidy up her flat, and put a load of washing on, she has no clean clothes left.

Bea Britt stands in the hallway and makes to put on her raincoat. I'll walk you down, she says, you shouldn't be out alone around here now. Do you want to borrow an umbrella?

But Beate does not want her to come, suddenly she does not want to spend a second longer in the company of Bea Britt and all she exudes, emotions outpouring everywhere, all the time, her breath and body heat, Beate cannot take any more of her presence, she needs to be alone, right now.

How quickly things can tip the other way. Lately she has taken chances she promised herself never to take, she has tempted fate and lost control. Like when she walks alone through Oslo city centre at night even though she knows it can be risky.

I'm a grown-up, she says, it's no more dangerous for me

than for you, I can go by myself. I just won't take the shortcut, and I'll keep my mobile handy. She thumbs in Bea Britt's number and pockets the phone. There, she says, all I need do now is press OK and I'll call you. She is on the verge of tears, maybe that is the reason Bea Britt gives in.

Beate turns and looks back after she has walked a little distance. Bea Britt is standing in the doorway watching her. Beate thinks about how she is far too visible from the road like that, lit up by the hallway behind, the darkened windows on the floors above, it is a big house.

Rain is still falling. Why does she have to think about Erik? She does not want to. He is too good-looking, he could not possibly be counted on.

The lights of the cars. The gusts in the trees. The wet tarmac. The mobile vibrating. It is Mum calling. Her place is always warm and bright, lamps all around, clean clothes, a spare room and Beate's very own soft, expensive duvet. She cries.

Oh, sweetheart, what's wrong, has something happened?

No, Beate sobs, I don't know.

Come on home for a little while, her mother says, and Beate does as she is told. She will not get to tidy up her own place now. She should not have eaten that chocolate. Everything is a mess.

6

The gravel makes a rustling sound as she walks down the driveway in her new shoes, they are tan leather with low heels. Ah, early summer, the lilac. The rumbling sound of the tram up the hill. She wants to walk arm in arm with Hartvig even though he does not like it. We'll fall out of rhythm, he says, annoyed, making her angry and ice cold: Can't we at least pretend to be married? Cutting. So he gives in and lets her link arms with him all the same. This is how a married couple should look. Her hand rests on the sleeve of his coat. It was nippy enough for her to bring the new gloves in light calfskin. Soft, unblemished, chic. Could have belonged to an actress for that matter.

They step aboard the tram, and she looks around. Sunshine fills the carriage as they go over Gråkammen. *I'm pretty, I know that I'm pretty.* A clear thought for once. Most of the passengers are in their best attire, going out to enjoy themselves. Hartvig sees several people he has to greet, tips his hat and nods. Good evening, good evening, people in different seats respond. Hartvig gives his trousers a punctilious pinch at the knee before sitting down, paying attention to the crease. The scent of perfume comes from the seat in front of them, lily of the valley, and Cessi finds her gaze level with a pink hat atop a bun of light blonde hair. Mrs Esther Heyerdahl. A swan neck, Hartvig once said, Mrs Heyerdahl is as beautiful as a swan. Some of the things he says are truly ridiculous.

Shush, she says, I do not want to talk to the Heyerdahls. But Hartvig does.

Oh, my word, what a lovely surprise. Esther and her husband turn halfway round in their seat, Esther as effusive as only Esther can be. As though she did not see them when the tram came to a stop at the platform and they got on. Rubbish, the lot of it. She knows Esther does not care for her. Oh well, the feeling is mutual. Fancy that, Hedda, is that not what they say, in Ibsen? Thank goodness the Heyerdahls are not going to the theatre but are playing bridge and eating supper at the Emmanuelsens' in Majorstua. They are Jews, of course. Esther likes to adorn herself with what is different. But only slightly different. The Emmanuelsens are not their next-door neighbours, that would no doubt be quite another matter altogether, having them live so close. *Jew riff-raff.* Of course, apart from everything else, Esther gets a discount from Mr Emmanuelsen, at the jewellery shop.

Heavens, are we there already. That is the way Esther Heyerdahl speaks. The swan arises from its seat, enveloped in soft fragrances and a pleasant smile, fluffs its feathers discreetly, places an eagle's talon on the seat back as the tram shudders to a halt at the station and says to Cessi: Now we'll have to see each other soon. Whenever things are a little less busy. I've opened a practice, don't you know. Yes, at home, naturally, and certainly not every day, but all the same, the children demand so much of my attention. But, of course, you know all about that, an only child needs no less looking after than three, that's what they say, that the difference between having no children and having one is the same as between one and ten. But your boy isn't at home for the time being, or did I hear wrong?

Cessi strokes her cheek with the finger of her glove. A cool, tender and restrained caress.

Damn her. Damn her to bloody hell.

She likes the red, carpeted floors inside the theatre. The gilded frames on the mirrors, the wall lamps. And the chandeliers, they are simply divine, she says to Hartvig, who refrains from replying. She no longer thinks his silence is due to any unwillingness on his part, but that he does not know what to say. He is only capable when he himself comes up with a comment, something he thinks appropriate to the situation. In which case he would say 'delightful chandeliers', and 'spick and span here, quite immaculate'. Something like that. He nods and smiles to acquaintances, catches sight of supreme-court lawyer Rachløw and his wife, whispers to Cessi: You remember we ate dinner at Blom with them? Come, we must pay our regards. So they stop and shake hands, smile and chat, but Cessi can see by Mrs Rachløw's expression that she wants to get on, she is not interested in them. Moreover, Hartvig is so long-winded, has so little of interest to say. Mrs Rachløw, incidentally, is much too plump, and really not well turned out, she has poor taste and no reason to behave in such a high-and-mighty way. No, Cessi really has no desire to stand talking to her either, nonetheless she is embarrassed by Hartvig. He drags her down, makes her appear boring and uninteresting as well. Something that by nature she most certainly is not, on the contrary, she has always been praised for how lively she is and for her sense of humour. She used to socialise, was popular, was invited here and there, a person naturally at the centre of attention. If she could not attend a party her friends would badger her. A bevy of them outside knocking on the door: Oh, Cessi, can't you come, it won't be the same without you. And Cessi threw on her coat and went with them for a while, I'll be back within an hour, Mama, she called out, and her mother stood in the hallway in her black dress endeavouring to look helpless. Which she managed very well. But she should be perfectly capable of going to the parish meeting unaccompanied. Had she perhaps not given birth to two children? Had she not been half beaten to death by Papa and survived? How could it be so difficult to walk the few blocks to the parish hall alone? The pavements were not icy, neither was it particularly late, and the streets of Majorstua were safe enough. Oh, no, Mama's 'heart was so anxious', Cessi had to be so kind. But Cessi clattered down the stairs with the others, through the covered entryway and out onto the street. Just an hour, Mama, I'll be back in time to make it. But she was gone longer than an hour, they ended up arriving late for the meeting after all, and Cessi's clothes smelled of cigarette smoke. Mama remarked upon it, that women smoking is an abomination: there are no two ways about it, Cessi. What kind of morals do you actually have?

But morals were a flexible notion. Not that she said as such to Mama and on the whole they just had innocent fun. Music, cigarettes, a little beer and sherry, a flirt. Only now and again something flew through her, yes, everything fluttered and loosened, and she rubbed up against some of the really handsome boys. She felt indelicate and common under their scrutiny, but could not manage to cease the laughter that encouraged them to be lewd, she became lewd herself, and the boys looked at her, laughed, stroked her rear. Hussy.

But the music, Mama, from America, you remember that? The Negro voices. I'm the only one of my friends who's been in America, I'm able to describe the wide streets to them, you can be sure they're thrilled. Of course, I can't depict how it truly was, but I try. The streets were dusty on hot summer days and I protested because I had to wear the straw hat with the string that chafed beneath my chin. Everyone could hear Papa's gramophone music through the open windows. He swung me around and said *she's musical, the little one,* do you remember?

But Mama will not answer. She wants Cessi to eat her supper. Tea, scrambled egg and white bread, as well as an extra treat for little Cessi, smoked salmon.

Now it is different, she is in the vice, stuck in that big house with Hartvig, who does not like to socialise with anybody other than those boring colleagues and bridge friends of his. No doubt because he can only shine in their company. Since he registered them as Friends of the National Theatre they have been constantly attending productions, where she seldom gets more than cold conversation with the likes of the Rachløws. If one really is to take the gloomy view, that is. Because there is a better sort of person here too. Doctors, professors, of old stock, good lineage, so much so that they still speak Danish. The kind of family Cessi's mother-in-law would have liked her to come from. Mean old woman. Money was the only thing on their minds in Hartvig's family. And to think at times he could bring himself to call Cessi a snob. But she could have married into a better position than her mother-in-law dreamt of for her Hartvig. If she had wanted. If only she had not had a *hussy* within. If she had been able to overcome that blank feeling. Like drowning in fog. She went under and came back up, but then people seemed so far away, she could not speak to them. She had such abdabs. Faces seemed to pile together and stare at her, either beautiful and unattainable or fat and uncomprehending. Spiteful. She froze. What was she supposed to say to people such as them, those on the right side of everything, who were completely stuck-up? Not that this applied to Mrs Rachløw, mind you, she was of the kind Cessi could easily run rings around.

Mrs Rachløw's dress is off-the-peg, expensive no doubt, but the cut is unbecoming on her. If one has such an ample form it is better to employ a seamstress, one who knows which materials to use and what cut conceals and accentuates at the right places.

What a lovely dress, she says to Mrs Rachløw, such pretty material.

Mrs Rachløw thanks her with an expression that says that discussing dress material with Cessi is the least interesting thing she can imagine.

But I can see it could do with some slight adjustment. It would sit a little nicer if you got it taken in along the upper sides, and let out somewhat at the waist. It's fitting a little tightly around the waist as it is, while puffing a tad beneath the bust. I can do it for you if you like.

Really, Mrs Rachløw said, looking her right in the eyes, you still sew for people outside the family? Well, I dare say it's a good thing to augment the family income a little.

She tries her hand. But Cessi has her now.

No, the very idea, no, she says. I just sew for the family and for friends of mine who have never quite mastered it themselves.

Now, now, Hartvig says, don't take on more than you can manage, Cessi darling.

She looks Mrs Rachløw's body up and down, as though studying the dress with an expert eye, but Mrs Rachløw is doubtless aware that Cessi is scrutinising her in order to express her contempt, which is after all the point. She notices that Mrs Rachløw has the same brooch as her. White pearls in the form of a bunch of grapes. It is boring, but no more boring than what most other women wear. What is worse is that Mrs Rachløw has the exact same. The brooch on Dr Vold's desk, on the other hand, that was distinctive. The green colour, the curve of the leaves, its size. A brooch one could not help but notice.

Hartvig buys a programme and they stand with heads close and peruse it. It probably looks romantic, as though husband and wife share a particularly trusting relationship. If only he was not shorter than her then they would make the perfect picture. But she is three centimetres taller and is also wearing high heels, fearing they look ridiculous, she pulls away, taking the programme to flick through it on her own. One of their bridge acquaintances passes and Hartvig tries to crack one of his stupid jokes: Well, here we are standing waiting to see *While We Wait*. They both chuckle, but Cessi does not for one minute believe that high-court lawyer Berg found it amusing, she could see it by his expression.

The play is about waiting, it says in the programme, and about how nervous that can make one, because that brings all one's worries and anxieties to the fore, the things that are set aside when one is in a hurry. Yes, that could be true all right, busy days can make her forget, calm her down. But then, at night, she can still burst into tears, because she is simply worn out, and she cannot bear it, no, she cannot.

The play is both a tragedy and a comedy, it says, tragedy and comedy are closer than siblings, *they are the same person turning a face from morning to night.* That jumps out at her. Is that perhaps how it is for her as well? She is not the same in the morning as at night-time, everything can change in the course of the day, becoming utterly wrong, she can be beset and torn to pieces by an uncontrollable rage.

The people around them saunter slowly across the soft carpets, or stand in groups chatting. She cannot say a word to any of them, not even those she knows a little through Hartvig. It is as though they do not actually exist, that no one of flesh and blood is going to come either, no one is suddenly going to appear and walk towards her. She is married now after all.

She would have felt different with that brooch in her lapel.

She could have been an actress, she really could have. Hartvig hands her a glass of sherry. She has never really liked him. The sexual side of things is so disgusting. But how could she get out of it, she had no idea at the time how that kind of thing was supposed to feel. Intimate relations. Is it perhaps merely Hartvig that makes her feel there is something repulsive about the whole thing? No matter, she is not going to do it any more. Neither will she share a bed. Hartvig snores and farts so at night, and she sleeps badly enough as it is. There is something foul about him, it goes together with his erotic fantasies in a way. All the things he can bring himself to say. Is that good? Do you like that? Will I do it like this? Or he asks her to do things that never would have entered her head. She does not like it. She can picture doing unmentionable things with other men. With Dr Vold, for instance. But with Hartvig, no. She feels like crying. But is she happy or sad? She really does not know, or whether it is good or disgusting. Knows only that she needs to control herself. That she must not cry. Because it is worse to cry with relief than with anger. She loses energy then. And Hartvig pulls her down to the bottom afterwards. Even though he may console her at the time. Because the next moment he has forgotten. And she goes around and around in that house while he is at work. There is no end of chores and he does not understand how much is resting upon her shoulders, no, he thinks things are as they should be. And he does not consider asking for a pay rise. They save a lot thanks to her being so nimble-fingered.

No, but Hartvig is kind too. Considerate, patient. He comforts her when she has her 'spells'. She hates it when he says that. Are you having one of your 'spells', he asks. As though she did not have a valid reason to be the way she is, as if what she is screaming at him makes no sense, has no meaning. If she only knew what the reason was. Is it Hartvig's nature that upsets her so much? He is a skinflint. And the responsibility for that big house, that unruly boy, the housekeeping. She wants to divorce him. No, Hartvig wants to divorce her. He was the one who said it first. She does not know if it is a threat or if he really means it. Besides, she could never have said so herself, not said it and meant it seriously. She may have said something similar while in a rage, she likely has, several times, but Hartvig knows well she does not mean what she says. One should not pay attention to words spoken in anger. It is different with Hartvig. When he says something like that, it is serious.

Oh, yes, she may want to be rid of him at times, or wish he was somebody else. But not really. The two of them are meant to be married. One should marry, settle down and start a family, it is best that way. Hartvig is dependable, comes from a good, upper-middle-class family, that offers great security. Besides which, she owns nothing herself apart from some furniture, inherited jewellery and silverware. No, divorce is not an option given her financial position. Nor should anyone find fault with her life. The lawn, the garden, the housework, the boy. She feels black inside.

No one can console her like Hartvig. Only Mama. Anyway, where would she go? Hartvig is not able to take any more of her outbursts, he says. What can she say then? She is speechless. Because one would have a hard time finding anyone as boring as Hartvig. The pedant. He is not how a man ought to be. And then he thinks he is the one who will leave her. Perhaps even feels sorry for her. As though he were the attractive one. Talk about back to front, and she cannot even say it. Still, maybe she will speak with Dr Vold about it.

The desk is brown, the chair, the walls, everything is brown except the Persian rug, and the cushions on the chair which are dark green. The traffic rushes by on wet cobblestones outside. There is so much she could have said, but as soon as she is sitting in Dr Vold's office, it all collapses into something soft, jelly-like. Tiredness overwhelms her. The images move too quickly for her to see them clearly. Rooms, houses, directions. The words conceal something. Or is it the faces?

Hartvig is just a name.

Imagine, she said. Hartvig is just a word.

The doctor thinks she seems agitated. Not so strange perhaps, divorce is a serious matter, he says. Or is it a question? She just nods, cries a little. But it is the doctor's office that gives rise to her anxiety, not Hartvig's talk of divorce. There is something here and she does not know what it is. Something she visualises as a scorching hot liquid. Gas. A laboratory. Is it a hospital, is she being admitted now? She cannot get hold of it. Is it something impending or something that has occurred? Is this perhaps the closest she will get to anything resembling the feeling of God? Dr Vold? He is neither good nor evil. But the sight of him is the sight of something to come. Future. Help me, oh, help me. She does not say it, but on the inside, oh, on the inside she is a solitary scream. Not enough allowance is made for how mentally weak she is, they should know better, all of them. She has no one.

The manly, trousered legs under the desk scare her. But then she is not a child either? Everything is very confusing. Hartvig is not enough of a man, that is what it is. He does not frighten her the way Dr Vold does.

The smell of medicine. Seething. Like it said in the newspapers. The world is seething, Europe is at war. That may bloody well be but what good is that? Her thoughts spin on the same wheel. Rat in a cage. This room cannot disappear. She feels she is connected to Dr Vold's brain, but what is inside it? When he writes in the journal, she no longer knows what might happen. Perhaps Dr Vold is only the beginning. The office is a waiting room. A big city awaits her. Not that huge, unfinished house in that dismal garden between the pine trees. She reads the newspapers, she knows that certain women can also accomplish great things. But to be alone? No. Dr Vold is not considering admitting her to hospital? No, he reassures her, only should she wish it herself, he does not perceive the situation as being that acute. She just needs to ensure she gets sufficient rest.

They used to joke about it. That the house would take as long to build as City Hall. Neither it nor their own house are finished yet. The claw-foot table and six matching chairs were delivered on the back of a lorry. All the furniture standing in the snow in the garden when they returned from town. It was a wedding gift from Papa. She did not know if his intentions were good or bad. If it was to make her feel guilty for not having invited him. Or if it was to make up for something. In which case it would have to be both at the same time. Papa would never do anything for her without at the same time wanting to torment her, confuse her, laugh at her. He enjoyed it. Anyway, she did not care about the table. It could go in the dining room as far as she was concerned, she would never feel at home here. And Hartvig was absolutely delighted to save the expense on furnishings. Naturally.

7

Beate is going to the lecture today. It is easy, all she has to do is get into the car with Mum. She works in administration at the university library, in Georg Sverdrup's House. Once Bea Britt had said that she wished her surname were Sverdrup. Sverdrup or Seip or Vogt or Bonnevie, or one of those kind of names, you know, she said, when you're born into a family like that there's no doubt you'll go far. Why, Beate asked, why's that, everything's different now, anyone can get an education and be something if they want. Bea Britt was not convinced. It's to do with confidence, she said, with a gloomy look, it's passed down, in the blood.

But isn't that almost how they thought in the thirties, Beate asked, who had just read about the inter-war years, only they spoke about genetic inheritance and gene transmission? They believed that intelligence and all the best qualities were concentrated in lineages that could pass them on. By selection, or something like that, I didn't quite get it. But that's probably where the saying 'in the best of families' comes from.

She was proud of having learnt so much, of remembering and understanding it, of speaking like a grown-up.

So what? Bea Britt said. No matter what you call what's passed on to you, it's still yours. And coming from a good family has always helped.

Not me, Beate replied, I'd sooner have freedom than inheritance. I can be whom I want.

Christ, Bea Britt said, and went out into the garden.

What's with Bea Britt? Beate asks her mother, a question she has put previously, without getting any clear answers. Her mother shrugs, says something about how talented Bea Britt is. It was too bad about the divorce, she will say, but her two kids are extraordinary. Then she will talk about Tuva, who is so intelligent and funny and outgoing, she always brings her up. As though Tuva's cheerful temperament can make up for Bea Britt's gloomy disposition.

Mum wears tan leather gloves when driving. Driving gloves, she says, they give *feeling*, and *feeling* is the big difference between boring and fun. Her hair sweeps over her chin and mouth as she twists around to reverse out of the parking spot.

Beate thinks Mum working at the university library complicates things. For instance, she does not want to sit there to study even though her friends do, does not want Mum to see how she lives her life. Erik usually sits there, on the third floor, and Beate would like to go up, pretend not to notice him, walk slowly between the rows of desks in the reading room, keeping an eye out for an empty spot, act like she does not see him before he has had ample opportunity to look at her body. She knows it looks good to boys, and reckons Erik is a boy who is used to hooking up with girls who look good. Who *only* wants girls who look good.

She also likes walking around Akademika, the campus bookshop, browsing the titles, taking them off the shelves and leafing through them, looking at the pictures if they are art books. But Mum does that too. They have often run into one another there. In wintertime, Mum wears her red coat, the same one as when Beate was small, it never seems to wear, Mum says and laughs, because in truth it is practically hanging off her, the lining is torn, there are buttons missing and the wool is nubbled. All the same she still wears it, wants to feel young, she says, and that is daft, Beate tells her, because the coat is old and makes her look old. But Mum is not bothered, and when Beate rounds the corner of a bookshelf, she can sometimes be standing there, in the red coat, concentrating deeply on reading. If she looks up and catches sight of Beate she smiles so as to melt her, at least that is what happens: Beate loves *Mum's smile*. That is the reason she needs to avoid her up here at Blindern, she does not want to feel like going home with her mother all the time. It is impossible to be angry with Mum.

Mum drives fast, but not too fast, Dad says she is an amazing driver. She puts music on, Lady Gaga, loud of course, rolls down the window and sings along.

You and Tuva are actually quite alike, Beate says, and I bear a resemblance to Bea Britt, isn't that strange, we're not related after all? And I'm named after her and everything.

But that makes Mum cross, and she says she completely disagrees, not at all, she says. Tuva takes after Bea Britt, no doubt about it, and only you could have been mine, are *mine*, she says. Well, and your Dad's, of course, but it sounds as though she thinks that is neither here nor there. Mum and Dad are so different, and Beate does not know why this is, but they both feel like something she can sink into at any time, like sleep. What stands out most about Mum is her smile, her face, and her smell. When she was small it was just as if she and Mum were one and the same. When Mum was nearby everything was good. When she was gone things could become scary and unpleasant. She could begin to get cold. Get a lump in her throat. Not manage to say anything. Not if Dad was there of course. He would pick her up and carry her away from any difficulties, whether her mittens were cold and wet, or some older children spoke to her whom she did not dare to answer. She would sway off on his arm, and leave the problems behind them, she would not see them any longer. Sometimes he carried her around the living room while she rested her head on his shoulder. He looked at the TV and spoke to Mum at the same time, and his voice rumbled and vibrated in her body. He would hold her like that whenever she asked even long after she had begun at school. She remembers him helping her move last year, seeing him carry her boxes and furniture up all the steps. Dad can carry a lot, and she tells him things she never says to Mum. About what she is worried she will not manage. That she wants him to teach her to drive, but does not want Mum to know. Mum is so good at everything, she is sort of everywhere and knows best, but it cannot go on like that.

Beate does not *need* Erik. She thinks about it as she cuts diagonally across the quad, that Erik is probably the opposite of *the right one*, that he will act as a poison in her body, she pictures sperm spurting out of a hole in his penis, and it is *the dark gate to hell*, I am afraid, Beate thinks, I do not understand any of this.

She gets there late and sits at the back. The lecture has begun and she cannot concentrate, she looks for Erik, his brown head of hair. She cannot see him. She looks slowly around the auditorium once more, lets her gaze sweep along row after row, the back of every boy's neck. Her hands around one of them. No one knows what might happen.

Erik is not here today, she can imagine where he is. In his room at the student residence in Kringsjå with a girl. Definitely. The communal kitchen swollen with sunshine, the cheese slicer cutting deep in a block of yellow cheese. She has been at Erik's, to a party on his floor, but it was chaotic. She saw him snog several different girls, at one point he looked her in the eyes at the same time as he stood kissing Sølvi in a doorway. When they broke off he smiled to Beate, and raised a beer bottle by way of greeting. Even Sølvi, who is willing to do pretty much anything to land a boyfriend, and therefore never gets one, had the brains to leave. Fuck's sake, she said, and marched off demonstratively into the kitchen where there was some sort of quiz going on. Still, Erik did not come over to Beate, he just stood there, leaning against the door frame smiling, but not long enough for it to be embarrassing, for her to get something on him. Is this some kind of game? Beate thought, as she watched him disappear, off into another room, or maybe he left, because she did not see him again that night.

Someone opens the door of the auditorium. It could be him. She turns her head slightly, but keeps her eyes fixed on the lecturer. Everyone says she has a beautiful profile.

Whomever just entered has not moved, is still standing by the door. Jesus, then it is him, she thinks, it is happening now, it has started. She feels an uncontrollable pounding inside. Sometimes things are just like this. Everything just happens, goes quickly and turns out exactly as she imagined. As she is imagining it. No, right before. Like when she is writing assignments and the words come before the thoughts, or is it the other way around? Her thoughts tear down barriers, she is in any case in front of herself as it were, ahead of what is going to happen, like now, as she turns and sees Erik over by the door. He lights up and waves, squeezes past the person sitting at the end of her row and comes toward her with his jacket open and his bag in his hand. She smiles and holds the folding seat beside her down so he can sit. He smells of soap, deodorant and aftershave, boy's smells, she feels a tingling in her chest. He bends over his bag to take out a ring binder. He cannot find a pen and asks to borrow one, she gives him her own and takes out another for herself from her pencil case. They smile to one another, then he turns his head and looks towards the lecturer. He seems to be listening but does not write anything down. She glances over at his notes from yesterday, they are going in all directions on the page, some are boxed off and underlined, others are crossed out in heavy pen. After a while he places one hand on the table. She understands that it is a signal, that it is for her if she wants it.

8

It is her nerves. They are overstrained. So Dr Vold says. He has not said anything else so far, not even after she told him about Hartvig's plans to divorce. Only that it would probably be best if they both came in to talk to him.

She remembers one time in late winter, standing in the wardrobe among the winter overcoats and jackets. The sun was shining through the little window and it was warm. It was time to tidy away galoshes, pitch-seam skiing and winter boots. But it was as though she were paralysed. How was she to manage all this? Finn and Hartvig. The house. It required too much of her. Could she not just – what did all this have to do with her? The house, clothes, the roads up here, the large gardens.

Sometimes she sees Papa down on the road. He wears a dark coat all year round. Stops at the gate. He takes the underground from the city for the sole purpose of standing to look at the house she lives in. Then he walks off. She cries. She is never going to say what he did. What was it anyway? There does not seem to be anything left of it other than the images she has of his big white face. The feeling. The anger, his or hers. The hatred in his features. The leather seat of the chair, his hand. Papa was horrid.

It was completely dark. She could not find a door, the floor was cold and scraped the skin on her knees when she fell. Weeping, scrambling. She could not go anywhere, could not go out. No Mama, nothing. When he finally opened up, it was too late. She was empty, blown clean through. He sat her at the table and made her eat the cold leftovers from dinner. It was something in thick gravy. The sun shone right in the windows, the surface of the table was scorching hot. She thought the room was visiting the house and that she would never come home again. Now and then they heard the black children yell and shout in the blocks beyond.

Sunday. Heat everywhere. White Sunday dress, white socks, sweaty shoes. Boredom. She has been told to wait, not to get dirty. The stairs have two planks on every step with a little gap between each. She jumps up on the first step, hops on one leg to the next, alternates between two feet and one. Up on the veranda she turns and does the same back down. The grass is bare at the bottom of the steps, a little hollow formed by all the feet walking here every day. Dry sand is sent into the air when she lands in the sunken patch, covering her shoes in a thin layer of dust. She draws a line with her forefinger, one on the tip of each shoe. Her back is sweaty and hot. Her dress tight and stuffy, her stomach quivers when she jumps, and her socks are warm and itchy. It is hard to breathe. The heat makes her throat feel thick. The windows in the house are open. Cessi hears their voices, not what they are saying, but what Papa is doing, that he is drinking, from both the big and the little glass. Hears him moving around the living room, raising his voice to Mama, he is teasing her, in that way she does not like. Why are they not coming? She clambers into the hammock on the veranda. It is lovely and shaded there, and she wants to swing but her feet do not reach the ground. She pulls herself up and stands, holding on to the frame, she sets the hammock in motion by bending her knees. Up and down, up and down. She is not allowed to stand in the hammock with shoes on. Not in her bare feet either. But she only does it once, to get it moving. Then she slides down into the seat. The speed is such that the frame lifts a little from the ground. She sits with legs outstretched and the tips of her shoes touch the edge of the table when the hammock swings forward. Then the table lifts a little too, the legs scraping on the veranda floor. She bends forward and backward, throwing her back into the seat and bending far forward to see if she can manage to keep the speed up that way.

She does not know how long he has been standing at the veranda door watching her. He is smiling, but is angry. She notices he has taken off his jacket and rolled up his shirt-sleeves even though they are to go for an outing in the park. Her brother Finn cries in the living room and Mama says a few words to him. Papa has probably said that they are not going. Or that Finn cannot come along. Then Mama calls out: Johan, can you please come in? And bring Cessi with you.

Papa does not answer. He looks at her as she sits unmoving in the hammock. It is only rocking ever so slightly now.

Are you bored, Cecilie? Papa smiles and smiles.

She nods.

I gathered that. *Since you were standing in the hammock with your shoes on.* He roars the last part. The fear gives her a bad taste in the mouth. When he is like this it turns white, cold and flowing in her all at the same time. She sits completely still so as not to do anything that could provoke him. That is what Mama says: Try not to provoke him.

Get up. His voice is calm but not kind. She waits a moment. Then he comes towards her, takes hold of her arm, squeezes it, lifts her up, hurting her under the arm and in the shoulder. He puts her down hard on the floor, and she stumbles, has to take a step backwards and feels the seat hit the backs of her knees, making them give, and she falls back onto the hammock again.

Stand still! he roars, pulls her up from the seat but does not strike her. He seldom hits her, but it can happen, and she never knows when it is coming. Usually not when Mama is at home, not when she can hear in any case. Now she is standing in the doorway with Finn on her arm shouting something to Papa which Cessi cannot hear because her heart is pounding so loudly in her ears. But Mama says it again: Papa has to come now. They're ready to go. Papa does not want to. He tells Mama to stop nagging. She can take her mummy's boy with her, yes, she and Finn can go to the park on their own. He is going to cure Cessi of her boredom, they are going to take a walk. He pulls her down the steps. Mama follows after, she calls out for him to stop with this foolishness. And Cecilie doesn't have a hat, she cries out, you can't take her anywhere in this heat. Finn wails, but Papa leaves with her. His hand is angry and squeezes hers much too tightly. He walks too quickly as well.

A hat, he says, surely you don't need a hat when it's this warm, Cecilie. And then he laughs. He is mean. He knows all too well that you need a hat to protect your head from the sun. Mama and Finn are good, they get to stay in the shade of the house, rock in the hammock, drink squash. It is nice there when Papa is not at home. Papa is here with her. She was naughty and stood with shoes on in the hammock and made everything nasty and white and wrong. They walk and walk.

At some spots the trees cast shadows on the pavement, but mostly the sun beats right down on them. She sweats and is both thirsty and sick.

Papa, she says, Papa. He walks so quickly she needs to run alongside him. If she stops he tugs her, pulling her on. Eventually they come to the café. They have taken a roundabout way, because she knows it is right by their house. Papa's friends are sitting around one of the tables. The sunlight outside makes the room seem dark as they enter. Two big fans turn in the ceiling and the door is open. There is a draught and it is airy and had it not been for all the tobacco smoke from the pipes and cigarettes it would have been lovely. The men wear white shirts with sleeves rolled up, just like Papa. They have hairy arms and large bodies, powerful legs in dark Sunday trousers, shiny shoes that scrape the floor beneath the table when they move their feet. Their voices are deep, they almost shout when they speak, and when they laugh it is much too loud and does not sound like laughter. More like they *want* to laugh than actually laugh. When they catch sight of Papa they bellow *oi! Johan* and wave him in the direction of the table, move to make room, the legs of the chairs scraping, and the owner comes with one big and one little glass. Beer and spirits. Papa lets go of her hand and sits down. She recognises the faces of Peter and Robert. They work with Papa at the *shipyard* and have been to visit the house together with their wives. Their children were still only babies and she could not play with them, only with Finn. They sat around the garden table drinking then too. Not Mama and the wives, but Papa and the men.

Well, well, Johan, such fine company you have today. A little lady.

Peter looks at her and he is not mean, but his eyes are strange.

Lovely dress, yes, lovely dress.

Peter has drunk many small glasses, they are on the table in front of him.

Oh, she won't be a nuisance. She's going to practise standing with her feet on the ground and not on sofas and that kind of thing. Papa turns to Cessi.

Go and wait by the door.

The skin on Papa's face looks as though it is heavy to carry. His cheeks and the bags under his eyes hang. He does not look directly at her. His moustache is really horrible. She can hardly breathe when he hugs her goodnight and it scratches and pricks her in the face.

Even though he was talking to her, it was somehow as if it was not to her all the same, but to the men around the table, it is them he is with now. So she remains standing for a moment.

Can I have something to drink, Papa?

Do as I say!

Papa strikes the table, but she is well aware it is to show off to Peter and the others.

Come, come, Johan, no need to make such a fuss. Peter laughs. Surely she can have a little water.

Peter turns towards the counter to attract the owner's attention.

But Papa shakes his head.

They only serve grown-ups here, he says, and disobedient little girls don't get anything. Nobody says a word. Papa looks at her and points at the door.

Papa is not right in the head.

She's a plump little one, Johan, one of the others says in a loud voice, is that what they mean by too much of a good thing?

Ah, she hears Papa say, come back in ten years, you'll be singing a different tune I'd say. There ought to be something to grab on to. She'll be a fine thing. If you behave yourself I'll let you borrow her, free of charge.

They break out in laughter around the table. Peter says, Johan, for God's sake, she can *hear* you!

Cessi stands at the steps. The sun is shining straight in the door and windows, and it is terribly hot there even though the awnings provide shade. She is sore in the small of her back and her feet hurt from standing so long, but as she goes to sit on the steps, Papa shouts from inside that she is to get up.

You were the one who was so eager to stand, he calls out.

She stands and stands. Now and again people pass by on the pavement. Women with parasols and prams. Gentlemen with walking sticks, and children in their Sunday best holding the men by the hand. They are their *daddies.* Papa is not a proper daddy, she knows that. No one can help her, people have to pass right by, and she has to stand there. She has almost melted and become invisible when Peter comes with a chair and a glass of water, and this time Papa does not say anything, not that she can hear anyway.

The sun is not shining on the house any more when he comes out, she thinks it must soon be night. Papa carries her, because she cannot manage to stand.

There there, little Cessi, he mumbles, lovely little Cessi, come to Papa. Papa is sorry. But now you've learnt. Haven't you? Papa is sorry. And he rubs her up and down the back. He smells of alcohol, staggers and steps off the pavement several times.

When they arrive home Mama is sitting at the table in the living room not doing anything. She has been crying. Finn is asleep. Cessi wonders if they went to the park without her, but does not ask, she is not able to speak. Nor does Papa say anything, just heaves her over to Mama, goes out onto the veranda and sits down in the hammock with his pipe and a little glass. Mama starts to cry again. Say something, Cessi, she pleads, say something. Where were you? What has he done with you? Are you hungry, do you want something to eat? But Cessi cannot open her lips, they are stuck together. Just like her arms, that are around Mama's neck. She just holds on, hangs on Mama, cannot let go. Even though Mama is so slight and pretty, and Cessi is already a big, heavy girl. Mama cries even more, and says: I'll take care of you, Cessi, take care of you, don't be afraid.

She dreams about taking the boat back to New York. Just to see. Just to sense the freedom. The relief when they left. She remembers the wind snatching at her breath when she opened the door out to the deck, the air pressure seeming to suck her out through the doorway. She stood by the railings and the sea just glided and glided by. She was going to get away! She walked to and fro in the narrow corridors, strangers smiled at her, many laughing and joking with one another. The stairs between decks were carpeted. And in the cabin it was completely quiet, it was just for her and Mama. They got hot chocolate in the dining room every morning. Mama was happy, it would be so good to come *home*, she said.

Cessi had been given a book by Mama to read on the trip.

The voyage took a good few days so she had read some of it, even though she did not particularly like reading. It was about a poor little girl who became a governess and married the wealthiest man in the parish because she was so exceedingly good and kind even though she had suffered greatly.

Mama thought the profession of schoolmistress might suit her. Within the practical area, mind you. Needlework, perhaps. But not a governess, Cessi said, having no wish to suffer. No, dear, Mama replied, not a governess. Times have changed.

Yes, for many years she had dreamt of returning to New York. Before she met Hartvig and they had little Finn. She would break through by sewing, that was what she would do. Start at one of the big fashion houses. With two empty but industrious hands. She would show them. After years of hard graft she would make a name for herself in the fashion world. Clothes by Cessi. Cessi's Dressmaker's Shop. Something like that. No one would dare make fun of her. It would be something else altogether from the unsuccessful year she spent at the sewing class. A wicked burning in her chest.

Papa accompanied them all the way to Kristiania. That was a fly in the ointment. But he was not staying. He had to get back to work, Mama said. She said that for several years, his contract isn't up yet, she said, or: Papa likes it there. Now and again he came to stay with them in the apartment in Frogner for a few weeks at a time, or a few months, and then he drank, hit, threw things around. On occasion he would come home drunk and roaring in the middle of the night, throw them out of the apartment and lock the door. The following day Cessi would walk arm in arm with her friends and tell them how mad he was, her father. Oh dear, they said, oh, poor you, but Cessi merely laughed, with the expression of someone who has suffered much and become hard and tough, that was how she wanted to appear, and how she became. Because her friends' horrified reactions mixed with compassion warmed her, but only in the moment. Once alone again, she felt how it was in reality, how everything she told them marked her. Inwardly they turned away, her friends, they were deceitful, it was only their curiosity and appetite for sensation that made them flock around her momentarily. Because she was sullied, vile, disgusting, they saw her the way she saw Papa, she heard herself talk like him when she told them what he had done. Oh yes, she was disgusting, and her frail mother had bruises on her arms. Not so strange then, that Mama wanted a divorce the day Papa came home to Norway for good.

I made my mind up that day, Mama said later, that time he came home with you, and you were completely white in the face, I thought you were going to die.

Cessi likes to hear about it, how Mama had to hold her, how despairing she was for her sake. At the same time she gets angry and wants to hit Mama. She knew damn well which café Papa usually went to at that time. There was no getting away from it. Mama was cowardly.

The next time she is at Dr Vold's she tells him that the nervousness is probably caused by natural changes in the body. She *is expecting*. Dr Vold must be well aware that— she breaks off in the middle of what she is saying. It must be the first time she has seen him look surprised, he always looks as though he knows best about everything. He even puts his pen down and looks. At her. Her stomach, her breasts, her face. Yes, it seems to be four months already, she says, hot in the face, hot all over, trembling, the blood flowing heavily down below, along the insides of her thighs. Those eyes. To be kissed by that mouth. Rasping stubble. Strong jaw. Firm lips. Hot, hot. Her breasts tingle. Even though she is with child.

Are you happy, Mrs Viker? Dr Vold is still leaning back in his chair.

Children are a gift from God. That is the kind of thing Mama says. People say that type of thing. So she does too. Dr Vold leans forward and picks up his pen, makes a note, his face has the usual, closed expression now: And what does Mr Viker say?

Hartvig? He's pleased. Children are what being a family is about. One child is not enough. It's how things ought to be. And the divorce? Hm, divorce? She is with child. She is not thinking. Her body is following nature's course. The doctor asks if she is apprehensive about how busy things will get. Busy? She does not know. It is an anaesthetic of sorts. She does not feel anything. Is not anxious. Does not know. But Dr Vold is concerned. He says so. Will they be able to afford help around the house? A nanny? More a question of if he is willing to pay for one. Hartvig is miserly, she says. Time enough to worry about that. Perhaps it'll do me good to forget myself a little more, she says. Those were Hartvig's words. She believes in Hartvig now. He wants to support her. Even though he is slight and feeble. She sits in the chair at Dr Vold's and leans heavily on Hartvig. Everything he says at the moment seems like the right solution to what she cannot manage to cope with. The doctor can do what he likes. Him and his aloof, pretty wife.

She looks at the desk lamp. The brooch is still lying in the little hollow in the stand, with a couple of binder clips and his fountain pen. Oh, she would like that brooch. Green, shiny, curved. Put the pin through her lapel, fasten the catch. She fixes her gaze on the carpet. It is not her brooch, she cannot have it.

The worst part about being pregnant is that she should not drink beer and preferably not smoke. She is well aware of it, they do not recommend it, no spicy seasonings, no strong drinks or powerful mood swings, it can be transmitted to the little one. But the one or two small bottles of ice-cold beer she drinks in the evening are precisely what keep her in balance. Hartvig speaks harshly to her about this, the improper urges she has for stimuli. It is not seemly, he says, and maintains she needs to work on her weak strength of character. At the least sign of adversity she reaches for something to help her, it is a trait in her he dislikes, he says, it is extremely unbecoming. Cessi laughs in anger, and says she can understand why he is so preoccupied with outward appearances and etiquette, what with those short, ugly legs of his. She does not say this to Dr Vold. Because supposing she cannot do without the bottles of beer, what happens then, what will they do with her? Dear oh dear, no, it does not bear thinking about, so many what-ifs, so many thoughts to grapple with, best to let it go. In the dim light beneath the desk she can just make out Dr Vold's shoes and trousers, she imagines his legs are probably quite hairy as well. The doctor needs her, if not he could not be a doctor. She does not know where that thought came from. That he must think healthy people are boring. That he himself is boring.

9

The helicopters hang over our heads. Hundreds of volunteers in yellow high-visibility vests search the vicinity. Advancing in rows, they use long sticks to poke the grass, heather and undergrowth aside, planting them carefully in the ground where it is hard to see. Every day new searches, but no finds other than the initial ones: behind Vettakollen station they discovered a nature-study book. A little further up in Huldreveien, her hoody and mobile phone lay in full view by the roadside. Nobody can explain why she had her schoolbag with her. The police have started looking through her activity on social media, checking her phone and talking to friends, and that part of the investigation is still ongoing. No witness observations have so far given any important leads in the case. The dog is also missing. The police are going door to door and talking to people in the local community. On the radio they said the police have also been granted authority to inspect certain gardens and private residences. Yet I still get a fright when they ring on my door.

Why are you here, I ask. The Red Cross search team have already been. Did the neighbours tell you I was a witch who eats little children?

The policemen do not smile. This is a serious matter. Besides, they are interested in the garden, not the house, and not because I am under suspicion but because the property is so large. There are a number of wooded areas around that need checking out, they say.

Yes, and swimming pools and underground wine cellars, I say, but they ignore that. I wonder what they are thinking. What they know about searching that I do not?

Awful lot of tarpaulins in this garden, one of them says.

He is right. But there are also a lot of bits and pieces. Dad has his stuff stored here. Firewood. The old snowblower. Broken lawnmowers. Planks, chains, cinder blocks. I cannot face tackling it, not until Dad and his sisters agree on what is going to happen with the house. There are so many steps that have to be taken. Can't you get rid of all this? I asked, but he responded by arriving with a carload of tarpaulins from Biltema, or some other catalogue store, and covered every pile. Won't the damp get in under those? I asked, but he did not answer me. He was at it for hours, pulling things closer and stacking them higher so there would be fewer piles. Then he threw the tarpaulins over and placed roof tiles along the edges to hold them in place. All the same, there were still seven big heaps by the time he was done.

Dad, that looks creepy. The way I spoke. Would I never get beyond twelve years old?

I don't give a shit about the neighbours, he said, so you don't need to put on any bloody airs either.

The police tramp away and set about pulling off all the tarpaulins. They do not ask if I mind, nor do they put them back in place. I begin to cry when I catch sight of a pink schoolbag against the snowblower. It must be Tuva's, I think, someone has taken Tuva. For a moment my child has been snatched from me. It's Tuva's, I scream, running towards the bag. But they stop me. Do not touch. I stand still and am in time again. Tuva is twenty-three years old and lives in an apartment in Grünerløkka. I was mistaken, I say. Sorry.

But now they want to see inside. One of them says: Are you the one who has her? Show us. Where have you got her? Let's go into the house. We'll help you. Then you can show us.

Are you crazy? I exclaim. Are you out of your mind?

I do not quite understand why I am so angry. I want to hit him. It is because of the questions. As though he is an adult and I a child. Perhaps he is not a policeman but some psychopath dressed up? Or is it a technique they have been taught? Catch people off guard. In case. Suspect people on the off chance. The other one does not speak. He holds me by the elbow, steers me towards the door. Come on. It'll be fine. The one who accused me talks on his mobile. I start to tremble, feel nauseous and get a ringing in my ears. Black specks appear in my vision. I try to tell them. Fainting, I say, or think I do. But then I am lying on the floor in the hallway and a moment ago I was not. One of them swears. They are standing a little way off now, talking. I call out. Hi, hello, I say loudly. I wish to be of help. Put things straight. Get up off the floor. Not lie here on my back. The one I was talking to bends his face over mine. The warmth under his uniform escapes through the openings between material and skin, I can feel it, mixed with the scent of men's deodorant, he is handsome, has kissable lips. He is too young, I think, has no sense of compassion, does not know that we are all going to die, that we do the best we can. Does not understand a thing. Is cold or matter-of-fact, I do not know the difference.

The other one is from up north. He is busy with something or other. Probably that telephone call. Arranging something between themselves, which I am not to get wind of. The police are always that way. Acting as though they know something more. Or maybe they do. Whatever that might be. The person who commits the crime knows most no matter what.

Can she stand?

They are not asking me but each other. Is she able to get up?

Think so, yeah.

Then we'll walk up this set of stairs here, he says to me. As though I am not familiar with my own stairs. One man on either side, one hand under each arm. Young men, strong men. If I were ten years younger they would be friendlier. But I am just a middle-aged woman now. A random body, in all its weight and helplessness.

I have to ask for a glass of water. They do not realise that I need one. Or is it because they suspect me? I am a suspect, not a victim, so I do not deserve water.

The talkative one is given a dressing down in the kitchen. Later on, this is, when the house is full of people and two patrol cars are parked in the yard. The policemen and the officer in charge are talking in the kitchen and the one from the north raises his voice: *What good was that? You just frightened her.* The officer in charge says something I do not catch.

Afterwards we sit at the big, heavy claw-foot table. One of them asks most of the questions, while the other one comes over now and again and sits down beside him. They ask about everything. What I write. Why I am not married. Not *if* I am married, but *why* I am not.

Is that a normal question? I ask, but they just put another one to me instead of answering. Do I like living by myself in such a big house? And why do I have a knife in the drawer?

Which drawer, what knife?

He holds it up for me to see. The old sheath knife with the black handle. It was in the desk drawer.

Because I sharpen my pencil with it.

Don't you have a pencil sharpener?

I do, but I like using that, my father taught me. We use a knife to sharpen pencils, I say, and picture the rugged wood at the end after the knife has been, the lead that turns flat if you whittle away too much.

They ask to see my pencils but I cannot find any.

It's probably been a good while, I say.

A good while since what? they ask. Since I used a pencil, I say. Since Dad and I sharpened pencils together, I think, a good while since childhood and adolescence. Yet it is always present, pulling and pulling.

They want the telephone number for Mum and Dad. For Tuva and Georg. For Knut. They ask if I have a good relationship with the children. If we are close. They ask if I can tell them something about my sexual orientation.

Now you're overstepping the mark, I say.

This concerns a kidnapping, he replies.

Have I had relationships with other women in the past?

I become weary. I don't know, I say. I don't know.

What is it that I do not know? Do I not know if I am a lesbian? If I am attracted to children? No, I don't know anything about that girl.

The same questions are put to me over and over, in particular:

Where were you the day she disappeared?

Here. In the garden. Or inside the house.

*

Someone else hid the bag in my garden, not me. Now we are at the police station, and that is what I tell them: somebody else hid it. Why would somebody do that? they ask. What reason do I think they might have? It must be the type of question intended to catch me out. They think if they get me to speculate around what occurred I might end up spilling the beans, it would be so natural, easy to talk your way into, hard to talk your way out of. I am aware of that and think they are stupid. Or that their strategy is clever but they themselves are stupid. Only idiots could have suspected me. At least they are nice. I am given coffee and a baguette sandwich wrapped in clingfilm. But they do not get it.

Just look at the garden, I say. It's huge and in a mess. Completely overgrown. And all that stuff, all those tarpaulins. You could easily hide there, or hide somebody else there.

Have you hidden Emilie in the garden as well? they ask.

No.

But you hid the bag, why did you hide the bag?

I didn't hide it.

You just threw it there, didn't care if anyone found it or not?

No.

But you did put it there?

No, I didn't put it there.

What about the tarpaulins? Why do you have so many?

They belong to my father.

Your father?

He doesn't like throwing things away.

Do you like hanging on to things as well?

No. I usually throw out junk, I don't like having too much stuff. I don't like clutter.

Did you throw out Emilie's things as well? Is Emilie a thing you'd like to get rid of as well?

No.

So you like Emilie, don't want to get rid of her?

I don't know Emilie.

They show me several photographs of Emilie.

Have you never seen her before?

Yes, I have seen her.

When?

On the road now and again. When she walks her dog. It was the dog that first caught my attention. I like dogs.

So you like dogs?

Yes.

Did you maybe want to take the dog from Emilie, did you think you could take better care of it?

No, on the contrary. I thought she was good with it. Taking it out often, going on long walks. And she did it by herself, even though girls that age rarely go anywhere without their friends.

So, you thought about that, her walking on her own?

No, that it was good of her to walk the dog even though she was on her own.

Did you follow her?

No.

How do you know she takes long walks?

I see her on the way back.

Couldn't she just have been visiting a friend?

Yes, she could.

So you keep an eye out for her, do you sit by the window waiting for her to come back the other way?

No.

Isn't it a little odd, your seeing her all the time, don't you have other things to be doing?

I didn't say I saw her all the time. Sometimes. My writing desk is by the window.

But it's been a good while since you wrote any books?

Yes.

Yet you still sit at the desk?

Yes. I'm trying. I have writer's block.

And in the meantime it's your parents who support you?

Yes, and I receive a grant.

It continues like this. It takes a long time. At noon I am given a break and another baguette sandwich. We switch interview rooms. Mum, Dad, Tuva and Georg are to be questioned in the room I have been in. I do not see them, it is the one conducting the interview who informs me, but I do not have the energy to ask him why. You can talk to Beate too, I say. Beate is often round. And her mother, Anita. She's my best friend. Actually, I don't see much of her any more. The interviewer does not reply. I wonder if he has so much to think about that he did not hear what I said. Or is it some type of trick: am I supposed to feel as though I have no power, as though nothing I come out with will influence the situation?

The room I am moved to is exactly the same as the last. White walls, no windows. Recording equipment, a PC. A rubbish bin beneath the table we sit either side of. I glance up at the vent on the wall. Imagine if I said that I think there's someone in the ventilation shaft watching us, I said. That in not too long my accomplices were going to spray poison gas through the ventilation system.

The man conducting the interview stares fixedly at me.

Do you think I'm daft? I ask. He does not answer. Everything is being recorded so he cannot say what he wants. Do you believe that, he asks, do you actually mean it? At the same time he types something into the PC. I am guessing he is writing a comment on what I said. What, I do not know.

No, I say. But do you really believe that I have something to do with Emilie's disappearance? Anybody could have put that bag there.

This is an investigation, he says.

Yes, I say.

In the evening I am allowed to go. I have been cleared of any involvement in the case, they say. For the time being. The pleasure was all mine. I told them everything there was to tell. Almost. I was reluctant to tell them about Emilie while I was sitting there. Not that it was of any significance. I just had a feeling that they must not find out that I often stuck close to the gate around the time Emilie took the dog for a walk. That we sometimes spoke. That I opened the gate and went into the road to say hello to Skee, who would jump into my arms, the way miniature poodles do, to be better able to lick my face. I was so soft on that dog. His name is actually Skeeto, Emilie told me, as in *Skipper & Skeeto* on children's TV, you know, Mummy says he's as small as a mosquito, and when we cuddle him we just say skee, skee, skee, she said, laughing, while the dog hopped up and down, squeaking with joy at hearing its name.

Emilie reminds me of Tuva that way. The way she rabbits on. She is not like her in other ways. I would never have been able to get Tuva to take Balder on such long walks, or to have her do homework before she left, for that matter. Emilie does, she has told me so. But Emilie and Skee are gone now, and on the late-night news they say that the police have interviewed numerous people in connection with the discovery of Emilie's bag, but are still following several lines of inquiry with regard to the case.

10

I watch all the news broadcasts that night. Georg is with me, Tuva too. Mum and Dad. And Knut, even though he has not forgiven me. I was not the person he thought, he is still bitter about that.

Now, you see, I say to Dad, when you have an odd dress sense and have strange stuff in the garden, it makes people suspicious. Not just the neighbours, the police too, look at the way they're acting.

It's true, Mum says, I've been trying to tell you that for years, Finn, but you just don't want to listen.

No, Dad peers at the TV screen, neither listening nor responding. He'll hang on to whatever junk he wants, after all, the things are in his house, aren't they, in his garden.

In any case, Tuva is quick to defend him. What are you on about, she says, odd dress sense? They brought you in for questioning because of Emilie's bag, Mum, not because of the garden or what clothes Granddad wears, they didn't even know who he was before that.

But the bag was only there because of the garden, wasn't it? Huge piles covered with tarpaulins. Chaos and clutter. And not mowing the lawn or cutting back the hedge, it's just asking for this kind of crap.

Well, you're the one who doesn't tend to the garden, Mum.

The newsreader in the studio is talking to a reporter who

is standing outside our house. In the background we can make out the red-and-white barricade tape and police busy in the garden, wearing headlamps. What are they doing now, I ask, I thought they were finished searching here?

When Tuva pulls the curtain aside to look out, we see her on the TV screen, a dark figure in the light of the window. The TV crew's lights shine on the neighbours who have turned out and the assembled journalists.

This is nuts, Tuva says, standing looking at the screen again, I can look out and see what's happening at the same time as it's on TV. She turns up the volume. NRK are reshowing the footage from earlier in the day when the police searched the house and garden. They had three dogs with them. Alsatians that unrelentingly sniffed the grass and Dad's scrap piles.

It is a question of time, the police say. When Emilie walked past my gate with Skee on a lead, what time could it have been? They have tried to work it out. When she was last seen. When she took the dog's lead down from the peg on the wall, when she locked the door, shouldered her schoolbag, when she walked down the hill and crossed the tramlines. At times the dog has tugged on the lead, and she has stopped to let it sniff around or pee.

If she took her usual route, she would have passed by my house around two o'clock, they reckon, and minutes later she is gone. Or at least nobody has seen her after that, neither in Skogryggveien or Huldreveien, where they found her things.

If I had been standing at the gate then. Or if Emilie had walked a different way. If someone had looked up and seen what was about to happen. That a car pulled up, yes, perhaps that is how it happened: the car stopped. There may have been more than one so they could lift her into the car, two, maybe three. No one heard her shout, the dog did not bark, nobody saw a thing. It must have happened quickly. If only I had been by the gate, then time would not have changed the house and garden so radically. Now nothing is the same any more.

The policeman from the north is standing on the Persian rug in the living room still wearing his boots. I have not heard the doorbell and do not understand how he has come to be standing there. For a moment my thoughts veer off course and I think it is he who has taken Emilie, that he has only dressed up as a policeman. But that is not how it is. So how is it actually, why are they plodding in here without any warning? Is it because they are in a hurry or due to a lack of respect? Do they think I am worthless? Perhaps I do not exist, I am someone other than I have always thought, and they have cottoned on, realised who I am and what I have done. Jelly-like.

Am I under suspicion, I ask crossly, seeing how all of you traipse in and out as you please? He does not reply. Or at least I do not remember what he said later, not to that. But I do remember him saying they needed to conduct several more searches of the house. New finds in the garden necessitate it. What could that be? I think. Blood? Are you going to look for evidence while we're here? Tuva asks. Detectives on TV never do that. But maybe you view us as a part of the evidence?

He shakes his head, they do not. Naturally, we cannot be here.

Your mother shouldn't take it personally, he says to Tuva.

He was *gorgeous*, Tuva says, watching from the window as he trudges over the gravel towards the gate and the waiting patrol car.

I go up to the bedroom to pack a bag. The window is open. Outside, a strong wind is blowing. Is it Emilie's wind, her solace? Is she lying out there in the forest, her face expressionless, empty, while it soughs in the trees above? And in the morning the sun will rise and shine upon her, the grass will be green where she is lying, and the blades will sway, a new day with warm wind over her, while her body is still here. And the dog. It is terrified.

I am staying over at Tuva's place. We are sitting on her bed and she is showing me her exam paper in archiving. She is going to be a librarian, but only as a temporary solution to what she terms her employment problem.

This is a keyword hierarchy, she says, and here are the references. You can't refer to something you don't have an instance of in the literature. You can't write *Elephants*, see also *Tusks*, if there's no documents about tusks in the library. However, from *Tusks* you can point in the direction of *Elephants* if the library has books about elephants, which they no doubt have.

Tears well up in my eyes. It seems so beautiful. To cross-refer from something that does not exist to something that does. Well, tusks exist, of course, it is the documentation that is lacking. I picture hierarchies with loose ends that cannot be brought together. Love hanging, dangling.

Before going to bed I put my arms around Tuva and hold

her body against mine. Our kneecaps, hips and breasts touching. She is four centimetres taller than me, and holding her like this, I feel the child's form within the larger body, a gentle weight, the small, soft arm around my neck, the hand playing with my hair.

II

They did not go to the halls of residence in Kringsjå, but home to her place on Observatorie Terrasse. She did not know it was supposed to be like this. That it could feel so good in her body she had to scream. That it did not stop. That tears would come. That he would shed some too. That her lips would sting. That he would cry out in her mouth. Now they will not let go of one another. They are naked, neither of them has the upper hand. Now nothing bad can happen, Erik says, his mouth against her throat, no one can get to us here, it's just you and me.

Mum rings the following day and attempts to rope her into the possible purchase of a Persian rug. I need something beautiful, she says. It is just that she feels so restricted, finds it difficult to change anything in the house when everything found its place so long ago. Besides, Dad won't hear of it, he doesn't like splurging, and one of those carpets, it could put you back a few thousand kroners. She *really* wants it though. And she has her own money, but Dad's views are holding her back, she doesn't want to rile him. True, the rug would be for the floor of *her* study, but still, he is right about the cost, and they do have the constant expense of the upkeep of the house to think of. But, Jesus, on the other hand, they do earn good money after all, her and Dad, there is no question they can afford it.

So what do you think, Beate, Mum says, would you like to inherit a Persian rug some day or not? And then she laughs.

Bea Britt has lots of Persian rugs, Beate says, and that gets Mum going: yes, exactly, have you seen the one in the first-floor living room, it's lovely, I'd love to have one like that. Bea Britt doesn't need to ask anyone's permission, she's lucky, she can do what she wants in her house, and she has good taste. Mum laughs again. Bea Britt is Mum's best friend, or at least she was, now they hardly ever see each other. It is Mum's fault, Beate thinks, she avoids Bea Britt, becomes distant if I bring her name up and does not reply to her text messages. Is Anita very busy, Bea Britt will ask, or has she changed her mobile number? I never get a reply from her any more.

Bea Britt is so serious, Mum says when Beate asks why they have lost touch, I don't know, I feel kind of *stuck* with her, and she bores me, she doesn't have a particularly positive outlook on life.

Beate has been standing in the kitchen looking out at the lawn, but now she is so tired of the talk about the Persian rug that she has to sit down. She has never noticed it before, how the thought of the rooms in Mum and Dad's place makes her empty and tired. All their things, it is as though they cannot be budged, but stand where they stand. The restrained energy in Mum's voice. Dad's resistance. Mum's thoughts revolving around the same thing, her doing the rounds of shops that stock Persian rugs. Bea Britt's rooms are different, even though they are also filled with things she seldom moves. Old, worn-out things, giving off a sense of unease, Beate thinks, as though they should not be where they are if they cannot demonstrate having *purpose*. Is it because Bea Britt does not think about them, does not dust, just leaves them be? Or is it the disquiet in the house, something in the atmosphere, the stories of those who have lived there, or just Bea Britt herself?

Beate believes Bea Britt is unhappy, but she does not quite understand why.

I'd love to inherit a beautiful Persian rug, she says to Mum, feel free to tell Dad that, maybe that'll convince him.

But I do not want to, she thinks, why did I say that, I do *not* want to inherit it, why do I give in?

Mum sounds relieved when they hang up, but will probably continue dithering, Beate thinks. She will buy the rug but only after a lot of back and forth, and after buying it she will regret it and be ashamed of her extravagance for ages. Then she will forget both the doubt and the regret.

The purchase of an expensive rug is hardly going to be what I'll think about on my deathbed, she would say, but maybe I will picture the colours and pattern. You have no idea how much I love that rug, I look at it every day and the joy it gives me, Beate!

There are so many things about Mum like that, Beate thinks, way too many. It is not wrong, and it is not right, but kind of vague, not quite as it should be. Not the way Beate wants it to be.

She and Erik have been a couple for three days. Together at his place, at her place and at the campus at Blindern. During lectures they sit right up close to one another, in the breaks they hold hands. Erik does not joke about as much as usual. They stand in a circle with the others outside the auditorium in the breaks, and every time he says something he will glance at her. Is he afraid she will think he is stupid? But she hardly listens to what he is saying, is only aware of his body, of his breathing, of his wrist brushing against her arm.

She feels she can see right through everything and everyone now, that she can read other people's minds by the expressions on their faces. Several of the girls are jealous, resentful almost. Sølvi will not talk to her. Some of the boys blush and look away when she says something. She sees the coherence in what the lecturer is saying as intricate patterns in the air, and she draws them more than she writes. Colours seem so strong. Smells. And food, it is almost impossible to eat fish balls in white sauce at Frederikke canteen, the floury taste and pudding-like mass in her mouth makes her nauseous. Erik laughs when she complains about the fish balls, goes to the counter and buys chicken salad and a cake for her instead. Now it is almost seven o'clock and there are not many diners left. They sit by themselves in a corner and Erik feeds her with a white plastic fork. He wears a red and blue checked scarf around his neck and smiles the entire time. She needs to tell Mum and Dad about Erik before Mum runs into them somewhere on the campus. It annoys her that she cannot be in peace here. Mum has had her time, now it is Beate's turn, she feels Blindern should be hers alone.

12

Cessi has called and ordered groceries from the shop in Majorstua. For Mrs Viker, the wife of high-court lawyer Viker, she said in a high-pitched voice, and slipped in an order of five bottles of beer between the butter and oatmeal, as though nothing at all. She had thought about sending Finn to collect the shopping, but there was the matter of the bottles to consider. He noticed things like that, tattled to Hartvig. Not that she could conceal that she had been drinking, it did smell after all. But five bottles are not the same as one. One in the cupboard and four hidden in the cellar. Besides, there was a lot of snow on the ground, and Finn would most likely take his sledge, she could picture the cardboard box turning over and the bottles sliding off into the snow, such that everyone alighting from the tram would see. She put on her coat, lit up a cigarette, left her gloves, it was mild, the weather was foggy, the snow dripping from the dark pine trees. The snowplough had not been around yet, the heels of her winter boots sank into the wet snow and made walking difficult. Still, her body felt light, her waist had got so thin lately, the nursing after the last birth had taken a toll, she was weak, but all the same, she looked better now she was slender, and maintained her figure with cigarettes and coffee. The cigarette smoke tore at her chest, it felt good. Her blouse material was smooth, she felt it rub against her stomach as she walked.

She could see in the mirror that she was attractive, oh yes, her face had a sort of natural flush these days. One noticed it in the glances of men. A slight tingling in her breasts, as though something was on the way, milk, or her monthly. She felt so hot, undid a couple of buttons on her coat. If it had not been for Hartvig, and that infernal house. How she yearned for the city. For life. For something to relieve the bubbling excitement, to fall in love if possible, life, life!

The conductor helped her off with the box on her way back. I simply can't carry anything, she said, I have an inflammation in my arms.

He did not reply.

Oh, goodness, you are well able, I'm sure your wife is more than happy with you. I hope you spend more time at home than my husband, he's overworked, poor thing, and my son is no doubt out running around somewhere, or else he could have helped.

Right, the conductor said, placing the box on the sledge for her, and fastening it tight with the rope she held out.

She saw several of the men on the tram looking at her through the open door as it made its way up the hill, one of them even lifted his hat. Granted they were simple working men, platelayers. Nevertheless.

13

I am allowed to move home again, but cannot manage to think of anything but the disappearance. It taints everything. The rustle of the leaves in the trees. The grass, the roadsides, lamp posts. The empty street. This is where she walked. I picture her arm being tugged as the dog made for my gatepost, as it always does. Perhaps she had her mobile phone in her hand and took a selfie when the dog stopped to sniff. But there is nobody out there now. The air she moved through is transparent and gives nothing away.

I look over at the boat in the neighbour's garden, the police have taken off the tarpaulin which covered it, just as they have removed mine. They have searched outhouses and scrub, copses and down by the stream. But what about all the cellars and garages, not to mention the cars? She could be lying in a car boot. Or she might have been moved and placed in a garden after the search parties had been.

The helicopters hang almost stationary in the sky, then go lower, descending towards the rooftops. The noise is piercing, alarming, and lends to the feeling of disaster, but their sound fades as they move onwards over the forested expanse of Nordmarka. After a time they return, and now they appear to be circling over large parts of the city, not just the heights of Holmenkollen. She could be anywhere.

The aerial searches are being called off, they say on the TV news, they serve little purpose, too much time has passed.

The man from the Red Cross rescue team, the one who was in my garden, is interviewed. We're not giving up, he says. The local community are giving their support, hundreds of volunteers will comb the area, it's heartening to see.

I do not catch his name, but study his face on the screen. His hairline, lips. The two open buttons on his shirt, his throat, the thin skin in the depressions by his collarbone. His jaws, shoulders. His teeth, shiny with saliva. Those blue eyes. His nose, pores, the dark nostrils. The gleam of the lenses in his glasses.

Beate asks why I have stopped writing. It comes as a shock.

I haven't stopped, I say, authors often spend several years on a single book, the intervals between publishing can be considerable.

I hardly ever see you writing, Beate says, are you? Writing?

What does Beate know? I think, looking at my bookshelves. They are filled with books I constantly peruse. I listen to the radio, and the sentences dance all around, I lean back in the chair and close my eyes to really take them in. Besides, I receive an income from the state. I have it in writing: Arts Council Norway grant. And then there are my thoughts, they spur me ever onwards. All this falls under the umbrella of writing. That is obvious. It is just that no book comes out of it. But neither God, nor I or Beate can say that there will not be any more. I have tried to stop, but that does not work either, *and why does it not work? Because of the fragrance of the honeysuckle in the darkness.*

Imagine, I jot down the same evening in my notebook, I

do not know anything about how weather comes about. Yes, of course it is something to do with air and water and heat, but *how*, that I cannot understand. And photosynthesis, I recall having such a hard time getting my head around that. But now I cannot manage to remember it. I live inside images, as it were. Within the jungle wallpaper in the bedroom. In the dampness and green of the garden. They are pretty much the same thing.

These are the kinds of thing I write, the kinds of thing I think. So far within myself. Now I am getting there, I think, now I am closing in on something literary. But then the thoughts slip away, nothing seems important enough. I cannot manage to create reality. There are writers who can. But not me. So I do not write anything for a while. Oh, wine, raise me up, I think with relief, as it nears evening and I can sit down with a full mug. On the inside, then I am inside.

In the winter I started becoming forgetful. I mislaid things too. My new trainers disappeared, the ones I'd bought in the January sales. I reckoned I had probably left them in the gym locker at SATS, but when I went back they were not there. A brand new pair, Nikes, cost me over a thousand kroners. They were nearly double that price before they were reduced. I am constantly treating myself to things I cannot afford. Or, rather, I have the money, at least when the day of reckoning arrives, cash is more of a problem, because Dad is the one with the money, although most of it is tied up in property. Good old safe and solid property. Skådalsveien is a desirable address. Some day the house will fetch a substantial amount, by which time I might be dead, but in the meantime I have the grant money coming in, as well as the regular amounts from Mum and Dad. They want so much for me to be happy, for me to write and not slave away on meaningless work. But can work be meaningless?

For some people work is the only salvation.

All food is good, all work.

Yes, there ought to be a heaven waiting for me. Then I would not mind so much about being unhappy now. But *now* is the only thing that matters, that is how it has become, I live life like most people, desperate, in the now.

I simply do not want to believe it.

Reason lags behind.

Jesus. What is it a person does their whole life, apart from subsist, where does the joy come from? Work cannot be everything, it is not enough, I think, me, who cannot even manage to earn a living, but am supported by others. So that I in turn can provide for Georg and Tuva when they need it, which they do continually. I pride myself on helping them. My pride and Dad's ability to pay. He acted as guarantor when Tuva needed a mortgage. I help her with interest and repayments. Just as I supplement Georg's student loan so he does not have to work while he is in college. The children are to have the best. They are to have the same as I had. Does that mean the bill will come in the shape of an inability to tackle *not* having, if faced with those circumstances? Or is that inability a flaw of my own? Is it hereditary, a genetic void?

I remember that awful, exhausting day last winter. It began brightly, with a pale sun and some small snowflakes sailing through the air. The clock on the mantelpiece ticked. I felt in my bones I had forgotten something. What am I doing? I thought. Am I going to sit here and write my childhood or something like that? I, who do not know the difference between living and writing.

The clock was Granny's, and the desk beneath the only window in the room had belonged to Granddad. Dad did not want them. Their furniture, no thanks, no bloody way, he said. You can have them. But why should I be left with everything, the house, the furniture and interest earnings? I did not know how to maintain a villa and a garden, and besides, what was I supposed to do with all the stuff that came along with it? It filled the cellar, the attic and the old garage, and what there was not space for was piled up on the lawn. They were not mine and nor could I get rid of them. Why? Because they were not mine. But the emotions were. The sentimental value was sky high, too high for one person, and why did it have to be assigned to me exactly? I did not want to *have* all the time. I did not want to receive and receive.

I went to the shelf by the window, took out the laptop, unzipped its black case, found the lead and plugged it into the socket. It hummed, I opened a blank document in Word and wrote: *Owing to the fact that I have not published any books in the last ten years, I hereby wish to relinquish my stipend from the state.* And so on. Felt sorry for myself, added *such that the funds may benefit others,* and thought: ones with youth and promise. There were tears, of course. Over everything I had not become. Failure is also a possibility in life, and I had seized it. I got dressed and walked to the post office, on a clear-cut errand for once, a work-related one. So many times I had been to the post office with letters and applications, struggling with pushchairs and bags, hot in a hat, picking up packages with books and thick envelopes with manuscripts. Now most of it was sent by email, but still, that was not the reason the correspondence had petered out. It had ceased to be urgent, I had plenty of time, so little to prove. So little, so little, I was so little. And so close to *death, death*. I had got that from Astrid Lindgren. In her old age, whenever she or her sisters phoned each other the first thing they said was *death, death* in order to get that part of their conversation out of the way. They laughed at that. Lindgren spoke about it on a documentary on the TV, they showed the programme on repeat the day she did actually die. A game for life, right to the end. I was not playing. I slid the letters across the counter to the post office worker. The counters were not fronted with glass any longer, they were open and the money was kept in a safe behind the employees' backs. It had been like that for many years, but I had not thought about it, that a change had taken place. Even the post office logo was different, more like all the other logos, I found it hard to distinguish the brands, and God knows, perhaps there was no difference between them either, electricity suppliers, Internet companies, mobile phone firms, maybe they all belonged to the same gigantic network. But nobody knows for certain, that is the problem, supposing it *is* a problem, that the highest authorities resemble God less and less and yet we still believe someone exists with a complete overview. We have not realised that power moves sideways now, like crabs, no longer one at the top, but many alongside each another, moving around all the time.

I went to Baker Hansen and sat down on one of the high-backed, red sofas. Uncoiling my scarf and twisting out of my coat, I went to the counter, ordered and paid by card. Most of the times I had stood like that I had been young, which was how I had been longest, and in a way still viewed myself as being. But I could not look at young men. Nor grown men. The time for thrills and excitement was past. I was no longer a writer. Already too old for men in their forties. I could write what I wanted. Or refrain. The noises in the café: the buzz of voices, clinking of glass, plates and cutlery, mobile phones beeping, this warmth, this *hello, what can I get you* at the counter, would no longer prompt me *to write*. The sky was blue, that was all. The sun shone and the snow lay high and white on benches and atop wheelie bins, on the thin branches of bushes, on the head of the statue in Valkyrie plass. The blue tram rumbled past with snow on the roof, and I thought of the cross-country ski tracks, the heavy pine trees in Nordmarka, my children, of lifting equipment and carrying them, steadying them on their feet in the skis, flicking snow from between mittens and sleeves.

A man by the counter looked at me. He was around sixty, greying at the temples and stooped. His scarf was not knotted and his jacket hung lopsided, probably because he had too much in the pockets, in one of his pockets. It was disgusting. I knew the type, they wheedled their way in as soon as they got the chance, and I looked away, demonstrably.

A group of young mothers came in the door. Buggies, babies. I tried to smile at the women but they took no notice of me. I felt spite well up. Mothers of infants think older women do not know how it feels to hold a baby in their arms.

Dad could be tremendously angry at times. There was shoving and pushing against door frames. His and Mum's bodies. Things thrown and shattered. I hid in my room the night he smashed the folding table he had been given by Granny. It was not just the blows, the thuds and the sound of splintering wood. But the shouts, the cries. I pictured bodies. Blood and broken bones. I went into the bathroom, switched off the light and locked the door sometimes when they argued. A tender pressure in my stomach as I stood in pitch darkness, listening to the quarrelling outside, a tingling. Because I was safe in the warm blackness, behind the closed door. Finally something had happened. Banging, yelling and screaming.

The maelstrom had taken them. It was like that feeling of anticipation before a journey, joy. I could be anyone, on my own.

Something was erased, I think now, the moment, or the memory of what happened just before the smashing of the table. A rupture, I do not know in what, but it ruptured, cracked, yes, of course it was cracked, and thrust me out, of what I do not know. It triggered an urge that was productive at first, but later became reactive. Because when a trail is first trodden: large destruction led to new destruction. Thereafter, angst, remorse and on many occasions intoxication.

Wine, the blood in my veins, oil on the sea, but the moon hung over the water and tantalised.

Dad made something happen, and I cannot live without it. Life on an even keel is a deathlike condition. Depression. Tying me up and packing me in so tightly that drama suddenly breaks out. Driven by rage, a yearning so strong I cannot live with it. I cannot live with it and return to what is steady, to well-balanced life, to emptiness.

Inherited.

A black hell.

Come on now.

Yes, I am close to clearing it up, but not quite, I am not able, it is too simplistic.

Yes, what if there is only simplicity behind the blackness?

It does not make any sense, that there is no connection, that the rupture is just a rupture and does not hold something together. There has to be something more, there has to be something.

The black dog.

The scrape from the leg of a chair in a living room in Marienlyst. The room is cold, no fire in the grate, it should not be necessary to light a fire so late in April. The garden, sleet. Gravel paths.

Anxiety. Who experienced this? Not me, not me. I was a different person in a different time, but someone entered me. Reactivated.

I was sitting in Baker Hansen, but I was nowhere, me, but not me.

After the rain comes the sun comes spring comes summer comes the dripping wet gooseberry bush in August when the sun breaks through after drizzle.

Blankness, the body shakes, trams trundle past, shaking that propagates, movements, chaos, electrons, sound waves, something that could be systemised, but not to the naked eye. People were dangerous. They could disappear. Hands on the tabletop, mere atoms. All that could hold me tight was other people. The only thing.

The new trams were Italian. Sleek, but jerky. Not rickety, like the old ones.

The man with the scarf looked up from his newspaper.

I was standing, a pool of melted slush underfoot, put on my coat. Sunshine. It soon disappeared behind the crest of the hill. I walked to Majorstua and turned onto Harald Hårfagres gate. The transport museum was situated in one of the old tram sheds. I had to walk around the building to locate the entrance. The big, blue tram carriages. Not dirtied by exhaust fumes and splashes of mud, as they would have been outside. I placed a hand on the metal.

From Majorstuhuset you took the tram up to the heights of Holmenkollen. You fastened your skis to the outside, nervously, no time to lose. That was how it used to be.

14

Just a narrow track trodden in the snow, on the edge of the pavement. In her hand she holds a box wrapped in brown paper, bound by string, the shop assistant tied a loop in the end with which she carries the box of millefeuille, Hartvig's favourite cake. Because it is Saturday. And it is snowing. Upon her hat, her coat, the package. On her ice-cold fingers holding the string grocery bag – what good are gloves in the cold, they are no use at all, but isolate each finger, make them blue with cold, frozen stiff. The string bag contains fish, bread and half a kilo of butter. She does not usually do the shopping at Sundby's in Majorstua herself. The girl does it now and again, or else they order their groceries and have them sent up on the goods tram.

She walks down Schulz' gate in the direction of Bogstadveien.

There is the tram at the bottom of the hill. She stops, wavering. Will she ride it for two stops? It is not far to go, but the snow is hard to walk on with smooth-soled boots and she has a lot to carry. And so many tears bottled up. Anger! And the cold, good God, she is freezing. It is too much for her. All the same, she would rather have worked. Run a dressmaker's shop. Like Coco Chanel. Smoked cigarettes in the breaks with the other women, laughed loudly. Handled material and evening gowns, turned on her heel and smiled at customers, watched the day move towards night, the lights of the city going on. The sounds inside a tram are quite different then, full of people on the way to parties, to the theatre or the darkness of the cinema, to restaurants and clubs. She would walk through the city arm in arm with a man. Not Hartvig. A gloved, big and manly hand would rest upon the back of her small hand. One could only imagine what might happen, where they were going. Back to *his*. She would feel his forearm tense through the sleeve of his overcoat. He could barely control himself. He was madly in love, with her. Biting down hard on his teeth, making the muscles in his jaws visible. Because she, she, was the one he wanted. And he was kind, this man was constantly kind and supportive. Not like stupid, boring Hartvig. And yet she buys cake for him, why does she do that, it will soon be over anyway, the kind of relationship *they* have cannot last.

It is mild, around zero degrees perhaps, still her feet are freezing, because she has to wade through all the snow. Oh. Enough. The tram comes driving up the hill with heavy snow on the roof and she climbs on. Standing room only of course, even so. All these looks, women staring and staring. Well, it is not as if she has anything to be ashamed of. New hat, new hand-sewn coat, nice make-up, nothing is wrong. Nevertheless. She is a *Mrs*, she is out of the running. A Mrs buying groceries, youth is in the past, she has wrinkles around her eyes. She will soon be fifty and is a mother of three. She wants to get away, maybe to the mountains, to a hotel preferably, she needs to be waited upon. Cold, it is so cold. Her stomach aches, maybe her monthly is on the way, she cannot remember, has lost track. Such a sticky mess, but at least she still gets it, and she does still have a social life, a slim waist, slim enough in any case, the childbirths do not show yet, not when she is wearing clothes, only the varicose veins are visible, but at this time of year, underneath tights, they are not so noticeable. Yes, it is most likely the monthly, she feels so angry. The stupid pot-bellied men sitting on the tram. Not getting up, none of them making any sign of offering her a seat, not seeing her. The one sitting nearest raises his walking stick at regular intervals, tapping it gently on the floor. Exactly like Hartvig. Finicky, smug. Men adorn themselves with canes as though they were items of clothing, think they are something, even when they are nothing more than conceited. Trotsky was something, that is true. She thinks about the picture of him in *Årsrevyen*, a few years ago now, but it caught her eye. How he protected himself, as it were, with his cane, holding it in front of his face as he arrived in Oslo. To shield himself from the journalists. How idiotic. You cannot protect yourself, not in her experience. Whether it be against questions, looks or demands. Or the days, dragging her ever on. So you are better off gritting your teeth, defending yourself. Dear. What a grey day, and the start of the weekend on top of it. No doubt there will be ructions and racket in the house with everyone home, no, she really has no desire, does not want to do anything. Sit in a chair in peace, read the weekly magazines, smoke a cigarette, drink coffee. That is what she wants, nothing else. She wants to be left alone.

There is always a familiar face on the underground, today is no exception. Mrs Vange is as usual wearing all too much make-up, it is tasteless, and the way she speaks, so the whole tram can hear, about the most private matters, her husband and children, mixed with all kinds of gossip. The people in the seats around listen breathlessly. Dear, oh dear. She is looking forward to telling Alice about it, thank God she has Alice, there would not be much cheer without her, not a single person who understood her.

Mrs Vange may be foolish, but everyone envies her the husband she has. He is a surgeon and my word he is handsome. The son of a shipping magnate into the bargain, and a good family as far back as can be traced. A sensitive, slightly weak aspect around the mouth, but manly all the same, and polite, considerate. Rumour has it he is a homosexual. Because Mrs Vange is really not much to look at. But Mr Vange's gaze, she has noticed him looking at her, lingering on her breasts. Yes, it is women he likes all right. Oh. Her stupid Hartvig. Feeble, and short, the little legs on him. No, he is not hers, he is just something she happened upon, something that could not be avoided. Who else would have had her back then? She was already well over thirty and afraid she would be alone for ever, filled with anxiety, it was bordering on, well, God knows what. Things were not good with her, oh no, she could have been committed, could well have. If Hartvig had not turned up, cycling slowly by her at the tram stop on Niels Juels gate one summer evening, and she had not suddenly called out to him, hello, you there! Excuse me, would you happen to know the time?

Perhaps she had seen how proper and dependable he was the moment he passed, perhaps everything within her understood that this was an opportunity presenting itself. No, oh she did not know. Yet it was strange, her calling out to him like that, as though she knew that here was a man she could get. Here *he* comes.

For a long time she thought her innermost wish was to

start a family with Hartvig, to be a wife and mother, and maybe it was, but it might also have been something she chose to believe, pure self-delusion. All she wanted was to settle down, to put a stop to those evil feelings flaring up within. Oh yes, she wanted to be miles away from that painful pressure on her chest, away from everything that reminded her of the uncertainty about Mama's rented flats, because they never knew, her and Mama and Finn, if Papa had paid the rent for them, as he was bound to by law. Or if he would suddenly turn up and ring the doorbell, drunk and furious. True, these worries ceased when Mama got her divorce, but all the same, Cessi wanted something quite different, more solid than how it had been back then. Besides, Hartvig liked her. She found that hard to accept, finally someone who liked her, someone blessed with infinite patience, that was how it seemed. God knows she needed it, she was on the verge of going under. That the whole thing should tip over was something she could not predict. What had seemed proper became pedantry, patience resembled obstinacy more and more. His good family turned out to be patronising and narrow-minded, and Hartvig himself was dull as ditchwater. She could weep tears of blood, at everything, at nothing. Mama, if only you could come and help me. But she cannot expect that, neither can she ask her again, not this weekend as well. She has only just come from there after all, eaten lunch and been looked after. But everything comes to an end and she has to leave, she has to go back home.

Mama dear, can't I stay here?

She did not say that, but it was what she was thinking: can I not stay, be your little girl for the night, you and

I together here? No father, no brother – oh, my darling brother, who is never coming back – but you and I at least. Can I not sit quietly in your armchair and look out at the sky between the green plants on the windowsill, at the snowflakes falling, hear the city far off, the trams?

She is going in circles. One day laughter, the next seething rage, followed by remorse over everything she has said and done. It is not her fault, one thing leads to the other and it just carries on from there. Exaggeration, Cessi, you're exaggerating, Hartvig says. Because when she first strikes out, the bouts of crying and screaming are usually not far behind. Then it does not matter that it was the boy who provoked the whole thing. He has such a vile mouth on him. Jealous he is, jealous of his little sisters. But none of them listen when she tries to explain. Mummy is so tired, she says, all this bickering is bad for Mummy's nerves. Oh, that boy. Had it not been for his behaviour things would be quite different and wonderfully calm in their home. She likes the bedroom, for example, her bed, the curtains, the silence, she seeks refuge in there, rests while everything is going on, yes, she needs the house, so must endure Hartvig. That tyrant. It is exactly what he accuses her of being, tyrannical. You tyrannise us with your erratic moods, he says. He says this, him, the one who wants to control everything and everyone. You know I am hurting, she says, that my threshold is very low. And they agree to a new convalescence for her. That is what she thinks they have agreed upon. But then he comes home having spoken to Dr Vold about admitting her to hospital. After all, Hartvig says, after all your nerves never get into shape, truth be told they've got worse. That is the way Hartvig speaks. At first she is afraid, then she gives way, gives up, in fact, as long as she can rest.

> *The County Governor of Oslo and Akershus proclaims the following: as spouses, high court lawyer Hartvig Viker and Cecilie Brodtkorp Viker, née Brodtkorp Lütken, both Oslo, are agreed to annul married life, and as mediation in accordance with the Marriage Act § 44 has been attempted by the priest in Ris, authorisation is hereby announced for separation pursuant to § 41 of the Marriage Act of 31 May 1918 cf. Law on changes in marriage legislation of 25 June 1937.*
>
> *Oslo, 9 June 1950*

So nothing comes of the hospital admittance. Suddenly Hartvig does not want to be married any more. *Damn him damn him.* He stole a march on her. Not that she would have left him, she did not want a divorce. She just wants to be in the house, she misses her bed, the flapping curtains and the sounds from the garden. Hartvig does not understand. And what about the children? She had said that of course. How could you do this to the children? Your outbursts are far worse, he said. She knew he would say that, but he was so unexpectedly calm. Indifferent, cold. Have you met someone else? she shouted, he had denied it, but she can feel in her bones how foolish she has been. She immediately sees him with new eyes, as though she were another woman, and realises he is attractive. With his broad wrists, his hairy arms. Now he is unreachable.

She had cried, screamed, fainted and demanded meetings with Dr Vold. So they sat there in a chair each, she in a dark outfit with a pressure in her chest, she suspected what was coming. Still deep down she believed that the doctor would help her, take her side, make Hartvig understand. That was not what happened. It was worse than she could have imagined. Her marriage with Hartvig was finished. Did not exist. She understood that from the moment Hartvig opened his mouth, but at first she did not want to go along with it, because she did not feel that way herself, their marriage was not supposed to fall apart. But after that meeting she was certain he had met somebody else. Otherwise he would never have had the strength to leave, in the long run he never refused her anything.

God, she grew so angry, her rage almost got the better of her as she sat listening to him. She was, in his opinion, prone to pretence, highly strung, unstable and a bad influence on the children. Not a word any more about her lively disposition and beautiful hair. He described violent outbursts she herself had forgotten, striking out, and the time she had thrown a plate at the boy, but it didn't hit him, she interrupted. And your hysterical screaming, Hartvig continued, the episodes when she pulled him by the hair, shook him. The objects she had hurled at him, how she constantly called him repulsive, said he smelled, was a cripple.

Hartvig made things out to be much worse than they actually were. She found herself unable to describe the way he sneered. My God, what was that compared to a smashed plate? How he laughed when she became angry. The tapping with a fork or fountain pen on the table before he said something, the way he cleared his throat before making a big fuss out of some deathly boring point. How he pawed at her. The smell of him, the smell. How he had to decide everything.

The details. The rules. Written down to the letter. The long-winded explanations. Everything had to be done his way, whether it concerned her or the children. He held the purse strings, after all. So you had no choice but to stand and listen. She screamed it all out in the end, all of it, but afterwards did not remember how the words had fallen, only Hartvig sitting there in his chair with his self-satisfied smirk. That made her even angrier, because she knew what he was thinking and what he would say when they got home, that now Dr Vold had seen it for himself. Hysterical shrew.

Dr Vold made her lie down on the divan. It was the first and only time she got to lie on it. He fetched her a glass of water himself, and she was told to keep quiet for a few minutes. Hartvig had to wait outside. Dr Vold sat at his desk and leafed through some papers. The tram passed by beneath the windows. Her heart pounded, but most of all it was terrible to lie on her back that way, because she felt an awful welling of tears working its way up, the lump in her throat preventing her from breathing properly. God, it was so painful, but she had to hold the tears back, they were too great, contained everything she knew, everything that had happened and could not be undone. Everything had an explanation, yet she knew it was impossible to explain, there were no words and no one could understand. There were too many small paths and tracks running parallel or crossing one another, like all the nerve fibres of every single leaf on a large tree. And it was so painful.

When they took their places on the chairs in front of Dr Vold's desk again, she was calm, leaden, almost as though she were asleep, and Hartvig was indifferent to her, he was just Hartvig as usual. She was so much stronger than him, had been for many years, nothing could change that, there was nothing they actually needed to change and soon they would be going home. It seemed like such an interminably long way, first the walk to Nationaltheatret station, then all those minutes waiting for the train before departure, followed by the rattling ride uphill on the red seats, neighbours and acquaintances you had to greet, a journey as long as a bad year, with Hartvig sitting next to her. Then finally they would arrive home, and she could lie down in her bed.

The situation seemed heated, Dr Vold said, and Mrs Viker was overexerted, they could surely agree on that, so perhaps a break was in order. In his opinion it would not be wise to act too hastily regarding the divorce, but Mrs Viker did need rest, so perhaps they could be apart for a while, a couple of months say.

Hartvig could arrange for a stay in the country, he said, but he still wanted a separation, that he demanded. Enough was enough.

Yes, don't believe for a moment that I want to stay with you after this, she screamed, she had to, he was stripping her of all dignity. But she did not want to go away, no, she did not want to go anywhere, just to be left in peace. There, in the house.

But she was banished, to a little cabin on farmland belonging to a woman, a domineering, coarse and rude old bag. In much the same way as Hartvig was also coarse and shallow. And letters arrived from Hartvig, dry, businesslike letters. The following is an inventory of mutual household contents, he wrote, with a suggested division attached. She could look over it and come back with possible alternative proposals.

She changed everything around, rewrote the lists, rearranged the order of things. Because he always had to be the one who decided. He wanted to be right, and was right, because he was precise and his memory was accurate. But that list, oh, it made her sick. That man's level of painstaking accuracy. He had kept an account of their mutual possessions, but never forgotten that they were placed in his house. Now he shrank her, now she saw how little her contribution was worth. She was to leave their home, with the few belongings she had brought into the household. What they had obtained between them was to be divided and although she could claim sole ownership of some items, gifts and heirlooms that had come into her possession during their time together, there were not many.

Cessi, she wrote, drawing a thick red line beneath. Of course she did not have a typewriter as he did, her lists did not look as credible as his, but still. Hartvig, she wrote in red in the margin: I am the one who sews, certainly not you, so it is only fair and reasonable that I should have the new electric clothes iron. After all, I will be keeping your – *our* – children's clothes in order. I have been stripped of everything but the children shall not suffer because of it, they shall be well turned out in their clothes. I *want* the iron, even though it was your father who gave it to us as a present:

1 electric iron
1 copper pot – small – antique, 3 legs
1 copper pot with round handle
1 copper teakettle
1 pewter jug
1 porcelain standard lamp
1 wrought-iron wall lamp
2 table lamps, metal

1 lamp stand, broken
3 electric heaters
1 iron biscuit mould
1 waffle iron
1 alarm clock
12 demitasses
12 dessert plates
2 large serving dishes
1 antique white tureen
1 antique white faience bowl
6 antique crystal goblet glasses
1 antique crystal sugar bowl

The crystal jam bowls are mine, Hartvig, they come from my family. Likewise the crystal saucers. So you were wrong on that count.

3 antique crystal carafes
3 jam spoons
1 cold-cuts fork
1 cake server
1 baking tin
2 soup ladles
1 potato dish
3 fruit knives
2 ashtrays
8 flat white plates
8 deep white plates
1 wringer
1 vacuum cleaner
1 laundry basket

1 zinc tub
1 enamel bucket
1 ironing board with sleeve arm
1 electric kitchen stove
1 Jøtul wood-burning stove
2 antique travel chests
1 antique wooden food box
1 sewing table
4 mahogany chairs
2 Windsor chairs
1 escritoire w/ top
1 corner cupboard (birch, two parts)
1 drop-leaf table
2 armchairs w/ cushions
2 oilcloth chairs
1 large white mirror. 1 large bathroom mirror
2 yellow beds
2 yellow bedside tables
1 folding bed
2 kitchen stools
2 angel pictures
1 painting of my mother
2 photographs (my family)
Various vases and ornaments

There, but you must also find me a place to live. Whatever were you thinking? I have no means, no savings. I can hardly work, I am sick, Hartvig, being heartsick makes me bodily weak, one thing is a consequence of the other.

Only now does she think about the garden. They had sowed potatoes at the start of the war, there were berry bushes from before but they planted several more, Hartvig loved the garden, not her, it was too much, that goes without saying. Or rather, she was not sure. She missed it dearly now, that delightful, big green garden. Her garden, after all. They hired help to tend it, different sorts. Young men. Oh, to be young again, free to dream of healthy, firm bodies, tender, strong embraces. Not that it was so nice to be young. No. It was horrible. But when she saw those young bodies now – that soldier they had as help before they were all sent home. He came into her kitchen with potatoes in that big wire basket, small clods of clay sprinkling on the floor, but she said nothing about that, stood instead in the doorway looking at that slender, taut behind in blue overalls as he bent over to put the basket down. She would so dearly have liked to have taken hold of it. Squeezed it, had him between her thighs, yes. He had a broad upper torso tapering into a narrow waist, and powerful muscles in his upper arms that tensed when he was carrying something heavy. That was a lovely autumn. Big, soil-flecked carrots sticking up between the potatoes. The girl transferred them to a tub and began scrubbing them vigorously. The soldier's eyes on her, it was unavoidable, unfair. Men were brutal. They went for young flesh. Golden potatoes, she and Hartvig weighed them, almost 150 kg that autumn the soldier was there, in '45.

No, she liked the garden, anything else was a lie. Hartvig told lies about her, diminished everything. Said she was not bothered with it. But the soft, deep red raspberries she took lightly between her fingers and dropped in the bucket! Gooseberries were nastier to pluck, she used a fork, pulled the berries off the stalk with a careful motion. She liked the work with the berries. Jam making. The big pot, the steaming glass jars she fished out of boiling water before pouring in the jam.

Now it was lost. The garden, the work. That disaster could strike so easily in that house was another thing entirely. Endless screaming between the walls of the living room, things being broken, the images were blurry, but it was like a storm of sorts. She tries to see if there is anything within the storm and within that again, but it is indescribable. She attempted once to explain it to Dr Vold.

What happens, he said, when you sense this rage coming on? Try to feel it. You are here now and quite safe, but when you find yourself in a fury in the living room, as you describe, what happens within you then?

There is, she says, the living room and the light, the daylight, and within it there is a face and it is called rage, it is my father's face, but there is something more, that once I am whirled into, I am sucked back, in time, you see, lose the power of speech, it is as though I am in a place I have been before but can no longer see.

Are you a little girl then?

Yes, I might be, it is early in life, and what is sucking me backwards is a spiral, it is black or white, no, I don't know. But my mother.

Yes?

No, I don't know. One really just wants to begin over again, doctor. A kind of peaceful sleep. Snug, soft.

It sounds like a baby's existence.

No, maybe not. Yes, but no, if you understand what I mean. I'm older as well.

You are also an adult?

Yes, but not then. I am perhaps . . . upset.

You become upset.

Yes.

Then you scream?

Yes. Then I scream. And then the air turns cold, there is lamplight in the living room and darkness outside the windows, and everyone is running around in all directions.

Who?

The children. Through all the rooms in the house. It is far too big. We never intended having so large a house. Dark everywhere, impossible to keep heated. It's Hartvig's face. Leftovers from dinner. Lamb chop bone. The cold fat. I'm afraid. It is these words, doctor: unease, rage. Like falling. Not knowing where you are.

What is it that starts you screaming? Makes you furious?

The fact that I cannot hear myself think. That they're speaking to me. No, it can be anything at all. When I have a lot to do, when it's just like that, inside me. I don't want it to happen. It's outside me. I can't get any peace.

What do you scream?

I don't remember. All manner of horrid things. I tell the boy he is evil and mean. Changeling, I shriek, changeling. Because I can't make him listen to me. How can you be my child? All we are is kind and you respond by being mean. Won't listen won't listen. WILL YOU LISTEN! And to think you are blessed with such loving parents. Changeling. To the girls? I don't know. With them it is mostly that I am screaming. Not so much what. That they are to stop nagging, stop bickering. NONE OF YOU CARE ABOUT ME! CAN YOU NOT SEE HOW HARD I WORK? I scream that. You don't care about your own mother.

Do you think that's true?

I can't manage any more, doctor.

Do you want to continue screaming?

No.

What do you want?

I'm so tired. I don't get enough sleep. Even making jam is too much. The white spiral.

Where does it want to lead you?

I don't know. To before all the bad. All the bad that's happening, it's not me. So it isn't actually happening. The children will understand. I'm not like that. I'm just so tired and worn out. Sick, doctor.

15

On the way up the steps to Majorstuhuset, heading for the train, I felt I wanted to buy something. I did not want to go home, and did not want to think, but I wanted something, that is to say, I wanted to feel the desire for something, a direction. So I turned around. I could think of several purchases to make. Espresso coffee. Red wine and new trainers. I had a sudden sense of anticipation: now I had an errand to run, alternative courses of action, a task.

As I crossed the street, I saw the man from Baker Hansen standing outside the 7-Eleven on the large paved area next to the Vinkelgården building eating a hot dog. He had his scarf in his pocket, one fringed end trailing in the snow. He wiped some ketchup from around his mouth while staring at me.

I stared back, *do you want me to brain you, smash your face in, shithead?*

I passed close, wanted to spit on him, *your existence disgusts me*, but brushed against him with a rigid shoulder and hurried on in the direction of the coffee shop. There could be no hesitation on my part, that would only provide him with an opening, enough time to make contact.

It seemed dark in the shop after the harsh light outdoors. I ordered a bag of espresso-ground Blue Java. My hands trembled on the counter. The bag of coffee was warm and soft, the smell both penetrating and soothing. I felt I needed to sit down. There was a bar stool free in the corner by the window. I leaned my head and shoulder against the wall and looked out. He was still standing there. His stomach was sticking out over the waistband of his trousers in a tight, gaudy jumper, visible beneath his open jacket. What was it he actually had in his pockets: keys, a mobile phone, a wallet, change, screws, a tape measure, a bill plucked from his letterbox as he hurried out? Things like that, no doubt. A fitting for a water pipe, car keys, a padlock. Only wellies on his feet. What made him think that I was interested? Was he actually interested? His type, did they not just want to latch on to someone, avoid being alone?

I was cut from the same cloth, it must be written on my forehead: better to be kind and docile than rejected and abandoned. Why else would I attract nutcases; whether they were straggly and clingy like small puppies, or snorted and raved, had all kinds of crap on their mind that they wanted me to take on board, they followed me, stuck to me, God knows why, what did they achieve? I just let them talk. Answered if I was able, but it did not seem as though they listened, I was the one who was supposed to listen, that was what they wanted. Jesus, Mum, Tuva says, why do you do that? Someone has to take them seriously, I say, they're human beings, just like us, but Tuva waves my explanation aside and says, then they ought to behave like people, you have to show them you have respect for yourself, Mum, or they won't show you any respect. Set boundaries, y'know.

When I was young they were constantly following me, and they were often as old as Dad. Horrible sights of naked, white backsides, all too slack and wobbly, boneless, I wanted to vomit, really. But now I could not shudder in disgust or be insulted, soon I would be just as old.

I was like them.

So which of us was less human? Me or the man with the scarf? The contemptible one or the one showing contempt?

But for God's sake. Can you be more or less human, can a human lose their humanity, is that not just a theoretical delimitation, a play on words? And perhaps the words make sense, but not when I am among people. Out on the street. Then I am always afraid. The empathy in a face impossible to grade. He followed me down Bogstadveien. I crossed the street and walked back up on the other side, went into United Bakeries and found my way to the toilet at the rear of the premises. Once in there I locked the door, sat down on the toilet seat and did not open until someone rattled the door handle for the fourth time, a customer had fetched one of the employees. On my way out I brushed against the jam bowl beside the cutlery and napkins, making it fall. Shards of glass and strawberry jam splattered on the floor and the meddlesome customer called out after me, hey, aren't you going to clean up after yourself?

My scalp itched beneath my hat, my head was unbearably hot.

No, I thought. No. I am not my best at the moment. Look at me. I am not up to it. Someone else can clean up.

I hoped he was gone, but when I got a little way down the street, I spotted the sagging jacket over the stooped back, the wellies slipping on the snow-covered pavement. For fuck's sake, did he not have a job, was he on benefits? Feeling hatred, I ducked into the nearest clothes shop, Yoko Loko or whatever it was called. There were no customers and the girl behind the counter left me alone. I tried on dresses, trousers and tops in the cramped changing room while my eyes and nose ran, I began to blubber because there were too many clothes to choose between and I was not able, I was not able, I lost heart, but at the same time the longer I kept at it, the more important it became to make a decision. The pressure of thinking made my temporal arteries thump, I tried to weigh up the pros and cons of each article of clothing, be efficient, because this was a task requiring a result within a certain time, if not there would be no purchase, I would end up paralysed and leaving the shop empty-handed. In that case I would have wasted time. What a waste, what a failure.

Eventually I decided on a pair of tight jeans and a blue denim shirt. The clothes fitted well, I looked youthful, a little cowgirl-like, Joan Baez-like, but not too much.

What a cool combination, the Swedish shop assistant said, *really worth the money.*

Christ almighty, money. Could I not get away from it?

'Working Class Hero' by John Lennon was playing as I paid, and for a moment I wondered if it was supposed to be ironic, but I noticed they also sold Mao jackets and Che Guevara hats, and realised the music was only intended to associate the clothes with the right attitude, it was as basic as that. Most things are simply thought out.

But I did not belong to the upper class, did I, even though I had access to money? I was outside everything. Me and the money were floating somewhere outside it all. I was an artist. Kept by my parents. Supported by patronage. I could not manage to escape. It was too late to break with that. *Poor thing.* The children were born and had grown up. The work was done and the books written. Loss after loss. Even if I gave up the grant and refrained from writing another word for the rest of my life, I would still live off Mum and Dad's money. Advance inheritance, followed by inheritance, a house worth millions of kroners, but you cannot call privilege like that *incarceration*, a closed loop, it would be unethical *in a world such as ours*, ungrateful, but it could still be true. It was true: I was not outside, on the contrary, but I wanted out, I was filled with rebellion and the urge to break free.

I saw no sign of him, but guessed he was there somewhere, waiting. Further down the street, in a shop perhaps, out of sight, on the lookout for me. I crossed Schulz' gate. Jews lived in this area before the war. I do not know why that should pop into my head on this particular day, a day with all its sparkling snow that should put you in mind of Sunday outings on cross-country skis, Norwegian culture in its purest form, and by that I meant *pure nature*. Because nature is pure to Norwegians. We even regard a rotting animal carcass as pure provided the remains are located deep in the forest, that is to say, when the bacteria occur in a *natural* form. That is to say, not in a rubbish bin. Not in the city. We value pure, natural and undiluted forms. We are not mystics, we are not dark. We are us. On the outside we are easily recognisable. Inside, we are governed by emotion, but are also unemotional, distant from the world. We love nature, but not people. The others.

I did not get any further with these thoughts, hardly understood what I meant myself, but had a sense of seeing something double which simultaneously swapped places, almost the way down can be up, and up down. Something internal changing places with something external. But so what really? All these thoughts, and I was the only one aware of them, in a few years both the thoughts and I would be gone, so why was I so obsessed with them? This reasoning, the closest I came to something substantial.

I wanted to drown the man with the scarf in white snow, bury him, make him go under and disappear.

Deep down we ignore mixed forms, I thought, we do not want them, and consequently neither do we see them. We are not so indiscreet and rude as to bad-mouth our neighbours' mixed marriage in plain speech. But unconsciously we can be, like when we are two-faced.

Genocide so distant, external enemies, fear.

We attack ourselves with emotions instead, those closest to us.

Granny told me how she used to see the *Jew riff-raff*, that a whole community lived in tenements on Schulz' gate, they hung out the windows in the afternoons and were different, dark. Or was it Sorgenfrigata? I always mixed those two streets up. The irony: sorgenfrei, carefree. Granny laughed at the Jews, *hook-nosed hawkers*, she used to say. And when she did it made me think of something I did not dare to mention: Granny's own hooked nose.

At the junction with Professor Dahls gate I caught sight of him going into the Arabian café. I knew it well, had often sat there writing because the premises were dark and had an atmosphere that was hard to pin down, a sort of energy induced by restlessness. I think it was due to the owner, or rather the friends of his always coming by. One or two would sit on chairs behind the counter. Or stand hanging around the till discussing something in Arabic, gesticulating, visibly concentrating. Tight-fitting white T-shirts, Marlboro packets and lighters, a smell of aftershave, they brought all of that along with them into the café where I sat squinting down at my notebook. However, they usually sat at one of the tables outside, where they could smoke. The owner served customers at the till while talking to his friends at the same time, or he took his glass of coffee outside, sitting with them until a new customer was on the way in the door. He did not look at me when I ordered coffee, never smiled in recognition when I entered.

I did not know what they talked so intensely about, if it was football, politics or women, I did not understand what they said nor what I saw. Were they serious, earnest and upright? Or were they irresponsible and lacking drive? I really would have liked to know, but on the other hand, I thought, as I sat there writing, if I did find out then perhaps I would not have begun pondering the importance of talking, or have been able to long for conversations with more content than the ones I had with my own friends. I yearned. Which meant there must be something to yearn for, even if it only existed in my imagination, like the idea of perfection in other people.

I turned, walked a little way back and went into a shoe shop. There were shelves of trainers by the entrance. All of them were made in China and none of them cost less than twelve hundred kroners, I checked, held each one in my hand to gauge if it was light enough, bent it to see how flexible the sole was, longed to run on the roads. It felt good looking at new shoes in strong colours, I was almost far away, deep in thought, but then I began to sweat, my pulse beat faster, my hat itched, enraged I tore it off, unbuttoned my coat, left the shop, and suddenly: a large space around the mind, that did not know what it thought. I found myself far back in time, and I was standing bent over the drop-leaf table in my student bedsit, furious. All my youthful energy intact, but no direction for it to take, going in circles. A frightening person. Filled with sex.

I wiped the sweat from my upper lip and set off downhill. My scarf was moist and the back of my neck cold. When I reached the Arabian café I slowed down and looked in the windows. The man with the scarf was sitting at a table with a beer in front of him. When he spotted me, he rose quickly to his feet. I gave him the finger and broke into a run.

The following day I rang the Arts Council and Authors' Union and asked them to ignore the letters I had sent. Don't read them, I said. As though it had ever been necessary to ask someone to refrain from reading something I wrote. But it would not prevent me from assuming my fundamental duties, I thought, God knows what I meant, but I suppose it's possible to work it out:

Nobody has the right to be read
But I am not getting what I deserve
I reap what I sow
But I have no control over the weather
I cannot get away from myself
No *but*, nobody can.

It was not possible to leave, I still ended up inside, only in a different way: off kilter, wretched, easy prey. Yes, there were many words to describe a person back in the fold, in a community, even if it was a community composed of the misguided.

16

Beate is fashionable, her style is of the time. Beate *is* time, because she is so young. She is fluid. I am not time any longer, I am age. That means calcification, the death of cells. I do not mean much by all this, it is a stockpile of words I construct to keep myself down for the most part, that is how depression works: it produces thoughts that squeeze emotions together, force them down or push them away. I think this myself, because I am possessed of self-knowledge. This gives a double dimension to most things. Double depression, double longing, and in theory double joy as well.

Beate has freckles and long fair hair, tight faded jeans and a white blouse which she has tied a knot in on one side. Plucked eyebrows and deep pink lip gloss. When I am close to her I can smell different fragrances, some must be from the styling products in her hair, some from body lotion and perfume, and some maybe from the fabric softener on her clothes.

I recall a reader's letter on a page aimed at children and teens in a newspaper:

What's wrong with being perfect?

I wear Uggs, cool clothes and make-up. I am pretty, many people say I look perfect. What's wrong with that? Why should I be criticised for it?

I could have told her: nobody is perfect. Only babies, and

you are hardly a baby any more, are you? Or: what is perfection? Or: perfection is boring. But I do not understand exactly what I mean by that. I understand neither the girl nor myself. Deep down I think that perfection exists. But I do not want it to. Why can we not just say it is irrelevant, that we can manage without the word?

We say that we live, I write in one of my notebooks, but it is not like that, that is a very poor description. At any rate, *I* do not live. *It* lives me. As if that is a better way to put it. Idiot. My dreams have deceived me. They have no time limit, yet time leaves them behind. Sooner or later there will be nothing ahead.

But I do not speak to Beate in the same way as I write. On the contrary. I play her music, show her books, tell her about them and am even enthusiastic when I do. Beate shall have what I myself want. Beate's open, young face. Isn't she beautiful? Anita used to say, beautiful, I would say, she's lovely, perfect.

I take books down off the shelf when I am alone as well.

I have everything, yet it is still not enough.

It is humid outside, but dusty amid the books, I find it hard to breathe. There is a picture of a forest on one of the covers. A woman walks alongside a river in the forest, in a black skirt and white blouse. I look out through the window at the overturned wheelbarrow. The flies, the midges hovering above the water bucket. The spade planted in the ground.

I feel sorry for myself. I have not lived through the Second World War, have only had my own fear, the dreary notebooks and nothing at all to frame my life, give me direction and consequently a purpose, no complete collection of friends, ways of speaking and conventions, no distinct culture, neither ideals nor visions. Only the flowing past, the one I found in books, or my own, the one that comes drifting.

We live in an age where nothing is at stake, I am in the habit of saying amongst gatherings of friends, slurring slightly after too much red wine, nor is there anything to fight against, no oppressive morality or suppression, the meaning of life cannot be identified. That is what I say, but not what I am thinking. There is nothing wrong with time, I think, it is not us, it is me. I lack something, *I am not here*, I should take a master's degree, a doctorate, maybe two.

I can do anything I want, there are no obstacles, it all depends on me and me alone.

No, I am too tired. Tired of thinking. Tired of lacking. Whatever it might be that I lack. Greater spirituality, or a man, a love that shakes me to my very core?

Or an activistic attitude, a societal engagement. That would help me see the meaning of life. To be committed to a cause, along with other people. To work for the common good.

So I do mean what I say through the haze of red wine. I am going in circles. Nothing generates purpose in me. There are no limitations.

Only loathing.

Knut used to laugh at me and say I got too worked up about the most inescapable facts. You're Norwegian, he would say, you just have to put up with it. That's how life is for us. Security has its price. You don't pay heed to the fact that the very existence of the planet is under threat, nature, climate change, all that stuff, there's a cause for you, but you don't involve yourself in that, maybe you find it boring?

Yes.

I travelled to Berlin instead to look for Jews, but they had literally gone up in smoke. I cried, not for them, but because I could not stroll into 1933, into a bourgeois Jewish apartment, sit at the table by the light of the candelabra and break bread, dip it in soup. I suffered from a non-committal reverie, exoticism, that was me, distant.

The trip was confusing, lonely, my attention attracted to shopping centres, museums, their gift shops, cafés with nostalgic servings of Sachertorte and espresso, hot chocolate with real cream, this word 'real' actually meant 'old', old cream, yes, my awareness of the present interfered with everything. The camera shaded my face. The text in the tourist guide never stuck in my mind.

I do not even know if I have utilised my books as well as I might have, if burying myself somewhere in the story might have helped, remaining there, not moving, not watching so many films, not reading so many novels or forgetting to read them, just seeing them pile up and become titles I would one day want to penetrate, but which remained simply titles, something familiar I was nevertheless unfamiliar with, something I had obtained, but had not used.

But the self-criticism has declined, not because I have matured, but because my time is running on and running out, I need to hurry. What I do not have time to absorb now is never going to be of benefit to anyone, what I do not read will not be read by me and what I do not write will not be written by anyone.

Yes, that is how I am, me, Bea Britt Viker. Filled with self-pity that poisons my intelligence and emotional life, and makes me feel even more sorry for myself. I am without doubt a true child of my time. Every time I read in the newspaper about an underage asylum seeker the Norwegian government has sent out of the country I sigh and say: I cannot even manage to get upset about *that*, I do *nothing*. That is the way things are around me, passive, but simultaneously marked by excessive activity, excessive consumption, restlessness. We suffer from a lack of alternative courses of action, suffer. But what can I do? *Me?* The solution is not to be found on the level of the individual, I say. What an awful person I am. A cliché.

I have pondered it since the children were born. The black dog. The black sickness. Warm and sleek, it slips between the trees. Pauses, approaches, waits outside the house. A faithful friend. Standing guard. I am inside the house. Cannot get out. The dog can enter but I cannot leave. The dog is free. It does not have to speak. It was Knut who told me that Churchill termed his depression the black dog. Knut suffered a lot from depression. I did too. But I did not understand why that animal would embody depression. Smooth, glossy black dogs are beautiful after all. And as I stand looking at Beate, I have a sudden insight: the dog is not depression itself, but its companion, the opposite. The wonderful things there are no room for, the things melancholy has displaced. The dog is actually your friend.

Beate's skinny body. That was what put me in mind of the black dog. Surely she has not got an eating disorder, I thought, at the same moment remembering that Anita and I had once taken the children to a stage production of *When the Robbers Came to Cardamom Town*. There was something about one of the actors. She was playing Mrs Bastian, wore prim fifties attire and had long legs that were far too thin. Her kneecaps protruded. Anorexic, I whispered to Anita, but Anita was not interested. There is something about her stance as well, I thought, staring at the actor, she stands like a *little girl*. Even though she was strong and could both tap-dance and smile coyly, she moved her legs like a young girl. When she turned to the side slightly, or stood still. Something awkward, knock-kneed. I remembered how it was back when I was fighting to stay thin. That feeling of being in harmony with myself, that came from keeping my weight down. As though my body belonged to a stranger and was made ready for this ownership, another life. Every time I exited the house, I was out to tender, I only existed in expectation of something else. My body was as light as that of a child. Soft and supple. It was while I sat looking at the actor's anorexic body that I realised I was seeing something other than the childlike. It was the opposite. Which was perhaps not the opposite. I was looking into something complex. My head throbbed, my thoughts trailed off, and the three robbers came singing and dancing onto the stage. What coordination. Look, so strong, I whispered to Anita. Sexy, she whispered back, more interested now, we sniggered. My stomach ached. I wanted to have every one of the men on stage. They were in control. They could withhold or dole out affection. The unruly chest hair. The very thought of men like that taking care of small children turned me on. That was where the misunderstanding lay, the twisted factor. If it is a misunderstanding, that women want to be women-children. First they fight themselves free from the symbiotic sense of belonging with the fleshy bodies of other girls. After that they can stand alone in front of men. Visible. Something special. When no longer a part of their bunch of friends they can be plucked: pick me, no, no, take me instead. Be like a father to me, but fuck me. Lift me up, hold me tightly, deal with me. Know better than me. Control me. I need you. I *want* to need you.

Skinny legs and pointed knees. Mere swell of breasts. I cannot be more visible. It is sexy. Stomach flat between my hip bones, skin taut. There is space for a man's hand there. It can take up all the room. Lust after me, away, away into the darkness. The woman who wants to look like a child is desperate with desire. Men think women like that have no interest in pleasure, that they are only concerned with themselves, *that they must be roused*, but that is a misapprehension, on the contrary, on the contrary, I thought, and that was how I was. Misunderstood.

What is it about penetration that is so crucial?

Don't ask if you can't answer.

Why not?

17

The hallway lies in semi-darkness, even though the ceiling light is on, because the windows are small and set high up in the wall. I usually 'see' things when I stand here: wrought-iron and ivy, dilapidated parks, townhouse gardens, thicket, and shadows of houses across the tarmac, strips of strong, yellow sunlight. I know I am in Granny's time. There are no people at first. Just places. But I can tell by the light, the difference in how it falls, making things appear with a sharpness I would not ordinarily see, in the material of the attire, for example, the fibres in the weave of the woollen clothing, the burls, the shiny lining discernible on the inside of the coat sleeve. This is a winter's day. I am walking on the street, the dirty blue tram passing by. I come to a pastry shop, enter and stand by the glass counter. A heavy chandelier hangs above my head. The ceiling is high. Large windowpanes face the snow outside, the light is harsh, making me squint. A woman in a white apron and bonnet stands in front of a shiny metal drum. She turns the black tap and hot chocolate runs into my cup. She places the cup and saucer on a tray and slides it down towards the till. The cashier provides everyone with cream from a bowl beside her, using a large spoon, she leans forward and tips the cream into the cup. In the park across the street, heavy snow lies upon the trees, the benches and atop the litter bins, the railings, on the little bridge over the pond. Black open water, two solitary ducks, males.

Where is this park? And why is nobody there?

I come near the inside of a coat, the form of a large man on a deserted street. Johan Andreas Walter. Suit trousers beneath his coat, the lining moving smoothly over the knees. It is winter, an icy wind. Underneath the clothes his body is strong, but unfit, his stomach white and soft, legs and chest slightly hairy, nipples pink. If I am Granny now, then I do not like this body, it is forcing itself in. From a different time. The men from childhood. Granny is tired of men. The road leads neither forwards nor backwards. Snow, cream. Ice, crystal, it does not become anything else, as it were. A bad dream.

Johan Andreas Walter. Granny once showed me that name. She had begun to research her family tree and I was visiting, sitting on her red sofa and reading the names on the genealogical charts she showed me. She had handwritten them in black ink, entered years of birth and death, who was married to whom, and what kind of titles they had. She had transferred the two latest generations to a drawing of a large family tree. My name was included, with a dash after the year of my birth and a space for the year of my death. But I already knew that I was never going to die. Granddad's name had a big black cross beside it. Between his name and her own, Granny had drawn a knife dripping with blood. She had written 'Bastard' in large letters with an arrow pointing to Granddad. She had only put in her own past relatives.

Look, Granny said, our ancestors came from Schleswig-Holstein in the eighteenth century. She pointed to some names. Proper German sailors, she said, yes, of high rank and all, chief officers and captains, that kind of thing. Johan

Andreas married a Danish woman, and one of their sons went to Norway and married there, he was a merchant.

And then, after that? I asked.

No, everything gets hard to follow from then on, Granny said, lit up a cigarette, and turned towards the window, the blue sky, the apartment block across the street, the rows of white balconies. I don't really know if I'll bother doing much more on it. Nobody is interested in it anyway.

I'm interested, I said, but she pretended not to hear.

I was a very clumsy nine-year-old. Granny looked at my body, and then I understood I had a defect. All the same, she told me about her father. What he made her do.

Why did he do that? I asked.

Because he was mean. He was a mean, mean man, Granny said.

We sat in silence for a while, Granny in the chair, me on the sofa. I did not dare go for a piddle, because then she would see me from behind, and no doubt say I was stout. That meant fat. The sun was about to break through the cloud cover, only a snowflake or two still sailing through the air. The sunlight lay in warm strips across the wall opposite us, where Granny had her portraits, both paintings and photographs. One of the paintings was of her, in a white dress and dark high-button boots, her fair hair falling loose over her shoulders, the front up in a ribbon on one side of her head.

You were pretty, I said.

Yes, I was fetching, quite fetching, Granny replied.

I think I look like you in that picture, I said.

Really, you think so? Granny responded.

*

I get the red bucket from the cellar. Fill it with hot water and green soap. Switch on the light in the hallway and wash the floor covering, it is linoleum and depicts a Persian rug. I bought the art-deco lamp hanging from the ceiling in a second-hand shop in Amsterdam fourteen years ago. I was there with some friends and fellow writers. On a cultural holiday. We were at both the Rembrandt and the Van Gogh museums. My thoughts were unsettled, the museum spaces big and airy, I do not remember too much about the pictures. The staircase to the Secret Annexe where Anne Frank lived on the other hand was packed with people, we shuffled through in a queue and no one got to see the rooms properly. All that stood out to me was a firewood box, painted an optimistic shade of blue. Anne Frank used to sit on the box, I recalled that from the book, that she was a light-hearted girl. Memory is selective.

And what happens to our memories when we die? Are they arranged according to age, do they lose colour, float in a lake in a dark wood? Do they revolve in a circle, as in life, not leaving us in peace? Or do they become dazzling works of art in our abstract bodies? Maybe Dante was closer to the truth than he knew, maybe after death we no longer have any control over time, we are here one minute, and there the next, in forms unimaginable to us. Heavily regulated, that is the common feature. Controlled by poverty or wealth, age or gender: each body in its own cage, that is hell.

Anyway, I was in Amsterdam at the time, with a group of young, well-functioning women. Being young is an asset. Having many friends who live and think the same way you do also helps, a little apparatus of power.

In the evenings we drank red wine and talked about art

and men. It was easy. I was recently divorced, released. Does anyone really understand how important motherhood is? I shouted across the table, not of course that you're allowed to say that, the law of life isn't allowed to apply. Yes, my friends shouted, you are allowed to say anything, here's to motherhood, and we drank champagne, here's to Jesus Maria, I shouted at the top of my voice, and the bubbles rose in the glass, they are one.

The children and I lived in a rented apartment in Torshov, I was young and anticipating everything to come, not least admiration and recognition: I would take up my deserved place as an author. Not to mention love.

I rinse and wring out the floor cloth in the warm soapy water, fix it to the end of the mop handle and push it with long strokes over the dark, floral-patterned linoleum. It is dusk and I switch on the wall lamp with the red shade. A key on a string hangs from the brass fitting. They found it among Granny's things, Dad thought it was a house key but it did not fit. The lock must have been changed, he said, because he recognised the key. It was the one she took from him, the one he was not allowed to have any more, because Granny wanted to decide when he was in or out. He was not allowed in when she was resting, nor if he was petulant, or if his sisters had any little girls visiting.

18

16 March 1951. As though he were her solicitor. Yes, that is actually what it is like. She is now Miss, now divorced, but she still has to submit her accounts for inspection. The only progress is that she is spared that green account book he would insist on looking over every evening. I must enter my expenses, he would say, but that of course was a pretext, he had his own little book where he recorded purchases, tram tickets and restaurant meals. He was keeping an eye on her, like a factory inspector or some such. Was it necessary to buy the good butter again? he would say. Or ask if she could not sew the children's clothes from cheaper material. She laughed at him, called him a skinflint. And said worse things than that. Do you know, she said, we could save a few bob on your short legs. It wouldn't cost that much to make *you* a pair of trousers. Then we could still afford good-quality clothes for the children. That was nasty, but she got so angry, yes, really rasped. It was harder during the war. Naturally they had to be more prudent then, it was wholly necessary. They planted potatoes, and Hartvig hammered together a little henhouse, albeit in his ham-fisted way, at the bottom of the garden. Then they had chickens and could have eggs. He was right, of course, everybody had to tighten their belts. All the same, she felt like hitting him. His behaviour, like that of a headmaster. Stingy, miserly was what he was. No, words failed her. Now she just copies her own notes onto a sheet of paper once a month, in rough figures, and posts it to him. Naturally, often as not he will ring up to say he wants the different items specified. Did the children's school things really cost this and this much? And the figure for miscellaneous expenses was very high, was it not? Why did he have to give two hoots about it, why did they have to talk to one another at all? His cold, businesslike tone. There was no way back. Oh, but she was sure he regretted leaving her. When he heard her voice. She is after all the mother of his children. She knows how she ought to be. She can be like that, knows she can. Could stop being so demanding, discard her nerves. She says it to him: I am different now, I am much calmer. More patient. You know that I am kind at heart, that all of it was due to mental pressure, my temper. The boy is difficult, you have to admit that. And there was the war, and the girls, those difficult births. I know I have been wicked to you. But I am normal when things are normal around me. You are just being stubborn and unreasonable as always, surely it is possible to try again, to forgive. What is it you actually want of me? What? Charity, Hartvig, have you completely forgotten the faith you were brought up in? I promise things will be different.

Everything hurts.

The children belong at home, it is their childhood home. How I have toiled in that house, the miles I have traipsed through the rooms. Up and down the stairs. I know all about it. You know very well that I took care of the upkeep. What it has cost. What you have saved on craftsmen's expenses. Yes, after all it is your house, you must know.

She is aware of course of Hartvig's new lady friend, but cannot take her seriously. She does not think it will be difficult to forgive him, on the contrary, she understands only too well his need to seek solace with someone at this painful time, she does not begrudge him that, no, and she will make sure to tell him as much when the opportunity arises, then he will understand how selfless she is. Hartvig does not really want this divorce, even though he says he does, because she knows that, really, he loves her dearly. It should not, therefore, prove any great problem for him to disregard this new dalliance. Perhaps it will die out by itself, as relationships of a passing nature often do. No, Cessi is not concerned about that, and lets him know just as sincerely as she is able in a letter.

My heart is sick, she writes. I am devastated. You are being very hard on me. Soon we will have been apart for two years. I had hopes. I yearn for you. I realise now that my erotic feelings for you are alive. That I am alive, for you, only for you, my darling! You can come here at any time, I will welcome you with open arms. You will find everything a man could wish for, here, with me. You are the only one for me, I have told you that many times. Surely it cannot be too late. Have I really lost you? Do not be so hard. Think of the children.

Dr Vold says that she is physically strong. Nevertheless she is sick. Weak. It is her nerves. More than that. She is frail, yet all the same they think her strong. In that case, she says to Dr Vold, I must be too weak to bear my own strength. There must be something wrong with me. Yes, not that she cannot work. But suddenly she will just be lying there. Utterly spent. Like the time she dug up the plot to lay a lawn. I am being very, very, very good, she thought. But Hartvig just took all her hard work for granted. No, perhaps that was not quite the same. But the tears welled up, she felt so alone with everything. And no doubt you think everything is perfectly all right, she screamed at Hartvig. Then it took a bad turn. Oh, that screaming. But it seems everything rests with her. Everything is a critique of her. The children criticise her as well. They obviously do not understand a thing. What she does for them. All of them. Life is not worth living. She says so too. Life is awful. Upon hearing that, Dr Vold wants to admit her into care. She does not need to be asked twice. He is so strong, Dr Vold. Things just sort of fall into place when he talks to her, what he says seems so simple and natural. That she must have faith, and forgive herself. That she can seek forgiveness, not only from God, but from Hartvig as well. But Hartvig has been hard as stone since the day he produced the separation papers. That was when all hope was lost, she told the doctor. Dr Vold had then spoken to her about love and altruism. Atonement, reconciliation and humility. Things of that nature. She wept, it felt so good, finally it would be possible to rest. But afterwards she had to manage for herself. The effect of his words only lasted a day or two, thereafter everything tightened and tensed up again, and it was at least a week between appointments. She was really down, she cried and asked the doctor to take her home, take me home, she sobbed, but he misunderstood, thought she missed her home with Hartvig, but she wanted to go to the doctor's, wanted him to put things straight inside her, rearrange her head, like he said in jest once, how sometimes a rearrangement is what is needed.

No, she did not want to go to the doctor's either, but home, she did not know where and how, but home, to someone who loved her. But there was nobody. Not any more. And it had never been Hartvig. He was right about that. She had never loved him. Not sufficiently, with his looks, and how terribly punctilious he was, it was his weakness she could not bear. She was not weak herself, but he made her so, yes, then she probably was also. One had to keep one's own house in order after all. It was so very confusing. Oh, but she was furious. So Hartvig had met someone else ages ago but had not said a word until now. That was the reason he was capable of being so hard-hearted, she was no longer desirable to him. She was pushed out, discarded, had no home any more. The other woman was to come and take over her house. She had put an extraordinary amount of work into that home, shaped it, and put her stamp on it, unfair was what it was, grossly unfair. That her 'sins' should overshadow everything else, her illness should blind them to the good she had done for them. She could not help her nerves. And God and Dr Vold knew she worked hard on herself.

She pictured them in bed, how Hartvig now appeared strong all of a sudden. His clearly defined jaw and sensitive mouth, the strong arc of his nose, he was manly, if one ignored his lower body and his short legs, and she could do that if she looked at him through the other woman's eyes. That crabby, skinny, pale scarecrow.

Ah, it made no difference. She was so tired anyway. As for Hartvig, that fancy woman was more than welcome to him, she could have him.

She just had to face it: she had been downgraded. Removed from her own house. Rejected by her husband. All the same she knew she was the one Hartvig wanted. Not that other woman, all cold and correct. That was exactly what

Hartvig liked in a woman, the hot and fiery, he liked her, Cessi.

She was not as he thought her to be, not as he made out, she wrote to him, you do not understand a thing, you see, you know I am kind. And love you, my darling, darling Hartvig, do not think that I am unaware of having hurt you. She wrote in that way. So he could see for himself that she had changed. How she had suffered since their parting, been ill the entire time. Her nerves deranged. Was there no allowance to be made for that? But she did not write a word about his lack of consideration, he would not be able to accuse her of being bitter. Forgiveness, Dr Vold had said, reconciliation. There is no point coming with accusations, you have to show through your actions that you have changed. Yes, I have been chastened now, she said to the doctor, and he took a note of that, but made no reply, it was impossible to see if he approved. Would it have helped? Hartvig did not call upon her, on the contrary. So how could she demonstrate to him how different she was, that he could rely on her now? She talked to him in her head, about all the things she used to turn to him with. A great many practical matters, naturally, but also when she needed comforting and support. Because all those people, the maid, Mrs Heyerdahl, the neighbours, Hartvig's silly friends, they could be so nasty to her. Of course she did not take it lying down but afterwards she wept, and Hartvig consoled her. Don't take it all in the worst possible way, he said, don't mull over it any more. It felt good to talk to Hartvig about their acquaintances, it was a source of amusement to them. They related small incidents to one another and had a good laugh about them, particularly Cessi's friends at the women's circle. Women are dreadful, she said to Hartvig. He drummed his finger on the table, looked at her, smiled and said that he was fortunate to have a wife so unlike those cackling hens.

But now he did not want her any more.

She had a thousand good reasons to write to him, and did so, she was still in possession of her rights. There were the children, all the particulars relating to the apartment, and she wanted to try and make him see how wrong he was about her. She was everything he wanted. Yes, she was really quite a different person, but she needed the opportunity to prove it. She pictured it, how she would love and obey him, be humble, how her anger would simply dispel, how he would apologise for his former impatience, all the scenes, that were not really her fault, but down to circumstances. And now that Finn had grown up there would soon be more harmony at home, he would be around less, it would be her, Hartvig and the girls, so very, very much easier.

Finn, her adorable, darling boy. If only he had not been so quick-tempered, so testy. Still, the worst of it was all the nasty things he said to her, she could not take that sort of criticism, she was too sensitive.

Dr Vold mentioned something else, which had annoyed her. He spoke about getting outside the four walls of the apartment, introducing a little variation, applying herself. Her, apply herself, she was responsible for three children, one of whom was very, very difficult. Well, Finn lived with his father, that was true, yes, imagine, poor thing, together with that terrible woman, she was not kind to the children, she was mean, and mean to Cessi's dear, darling boy. She might not be responsible for the big house any longer but she was on her own, Dr Vold should not forget that, she was a lone, vulnerable mother who was badly off. A great deal of her time went on darning the children's clothes, making food for the two little girls, keeping house, cleaning, yes, taking care of practical matters. She could not afford a maid any more, after all. How was she supposed to find the time to work outside the home? She was so angry she almost screamed at Dr Vold, but managed to get hold of herself at the last minute and laughed, yes, you are almost speechless now, she said. But did he reply? Oh no, he sat there with that stony expression of his, utterly impossible to interpret.

Oh, it was actually lovely with the apartment, not that she let on, how good it was to sit on the chair with a cup of coffee and a cigarette when the girls had been safely packed off to school. In her own apartment. The only thing was it did not come free of charge. Hartvig's stern, businesslike letters followed into the bargain. She would never be spared having to answer to him, he oversaw all that was coming in and going out. Well, for the most part, to get back at him she wrote rather rough, illegible lists of income and expenses, and always to her advantage, naturally. But this month she accounted for every single krone she had spent on food, so he would understand that it was too little, she could not live on what he paid for the children. He was well aware that she drank beer now and then, so she could not very well leave out the measly few bottles she had bought last month, nor the smoked salmon she and the children had enjoyed the weekend Finn was visiting. She had fancied he might be so churlish as to point out what he referred to as her overconsumption, but had not wanted to believe he would. He wrote that she could no longer carry on feeding the children delicacies, not in the financial situation in which she now found herself. She must see to it that she found employment, yes, there ought not to be any hindrance to her finding work now.

I'm over fifty years old, she sobbed in Dr Vold's office, and for close to twenty of those years I have worked hard in Hartvig's house, for him and the children. I'm not strong, she said, look at me, I'm not strong.

It has been a while since the divorce now, Dr Vold said. What did you dream of when you were young? Perhaps you could look at this as a fresh start, an opportunity to breathe life into your dreams? You have spoken a great deal about the pleasure you derive from sewing and making clothes.

She sobbed, was not up to imagining any longer. She did not know. What did she dream about? Of getting away, first and foremost. She did not know where, wherever she would find love and beauty. Find peace from all the terrible agitation and disturbance, such powerful forces, as difficult to grasp as the muscles of the sea should it have any, because it does not have muscles, it is seething turmoil without let-up, squalls, chaos.

I do have an extraordinary sense of beauty, she said to the doctor, adore music and colours. But I do not know if I ever believed I would make anything of myself, not in any real sense. My emotions have always proved such a great difficulty, they have been in the way, as it were. But I was good with my hands. Everyone said so. Then Mama got me a place at the dressmaker's workshop, you know. It was what I wanted too but it was terrible, how they bullied me. I did not fit into working life. But it is true what you say. Back then I did think that perhaps, in time, I could start up my own dressmaker's. I might have managed to as well, had it not been for the circumstances. My father. My mother. And now look. A difficult son. Two girls at a vulnerable age. A husband who does not want anything to do with me. They just criticise. All of them. I cannot take it.

Oh, but you manage a great deal, Mrs Viker.

19

A writer cannot cry as much as I do, I say to Beate, and she looks out the window and says, at this time of year it's better to be outside than indoors, at least when the sun is shining. The cheek of her. Beate is coming round all too often, I wish the rain was splashing down on my white plastic chair, and on the radio, drowning the radio.

It has been two weeks since Emilie disappeared, and the police are keeping their cards close to their chest. I have been eliminated from their inquiries, but the man in the baseball cap has been passing by my gate every day lately. His huge form slowing down, his face gawking up at the house. Sometimes he comes to a complete stop. I get the feeling he sees me, even though I have withdrawn far into the room.

He stands there. Always wearing the red baseball cap, the same heavy army jacket. He has probably seen the house on TV, I think, along with everyone else in the neighbourhood, and they stare just as much, only not as openly. There is no danger. He is doing what he has always done, same as when he had the dog. It is because he has heard about Emilie, that is why, simple curiosity. It is human, completely natural, he just does not have the sense to hide it.

God knows what he is thinking. How deranged he is. What sort of fantasies he actually has. Sick ones that no one knows about.

Those arms of his, like ham shanks. I saw him in a T-shirt once. At the shop. Imagine he strangles me. Sits astride my chest, pins me down and squeezes. Easy as pie. Because he thinks I am the killer. But actually it is him, he is the dangerous one, maybe that is how it is.

Well, what do I know. He might be psychotic, his condition might worsen in the summer, that happens to a lot of them. It is the holiday period at the institutions, the psychiatrist is away, public services are keeping summer hours, it is hot and his confusion mounts. Then he stops taking his tablets and buys beer and spirits instead. Drinks more frequently, downs larger amounts. Walks through the woods in his warm clothes. Sits down on the grass up at the lake at Sognsvann and watches girls in bikinis. They lean their heads close and send him funny looks. He becomes angry. He walks the streets in the neighbourhood and stops at mine. Maybe he is furious. Believes it is my fault or something. He is going to get me, he thinks, get that fucking bitch.

I am imagining things, I realise that. But Christ, what am I supposed to think? Does he want to get in here, and why? Should I do something? But seriously, is that really necessary? I do not think I can be bothered.

I am prone to exaggeration, or so Tuva always says.

Maybe I should give her a ring and hear what she has to say. See if she makes light of it. If she does, I need not concern myself, then it is nothing.

An upset stomach, a metallic taste in my mouth. I do not know what is up or down. Is he dangerous or not? I am such a coward. Should not exist. So ugly, stupid and worried. Typical me, just thinking of myself.

I could mention it to Beate in passing, while she is still

here. Ask her if she thinks I should call the police. But she is in the toilet and by the time she comes back to the kitchen I will have changed my mind. The police probably know about him already, I am pretty sure they check out things like that, if there are any dangerous lunatics in the area and so on, and anyway the neighbours will have mentioned him already, everybody takes notice of the likes of him. I do not think I need to do anything.

I'm heading off, Beate says, standing in front of me on the landing with her back to the window, the sunlight making the outermost part of her hair glow, giving her a halo. I hug her. Your little angel, Tuva usually says, she is jealous. She has no reason to be. I tell her as much, there is no one I love like you. Do I need to have a reason? Tuva asks. It is just an expression, I answer, and she lets it go.

Take care, I say to Beate.

Mum always says that, take care, but how are you supposed to do that? Beate says, and laughs.

In the afternoon it begins to rain and I bring in the radio. I am fond of it, after all.

I wonder if he really thinks I have Emilie.

I have not seen any sign of him today. That means he might come tonight. In which case I should not leave the house. It would be all too easy for him to break in while I am gone. The veranda door is not visible from the road, nor are the windows at the back of the house. But I do not see any quick escape routes. Sooner or later, I will have to leave. So I may as well go to SATS to work out, that is what I usually do when I am going up the wall. Maybe give Tuva a call before it gets too late, I will see when the time comes, how scared I am, even though I know how scared I will be, how my heart will pound when I put the key in the door, how I will check all the windows and every single room, before going up and pouring myself a large glass of wine, before going down again to shove the big chest of drawers in front of the cellar door, since the easiest way to gain entry is through the cellar windows.

What about an alarm, Mum? I can just hear Tuva. That huge house, Mum. And in that snobby area, why don't you get an alarm?

Because I find it objectionable.

Because I find wealth objectionable.

Comfortable bourgeois wealth built on quality and stability. Solid wood furniture and an everyday marked by repairs and frugality. The expensive wine and the Persian rugs are just for show. Cut your coat according to your cloth, always. That is the consistent practice that has served to accumulate the money I am living off – *you're nibbling at your own nest egg, you silly little mouse.*

I do not know why I should view capital growth as so wrong, yes, what is the problem with that, wealth creation, looking after money and passing it on? Except for the fact that I am unable to do it.

I do not know.

Having to put yourself first.

Everyone not having the same, the shame in eating while others watch.

The urge to divide equally, the tendency not to do so.

That I am childish.

Immature and spoilt. I am over fifty years old, but still want an unrestrained life near the street and nature. Live simply, collectively and in solidarity. Like a young person.

Because, I do not know. When one thing is true the other quickly becomes a lie and vice versa: I love gardens and Persian rugs as well. I do not dare grow a single vegetable without a fence around me. Someone could come and get me while I am bent over the patch. I am afraid. I am very afraid.

The truth is I do not want to be alone. I do not want to live in the house and I do not want to need an alarm.

I love the house. It endures everything, contains everything and stays quiet.

I am being torn in two.

But, no matter, I know it is only a question of time, I know what will happen, and then I will no longer have a choice. Daddy and his sisters will pull it down. They will demolish the house and divide the site into several smaller ones, erect prefabricated houses and sell them at a high price to people who want to live at a good address near all that nature in Nordmarka. Thus Granddad's old fortune will begin to circulate and spread, among the grandchildren, the great-grandchildren, to be used on mindless consumption by some, acute need by others and perhaps invested by one or two more. Some people will make the money multiply, others will make it disappear down a dark drain. The wooded areas, the heavy pine trees, the roots. The squirrels, the fox. Stray dogs, crows, magpies, the woodpecker. Field mice who claw at the walls. The chickens.

Granddad and Granny made contemporary architectural choices, but the fundamental principle was in line with their upbringing: four solid walls with good materials in the laying of the foundations. The house was meant to last, to stay within the family, but the family no longer wants to be a family, we have forgotten ourselves: I have this much, I take this away, this is how much I have left. Until it is all gone, or has been converted and recycled so many times that we no longer remember how Grandfather's father considered carefully before investing in the large plot of land, and then passed it on to his children and impressed frugality upon them. It no longer works. The measured craftsmanship at a chosen spot in nature has become a restless stream of transactions and symbolic life, flashing and smashing.

Christ, so much dreaming.

I, Bea Britt Viker, have never liked bourgeois ideals.

I have never liked the norms, dogma and requirements of good manners and pretence.

So why am I not happy when they crumble? Because, God help me, it is the inheritance that has given me freedom from the world of waged work, from the monotonous.

I am the heir of the old capitalists.

Now I miss the ideals. There is a logic to that.

I miss long-term planning, property and solid buildings.

I long for sobriety and a toolbox.

The first was not freedom, but neither is the second.

It is the same as something else.

It always seems to be.

Somebody controlling others.

I place my hand on the door, pull it towards me, walk in, and am then inside. I hand over my membership card, the receptionist draws it through the card reader and a white ticket is printed out. I walk towards the changing room with the ticket in my hand, taking off my shoes before entering and placing them under a bench by the door. They are a relatively new pair of grey Adidas, I bought them after the Nikes disappeared. I push open the door. Choose a locker on the third row. Lean over the bag and unzip it. As it opens the odour of stale sweat, reminiscent of cat piss, hits me. No matter how much fragranced fabric softener I pour into the washing machine the smell lingers on my exercise gear. Not to mention in my trainers. I cannot even put them in the wash. The shop assistant told me the water would ruin the cushioning. The gel or air bubbles in the soles that keep the impact springy would be weighed down by the water. The fully cushioned running shoes to prevent injury to your skeleton and sinews, but do not, because age weakens the body more than the trainers can compensate.

Wearing sports gear makes me look younger, I can see that in the mirror as I fill water from the tap, in here I do not age, I am all alone. A white orchid stands in a vase on the bench beside the sink, I am wearing a pink T-shirt with Nike and *JUST DO IT* written across the front, I look like everyone else. Every gym in the SATS chain looks the same, I find that comforting: they are all alike, in a world that cannot come to an end, here everything is constant, and no one knows each other, even though you see the same people several times a week, year in, year out.

Everything I know is of benefit to myself. This is the way my life is organised, everything is about me, my own well-being. The wine I drink later that evening. The sentences that start to flow but which I no longer write down. The rain hits the ground, the stone steps, the leaves outside, water collects on the white plastic chair. Soon the brown killer slugs will come out. What is my life actually worth? Nothing? Nothing is threatening. From all sides. I walk through the house and barricade the cellar door. There is no sign of attempted entry or that anyone has been inside. Nevertheless, I carry my mattress and bedding down and lay them on the first-floor landing. If I leave the door from the dining room to the hall open, I can keep an eye on the veranda door from the mattress, while at the same time hear if anybody tries to get in by the front or cellar doors. I'll be lying in a cold draught but rather that than be surprised in my sleep. Something has dawned on me that should have been obvious from the moment they found Emilie's bag in my garden: I must be involved even if I cannot see how. In someone's head I am part of a terrible world. Someone is thinking about me. Somewhere or other, something is being planned for me that I cannot guess nor foresee. Christ, what is going on, who has taken hold of my life, and how is it at all possible for them to do that?

I have never realised this before. How many people cannot make their own choices. What that means. I do not understand what it involves now either, of course not, how someone appropriates everything that is yours. Your parents, your children, your house. Your life and your death. I am so stupid, have been stupid for over fifty years, and will in all probability remain so for the rest of my life, so ignorant, thoroughly lacking in knowledge, about people, that solitary individuals make up groups, countries and nations. Nations. That we do not decide over ourselves. I am very tired. I am fifty-two and have hardly begun life.

Because life. Is. See, I cannot manage to complete the sentence, is this for real? Not knowing what you are going to say, only that it is a sentence, a small sentence, and it is too complex, too complex to exist, it is the root of my tongue that cannot manage more, there is no movement down there. Life is

And then

Continues

I have not rung Tuva but that is because I do not want her to see how afraid I am. Helplessly alone. With the children I am feeble and filled with anxiety. I could have a man, but sooner or later I would want to get rid of him, or he could suddenly take off and leave me alone with the fear, it never goes away.

God knows of what.

Frightened of him leaving or of him staying.

Forcing his way in or pushing me away.

Both.

The criminal is thinking about me. I understand that now. He wants something from me or to do something with me. But why? Is there something in my eyes? Is it because I do not have a man?

No. I cannot face thinking any more. He can just come, whoever he is. The man in the baseball cap or some other bastard. He wants to get into the house. But you know what, I think, it makes fuck all difference. So I go up and open a bottle of red wine.

I drink. I float. Who is it I think I am with? Because I feel close, in communication. *Communicatio*. But with whom, there is nobody here? And yet, now, on the sofa with the radio on, under the light of the wrought-iron lamp, in the warmth, with the red wine both in my body and in the glass on the table in front of me, I am swimming in an ocean of security. As though nothing ever went wrong and I am not actually alone.

What does it mean to be alone?

I don't like 'em.

20

I was sitting in the kitchen eating when the mobile phone beeped. It was a text message from Beate: 'I got a boyfriend. Don't tell Mum. Love u. Bat.'

Slices of bread get a distinctive salty taste when they lie right on top of the surface of the table, I remember that from when I was small. It is the same kitchen table, I took it with me when I left home. I thought I would get a boyfriend straight away, but that was not how it turned out.

Emilie will never have a boyfriend, because Emilie is dead.

I lie down on the sofa and nod off. I think I am resting my head on balls of wool, the wicker chair in the corner creaks. It is the pills that do it. My GP gave them to me. You aren't ill, he said, but if depression is preventing you from writing? A little lift, that's all. These pills. They're a leg-up. But I am sliding down instead, am almost at ground level now: I can see the sides of a sledge sliding through crusted snow. Scraping. Cotton, snow. The illuminated carriages of the underground passing on their tracks. A queue of cars moving slowly through the slush on the road. It is to do with something, I know, but I am so drowsy, what is it that is sliding, the brittle sound of frozen slush against hard plastic. I am not on the way into the light, into the school buildings which the marching band and choir borrow in the evening, instead I am being dragged with a scraping sound that fades in the dark forest, and I tell myself I have to think, now I have to think, because if my feelings should glide more easily henceforth, my thoughts must find me in another place, if my garden has another meaning, then I do too. Or it could be my thoughts that are gliding, and my feelings have changed, become immersed? I will soon sink down to the vegetation in the garden, to pine cones and damp soil, mushrooms and grass, algae on the foundation wall and old rainwater in a flowerpot.

It is dark and raining outside, I hear the gusts of wind, something falling over in the garden, it could be the plastic chair being blown around into the bushes, lying there rocking. I sit up and switch on the wrought-iron lamp, the light bulb gives off heat, I feel it on my head, my hair getting warm.

Not only can the past lie in darkness, it can also *be* darkness.

Dad as a small boy, in a strange bed at night, at the children's home, sent away. That could not go well. I think about how fear transforms everything: the taste of a slice of bread, the sight of trees, snow, houses, everything flattens out, colours recede, the air becomes grainy. That is how it feels to be afraid. It is an assault on perception.

I need a glass of water and walk into the kitchen. The rain hits the windows, the wind cleaves the hedges and tears leaves from the trees. Everything is wet and viscid, the leaves, grass, the soil in the flower beds. Soon it will be summer and Beate is in love. Expectation is in the air, shifting from person to person, place to place, depending on whose turn it is, according to age and background. It is now in Beate, or she is in it, inside a force field where everything appears possible. *Creation*. I think how it is not the things around us that are good for us but we who make things seem good, we grant them potency. I walk into the living room, across the Persian rug and over to the desk. The rug was once Granddad's. There was a time when the sight of it made me light up, the tawny colours, the latent red. Now it is just a rug that fulfils its function. I am not radiant any more and things do not radiate back. Rather the earth beams in towards itself where I stand, pulling the heat back from the surface, God knows how things are within.

I hear sounds coming from outside for a while before I manage to get up and look, I do not want to. Because it is a new revolution, I feel it in my whole body, it seeps in gradually: this is not over, and is not going to let up. I am chosen and captured.

No. I will not. I am not budging. I want to sit on the sofa beneath the warm lamplight, the woollen blanket around me, looking at the fire in the stove. I want to watch TV and drink red wine. That is all I need. I do not need to think.

The sound of steps, of scraping and of things being disturbed, purposeful sounds, unlike those of an animal. Animals stop, listen and wait, move gradually and swiftly at the same time, are alert. People hurry, think ahead, want to get things over with. I stand up and walk into the darkened dining room where the curtains are drawn. Pause and hold my breath so as to hear better, but it is quiet out there now. Except for the wind. It has blown so much since Emilie disappeared. I draw the curtain back ever so slightly with my forefinger, enough to see out with one eye. Nothing. I then go from window to window on the entire ground floor, but there is no one to be seen. It is four o'clock, beginning to get light and I feel less jumpy, maybe it was an animal after all, a badger, I think, a badger's direct way of doing things that made me believe I heard human steps. I decide to open a window. My heart begins pounding again, but nobody can get in through the window when it is on the latch, it is not possible, I tell myself, and open it. At first there is nothing but the usual sounds; the rustle of the wind in the trees and the reassuring slam of the door of the paperboy's car down on the road, he is driving from gate to gate. But then comes a whimpering, a whining.

I wish I could ring Tuva. Not because I want her to come over, but because it reminds me that I am a mother. That Tuva is my child, whom I have protected and loved. Hearing her voice would be enough for me to understand how things ought to be handled. You need to do something, Mum, Tuva would have cried if she was still a child standing barefoot on the floor in her nightdress, her long hair down her back, upset.

Hurry, there's an animal out there we need to rescue. It's in pain, Mum. Mum!

An hour goes by and the sun is on the verge of coming up. The whimpering is still audible, but coming at longer intervals, weaker, I think, perhaps it is dying for me. I stand at the window looking out, listening, to see if someone is there, waiting, watching, spying on me? No one, I do not see anyone. Tears run down my face. Finally I go out.

Between the bags of firewood and the old snowblower lies Emilie's dog. I knew it, knew that was what it was. But I was so afraid of what I would find. A dog with broken paws?

With its eyes put out or brutalised in some other way? What I see before me is bad enough but not in that league. Its paws are bound together and its collar is tied to a short length of rope knotted so tightly to the snowblower that it cannot move. Skee, I say, and cry, lovely little thing. He snaps at me but is weak. Thin too, cannot have had much food in the last couple of weeks. You're just scared, I say, there, there, you're just scared is all, don't be afraid, it's okay now. I cannot manage to undo the knot in the rope so just remove the collar, whereupon his whole body twitches, I lift him up, hold him close, and he pees. There, there, I say, there, there.

Walking up the steps to the veranda I spot the man in the baseball cap, standing at the gate talking on his mobile. I hug the shivering, pee-soaked dog close to my chest with one hand, run inside, lock the door after me, pick up my phone from the living-room table and make it into the kitchen. The card with the northerner's number is fixed to the fridge door by a magnet. I am not wearing my glasses, and have to stretch my neck and squint to make out the digits. The fingers of my free hand feel slow and podgy, I cannot move them fast enough, and I have to punch in the number with the mobile lying on the worktop. As it slides a little across the surface a couple of times, the tears begin to flow, making it even harder. When I lift my head and bring the phone to my ear, I can see the gate and the man in the baseball cap. He is also holding his phone to his ear, but has his back turned to the house, I see him hunching over a little as he speaks.

The morning sun lights up the kitchen worktop and the brown ceramic jug where I keep ladles and hand whisks, a yellow streak of grease on the top of the cooker, the green glass jar with dry crumbs of cake.

The northerner does not pick up, naturally, it is not quite half past five in the morning, so I speak in a clear, slow voice to the answering machine. The dog, I say. The man in the baseball cap.

I then ring the main number for the police. It's about the Emilie case, I tell the duty officer, I'm a witness, I've found her dog. In the garden.

I see, he says.

It's frightened, I say. I'm frightened as well. There's a man at my gate. Every night. He's standing there right this minute. I know who he is, he lives in the neighbourhood. You probably know him too, he looks like a psychiatric patient.

I see, says the officer. Okay, there's a patrol car already on the way.

Already. Dispatched before I rang. I thought as much. He was at my gate ringing the police. Making up some lies. I will have to watch my mouth now. I must not let them realise that I know he has called. But maybe it is even stranger not to ask how they could be on the way before I got in touch. It is closing in, getting complicated.

Hello, the policeman on the other end of the line says, hello, are you still there?

Yes, so, I'm calling to report that a lunatic has been hanging around my gate every night since Emilie disappeared.

Emilie? I didn't think you knew her. Well, you can take it up with the officers when they arrive. I'll make a note of it here.

Everybody says Emilie, Jesus, the whole country knows who Emilie is. Which officers are coming?

Like I said, a patrol car first of all. Then we'll see.

I've tried to call Bjørn Eriksen, I'd very much like to speak to him.

Right, well, we work in shifts, we couldn't have one man on the same case twenty-four hours a day.

But he gave me his phone number.

Listen, I've made a note of everything. You take it up with them when they arrive, okay?

Okay, I feel I'm getting pretty short shrift here, I have to say.

Well, you'll have to live with it.

Yes, obviously, I say and hang up.

Fucking arsehole.

I find the scissors in the kitchen drawer, sit down on the floor with the dog on my lap and carefully cut the rope holding his legs together. He whines a little but does not get up.

Maybe you're thirsty, sweetheart, I whisper, holding him to my chest so he can feel it rise and fall and hear my heartbeat.

I fill an old ice-cream container with water but he will not drink. So I get a teaspoon from the drawer, lift him onto my lap again and, forcing his mouth open, tip a spoonful of water in. He tries to wriggle free and stand up but his legs give way. My eyes are so filled with tears that I can hardly see, but I manage to pour the water into a little saucer that I place beneath his snout. Then his tongue comes out and laps up a little. I stroke and pat him, cry and speak softly as I carry him around the kitchen, open the fridge and take out a tin of pâté. I sit back down and let him lick at it straight from the tin, he manages a tiny bit then tries to get down but I do not want to let go. You're so scared, I say, lie here, I'll look after you. With that he deposits his inky black diarrhoea in my lap. When the police car pulls up in front of the gate, I have just taken off all my clothes and placed them at the foot of the stairs. There is no time to do anything other than wrap the blanket from the sofa around me, like a sari. Then I pick up the dog again, holding it close, his muzzle to my throat.

The policemen are suspicious. They have not observed any man in a red cap, they say, and ask why I am not dressed. One of them wants to take the dog from me, but luckily he pees again, shivers and whimpers, wetting the blanket and giving me the opportunity to explain why I am not dressed. They offer to hold the dog while I change, but I will not let go of Skee, he's too frightened, I say, and go out with him into the garden as I am. They want to know everything in detail, and I have to explain twice what has happened, how I had been up late drinking red wine because I was depressed, how I was afraid of the man at the gate, had heard sounds outside, come across the dog and tried to call Bjørn Eriksen. I cannot tell what they are thinking by their expressions. One of them walks a little way off, stands by the old playhouse and speaks on the phone. While he is talking, he looks in the window, but must not see anything, because he just continues speaking. The other one takes a walk around the garden, moves a few things, looks behind the stacks of firewood and berry bushes, but does not find anything either. The man in the baseball cap suddenly appears at the gate again. Hey, I shout, there, look, quick. The dog, in my arms, gives a start. The man in the cap opens the gate and comes into the garden.

Do you see? I say to the guy on the phone. Yes, I see, he says, pocketing the phone. Come on, he says, as though to a child, you and I can go inside for the time being, my colleague will take care of this.

He tells me that both forensics and Eriksen are on the way. I look down at my bare feet. One step at a time up to the veranda, sand and the odd piece of gravel beneath my soles. The policeman holds me gently by the elbow. I walk slowly. He asks if I want to get dressed. I turn and look out over the garden. The light seems dusty, it must be due to the haze, a veil across the sky, and the wind perhaps, maybe there is something in the air that the wind has raised up, small particles, pollen. I look at the two figures down by the gate. The man in the baseball cap is gesticulating. The policeman taking notes.

I'll wait, I say, and sit down at the living-room table, holding the dog close, it no longer shows any signs of wanting to get down, I'll wait.

The other policeman comes in.

What did he say, I ask, what does he think he's up to?

He does not answer me but says he thinks I should get dressed.

Christ, I say, you must be able to tell me what he wants, he's terrorising me. I'm going to report him, I'll report him.

Let's just take it easy, he says, this will all be fine.

But now I have started crying.

I am handed a glass of water but I place it on the table. The dog is warm in my arms, his breathing regular. I bury my face in his fur. After a while he turns his head and licks my ear. I pick up the glass and take a sip.

You haven't been charged, Bjørn Eriksen later informs me, as he sits across the table, his mobile and notebook in front of him.

The two other officers have driven the dog home to Emilie's parents. His weight, fur, warmth, I can still feel it in my arms, that was love, but now it is gone, I am alone with Eriksen and God knows what he is thinking, nothing to do with me in any case, with the person I feel I am.

I can understand your confusion, Eriksen says, but you just need to relax. We're interviewing you as a witness and cannot provide you with any more information about the investigation than we release to the media.

But I might be killed, I say. Have you considered that, have you considered why exactly my garden was used?

What do you think yourself, Eriksen asks, what's the reason? he says, in his thick northern accent.

I do not know why. Maybe it has nothing to do with me, even though it feels as though it does, as though it is my fault.

21

She finally found a job. Stylish ready-to-wear garments for ladies. Well, there is stylish and there is stylish, it was, for the most part, nylon stockings and brassieres. And, true enough, it was part-time, but together with the sewing at home and the financial contributions from Hartvig, things went fairly well. The shop was close to Storgaten, she took the tram from Frogner plass in the mornings, but walked home in the afternoons, in spite of her swollen feet, she needed the air so desperately. Oh, standing like that the whole day smiling tired her out, and was so exceptionally hard on the legs, her varicose veins throbbed so. Even though it was not a full working day. Fortunately they went out of business after two years. So she was spared from handing in her notice, from the defeat of having to tell Hartvig, of seeing that smile of his, the one he so loved looking at other people with: what did I say, it meant, what did I say. Spared because she would scarcely have held out much longer. Mrs Rugstad was the worst thing about it. Old bag. Oh, she hated women. Always wearing those knowing expressions, coming up with little remarks. Mrs Rugstad! No, she had no intelligence to speak of, she was easily knocked off her high horse, did not understand Cessi's sarcasm at all. But Miss Espeli did, she tittered, and Mrs Rugstad went red in the face. But working there was not pleasant, no, it was not. Having to dance attendance on crabby housewives from the east side of the city. Who would have thought that Cessi could end up in such a desperate situation. You're courageous, Mama said. Mama, so kind, coming over to them in the afternoons back then, preparing supper and stroking Cessi across the cheek. My child, Mama said, and to think she has been in the ground ten years already. So strange, because it did not seem long ago, she and Mama sitting on the balcony drinking coffee and chatting while the girls, still small, ran around in the warm summer evening. Cessi was darning socks and the sky in the east was red as the sun was setting, she harboured hopes of things somehow improving. She was hardly meant to end up here, in a tiny little apartment in the city, she and the girls, who were almost grown, crammed together in these little rooms and her providing for them on the pittance she earned from a rotten little shop. She, who had once had a garden, run a household and been married to a barrister, there she was all of a sudden, being treated as though she were backward by some fat matrons. For shame. But rather them than have old neighbours or acquaintances as customers, having to stand there knowing full well they would backbite her afterwards, laugh maliciously. The way her friends in the club would no doubt do. Oh, she had such a lovely time with them, but they did talk, about one person after the other, and it was not always gracious, no, it was not. So why should she be spared, it was unlikely she was. Her with all her problems. She did not try to conceal them after all. They knew all about Finn, how it was her lot in life to have such a difficult boy, how worn out she was by him, yes, frankly, did he not contribute directly to her marriage to Hartvig falling apart?

Her dear, darling boy, her beloved Finn.

As he grew older his troublesome nature had become obvious to everyone. They had done what they could. Professionals had taken care of him at times, that sort of thing had to be worked on, agitation such as that, and his wildness, temper and jealousy were completely beyond the pale. Oh, how jealous he was. To say he was difficult was an understatement, so they had sent him to the boys' homes, on several occasions. Good, decent places they were, and the periods he spent there were not *so* very long. Finn makes it sound as though he was gone for years, but his longest stay was barely a school year. Minus holidays and a few weekends. She was so tired back then, tired, and angry into the bargain, about everything and nothing. Hartvig, the girls, the house. Everything just built up, merely thinking about it gave her anxiety.

But it kept happening. All the time he was at school and afterwards when he started working, he just was not able. She had not been completely off the mark when she said he was unruly and there was something not right about him. He began to find it hard to sleep, grew listless and her heart bled for him. She would have liked so much to care for and coddle him, he could have lived with her, if only he had not been so angry. Not that he wanted to, oh no. Besides he drank too much, at least he said he did. Standing there so defiant in the middle of her living room, of course he never took off his shoes. I've gone and got drunk, he might say, I don't remember where, don't remember what happened, but I woke up in Frognerparken. She did not know if he was telling the truth or not. Anyway it was a long time ago now, in his younger years, before he met Linda and they had that child. He might well still be at that kind of thing, and he probably does drink too much, she had a feeling he did, but fortunately it was no longer her concern, as it had been when he was young. Oh, she was so afraid then, because she thought of Papa, his drunkenness, his bad behaviour that went beyond all boundaries. She knew her fear was not unfounded. She and Finn, they had something in them, and that something came from Papa. Mean, nasty genes.

But she limits herself, she does. Even though she has no intention of covering up the fact that she is fond of a drop. It is for her nerves, and she does not care a straw about what Dr Vold said that time. Avoid stimulants, he said, alcohol, caffeine and nicotine. For God's sake, it was twenty years ago. He would probably have said the same thing today, but she could not care less, she knows herself what she needs, and it is not semolina and long walks, she needs to calm her nerves, turn down whatever it is that works itself up within her, the feeling of intense hatred. Of herself. You cannot live with feelings like that and she has never been in any doubt that she will live to the bitter end. If for no other reason than that sherry tastes good and makes the world wonderful. Yes, sherry is the best, because it warms your cheeks and your chest as it goes down, unfortunately it is much too sweet, so she can only manage two small glasses. Red wine, on the other hand, she can drink more of. She does not really care for white wine, it makes her feel sick and does not have the same soporific calming quality as the red. She does not mind beer, but preferably in the summer. Cured pork chops, potato salad and beer, they taste lovely together. She invites Finn, and it is a pleasure to see him eat. He comes on his own, she hardly needs to invite everyone, does she, just because she wants to see her son? She cannot face preparing for so many people, having to be bright and warm and keep the conversation going, that exceeds her energy. They do not understand how tired she is, and neither does she. Besides, Linda hardly wants to, you notice that kind of thing. So all in all it is best that way, for everyone concerned. It has always been easier with Finn when it is just the two of them. Her firstborn. He likes her food. He likes beer as well. That is something they share, a taste for food and drink, not that they talk about it of course. She does not know if he knows, if he notices that sort of thing. He is probably too busy with himself, too busy blaming her. Finn always has his guard up. But it is hardly all her fault. On the contrary. She has no control over nature. Or her finances. Or Hartvig, that wearisome person.

They sit on the little balcony. He tells her about his cars. It is like when he was a child. He has always told her lots about what he is making and how he is doing it. Which small parts he needs for the different things, where he gets hold of them and how he solves the technical difficulties that arise while assembling. When he was a boy, a lot of his chat revolved around his bicycle and the trips he took on it. He went off on expeditions on his own, with his sleeping bag on the rack. Then it was quiet in the house for the duration. Her inventive son, all the things mended and made. He was good with his hands. Steam motors, crystal sets and tree houses. Yes, he was practical, like her. She liked listening to him talk about it. Well, up to a point. This talk of motors could go too far. Now he had bought a car for parts, in order to fix up the other cars he owned. Yes, *they* rather, I should say. Finn, Linda and the little girl. The little one was adorable. A little shy, perhaps, and plump. But Linda, no, she was not easy to like.

Finn can say all kinds to his own mother. You can be very cruel, she shouts at him when he talks about how she is. You bundle of nerves, he says. Did you have to be so self-centred? It is mean of him to say it. But she knows him, her Finn is so terribly, terribly kind. A rascal, but the kindest of all her children. Reliable and devoted to a fault, she knows him through and through. He is like her. When they sit in the afternoon sun on the balcony drinking beer, and he taunts her, it is fun, she can sense they have the same urges, they want to be borne away, taken somewhere. When he drives her to the doctor, to the shops, or out to Bygdøy to visit friends and he speeds up, jams on the brakes, goes through a red light, he does it to provoke her. True, she is scared, but she likes it, that is how it is, she likes it.

It is peculiar however that he has never criticised her for being mean to Linda. She knows she has been, and in some respects she knows why. She is not well-born, that wife of his, but she puts on airs, thinks she is something because she comes from a bookish family. They might be bookish but when all is said and done they are blue collar, really working class when you get down to brass tacks, and yet so sure of themselves. No, she is not quite sure what it is, but she has felt ill at ease the times she has been to visit Linda's parents. They are lovely, it is not that. But my God, what do they know about her, those people who think they know everything? Do they actually understand that her life is in ruins? Everything she owned belongs to someone else now. The fancy woman in Vettakollen. As though all that time she and Hartvig spent building a home no longer matters, does not exist, has vanished into thin air. The children she gave birth to, the work she did, it is nothing in the fancy woman's eyes. Hartvig waves her away as though she were a fly, and Linda's parents sit there offering her coffee and cake. No doubt they feel sorry for her, divorced and living alone in a little flat in the city. While Linda's mother has been at home looking after her big family all these years, they have allowed themselves that luxury. Now she and her husband live in the same little two-up two-down and, what is more, it is on the east side. They have no business looking down at her, just because she is alone and has nothing, is nothing.

Anyway, the divorce was a long time ago, besides which she is only too happy to be spared Hartvig, ugh. It is just, no, see, she does not know. But, in any case, Finn has never upbraided her for that, for not thinking Linda is good enough. In her own mind she knows, a loud voice within tells her: and neither were you, Cessi, you with your alcoholic father, you came from a rotten background, and they saw that, they saw right through you, Hartvig's parents, how little you brought, how little there was to build on, no money, no means, no grace, you with your coarse, selfish laughter.

And there were worse things than that, everything is much worse than anyone could guess. But there are no proper words for it.

It is ironic. She still keeps the accounts, even though she has told Hartvig once and for all that she is never going to submit them for his inspection again, never. That had to come to an end, her mind was made up, and maybe that was the reason he gave in so easily, just muttered something about her being dependent on his support after all, so how could she expect to get a loan from him in the future, if she continued living beyond her means.

Living beyond her means, her! She does not know how to respond to something so preposterous. Liking the food you eat, is that living beyond your means? Buying good butter, prawns and smoked salmon at the weekends. Inviting the grandchildren over, dishing up hot chocolate and cream, inviting them to the cinema, was that living beyond your means? Because it was cosy to sit in that dark cinema at Gimle. It was actually a relief to admit to herself that she liked moving pictures a million times more than the theatre. You go to the theatre, Hartvig, together with that boring wife of yours, I am delighted to be spared that.

Perhaps she lived a trifle beyond her means when it came to beer and wine. She had made herself a solemn vow to enter all those kinds of expenses into the household account book, and she nearly managed to keep her promise, she wrote them up: wine, kr. 17 –. For special occasions and entertaining guests she bought a slightly more expensive one. It was only when she was at the Vinmonopolet twice a week that she neglected to write it up, because she did not think she could indulge in more than one bottle a week, preferably no more than two a month. But she comforted herself with the fact that it was so seldom she failed to keep her promise, so it ought to be possible to turn a blind eye to it. Anyway, some weeks she did not buy any at all, so it balanced out, as it were.

After all I have to stay alive, she said to herself, I am all alone here, it is just me, and I have to go on living, there are limits to how resourceful I can be on my own. Not that she was lonely. She had Alice, and all her other friends. The children and the grandchildren. Her correspondence to America. But inside, the gnawing never let up. She scarcely knew what it was, but it hurt so, almost constantly, and she felt such unease within. It was her lot and fate. Was she not then entitled to drink a little wine?

22

I walk down to the shops in Slemdal. Drab food. Good thing I have wine at home. It will make the bread taste a little better. I do not see him standing behind me in the queue. I have been getting so many looks from people. I am shrouded in suspicion after all. But as I stand bagging my groceries I see who it is. The man from the Red Cross rescue team. My heart pounds, I become instantly nervous, and do not know if I should cast my eyes downwards or look at him. I look at him. What a handsome man. He is about to punch in his code and pushes his glasses up onto his forehead. He must sense my eyes upon him because he suddenly looks up and right at me, his gaze sweeping my breasts. It happens quickly, but is unmistakable, I have seen it before, when someone likes looking at me. I nod to him, and he seems to blush, but he turns his head at the same time to accept his receipt. I am not certain he has recognised me. He shakes open a plastic bag, I glance at his groceries: full-fat milk, butter, wholemeal bread, crisps. Vegetable mayonnaise. Bachelor fare, I think, no woman would eat that much fat.

I finish filling my shopping bags, place them on the floor between my feet and pretend to rummage for something in my shoulder bag. When I lift my head he gives me a slight bow.

You were the one who was in my garden, I say, do you remember me?

Yes, aren't you the local writer? he says.

I'm the one whose house has been on the TV, I say. The neighbourhood witch. They think I eat children. You probably think the same, do you?

He breaks eye contact, but remains standing in front of me with his bag in his hand. They're only doing their job, I suppose, he says. It's an awful business.

Yeah, you just have to keep searching, I reply. Keep searching and hope for the best.

I am well able to do that too. Carry on that way. Not hop over the preliminary platitudes and get right down to business. Best to hold back a little, that is what Knut said to me at the outset of our relationship. But that was when we were having sex.

He looks at me and nods seriously. Things going okay with you? he asks.

Yes, considering the circumstances, I say, not too bad. Just think about the parents.

We walk together towards the exit. He stops right outside and takes a bunch of keys from his trouser pocket. I'm heading down this way, he says, motioning in the direction of Vinderen.

Does he live nearby, I think, so close to me that we go to the same shop, how could I have failed to notice him?

I hope things improve for you, he says, and I nod, say that if they could only find her, they would, and preferably alive.

I cut across the car park, and as I look back I see him throw his leg over a bicycle and freewheel down towards Vinderen. A tall, thin man with long legs in a checked, short-sleeved shirt.

I walk uphill and home. I put the food in the fridge and

cry. Pour red wine into the cup and sit outside the house. Sun-warmed plastic at my back. My toes in the moss. An hour passes. I cry some more, my nose runs, and I feel sorry for myself, but then the wine takes effect and I realise I am not as sad as I think, on the contrary. There is a throbbing throughout my entire body. It is happiness. Completely out of control. He liked me. I saw it. And now I have thought it. It just happens, comes, takes me over, consumes me. I cannot, will not, it is not on. But it comes: I am excited.

It is like rain falling inside my head. I try to think but my head is filled with drops. Clear, translucent drops. They contain everything I want to know, *insight*, but the rain falls quickly and heavily, I see, but do not see. That was the way it was in my relationship with Ketil M as well.

We got together after a members' meeting in the Authors' Union. I was a lot more involved in that kind of thing previously: turned up at meetings, festivals and seminars, went to publishers' parties and dinners. Driven by a longing, a feeling of not making it, ever. I do not know why I thought other writers could help me with that. Or that I would find a man among them to be happy with. Was I never going to be happy? Or if not happy then at least content. I told myself that: being content is sufficient. But my fantasies had greater ambitions, they were wild and uninhibited, I wanted bliss, orgasms, fusion, not a trace of loneliness, my other half was not to feel extraneous. Everything was to be harmonious, a fellowship, perhaps something even more lofty, a spiritual convergence.

My attraction to Ketil was purely physical. He was big, everything about him was big, his hands, upper arms, his chest. His legs were long, and you could just picture the size of his penis, and I did, every time I ran into him, which was pretty often, he was constantly to be seen at writers' events, as was I.

At first he showed no interest. I was not surprised. Ketil likes women who are tall, blonde and outgoing, well-endowed. And beautiful, of course. Not that I am ugly. But I am not striking either, and I am dark-haired, reserved. For the most part. Except for when I was chasing after Ketil, then I was neither nervous nor hesitant but chatted away. That was a red flag. Men whom I am not afraid of approaching are the most dangerous, they are the kind who let you down or will not let you go.

His books were boring. At least the one I read was. It was not the story that bored me, more the words. He wrote about the wonderful tranquillity of the forest and the dark mystery of women, something along those lines anyway, maybe not quite as bad as that, but still. Perhaps it was not so much the words that bugged me, even though they testified to literary weakness. No, it was his ideas about great literature, what was required, how a sentence should be sculpted in order for it to be art at the level of a master novel. I was more poetic, in his opinion, my work was about displaying the contents in the toolbox of language, and that was all well and good, but was still only the first step in the development of a writer. Ideally, the language of the novel should be *transparent*, he said, the craftsmanship should not be visible. That was his goal, what Ketil was aiming for. I was tempted to tell him he was mistaken, that I, as opposed to him, had come so far in my development that I did not know if I wanted to be a *writer* any longer, or rather did not know where the line went: when was I a writer, when was I not? No, I could not have said anything like that at that time, because I did not think so much then, or did not want to think, acknowledge my discomfort. It was the contrast between his ideas and those feeble sentences of his that made it uncomfortable, embarrassing, turning it into something I wanted to overlook, because it would most likely improve, I reckoned, when he became more confident. That was the way I thought back then. That love was not dependent on intellectual parity. It was not intelligence that mattered. But I was wrong about that. No, I lied about that. My ideas masked something else: the fear of finding an equal. The fear of the sexual side of things then eating their way into my soul. Into every perceptible aspect of me. That devotion would lead to self-destruction. Were not even my thoughts to be free? My very core.

We became a couple in November, at the closing party after the members' meeting. At the table, when the meal was finished and everyone was mingling. Some people danced, and we held hands on the white tablecloth.

I could see the very moment he decided upon me. His gaze stopped wandering, he began to flirt, or rather, he simulated flirting. So what, I thought, so what. The difference between flirting falsely and the real thing is negligible, nobody can tell them apart. I knew he would say yes, so I asked him if he wanted to go back to my place. My body felt so light, small and delicate alongside his large form, it never felt like that otherwise. A love affair, I thought, finally something that can work out. But something was ever so slightly amiss. Something in his eyes, not quite right. I think he felt that walking along with me resembled something that had been. As for me: walking along with him resembled something that could have been.

The last time we made love was also on my sofa. My body did not respond, I had no desire for him any more, but did not say anything. Instead I stroked him up and down his back and along his sides. He held out so long that I came all the same, and then it was like something in my head burst, something water-like, and for a moment I could see the past in one sweep, I smelled it, just as I could perceive the smell of semen long before Ketil came, I saw where it was coming from, a room I had been in, followed by a different room, a different man, several men, rooms, sofas, beds. In every instance I was much too young and an odour of soil pervaded, where did that smell come from? I remembered some coloured lights in a tree, warm night air, a market or a neighbourhood party somewhere in the south of Europe one summer I was travelling. A woman was selling paintings beneath one of the lights, she had hung them from the branches of a tree, they were pure kitsch. I passed by her with my arms wrapped around a man I did not know, gloating, poor her, I thought, does she really think what she paints is nice? But the night was dark and dense, music was playing, and the aroma of fried, spicy meat drifted from a shack. The whole scene resembled something good, everything about it, I made myself believe I was loved, I had sex with the stranger on the ground in a back yard because I confused the likeness with the original, I thought the image of what was good was good itself. And lying with this person on top of me. Ketil. I should have been able to love him, but I could not love. The drop burst and the water divided, the way back lay open. I saw how love lost. I think it's over, Ketil, I said after we had put our clothes on. It's good you say that, he replied, because I've also been thinking about it for a while, ending things.

When he had left I slept half-sitting up on the sofa, dreaming I had written a novel comprised of a single sentence: *You must search in the darkness for your dreams, not in your dreams for the darkness.*

Memory is dangerous. I am standing at the sink looking down at the dishwater. The red wine is within reach, the handle of the washing-up brush has soap-froth stuck to it. There is a programme on the radio about memory techniques. A researcher is relating what people did to recall events, names and words before they had a written language to rely on: *associated them with buildings, rooms and objects in the rooms.* It is dangerous, I sense: the rooms, the demands they make. That unexpected opportunity of understanding what is happening. The opportunity of transgressing the material, of physics, even though such an intellectual condition is of course physical, the particles that make the brain move beyond its own memories or right to the core of them, reliving. And something more. Suddenly over to something else. And the shimmer of light that takes me beyond a specific place and time. To another specific place, in a room next to my own time. To the Roman Empire, to Berlin, to the Middle Ages. To Lillestrøm.

A council house between the towns of Strømmen and Lillestrøm in the late seventies. Open plan between the kitchen and living room, pine-panelled walls, a fireplace. A mother, father and some teenagers – I am one of them. A wooden bowl, buffed and scorched with letters in one of the children's woodworking classes.

I am visiting a friend. She can play the guitar and I have a vague desire for something or other.

She lives right by the railway line. I went past the house on the train, before getting off at the station and following a gravel road back along the tracks. The sound of the doorbell resounded through the house. The hallway is full of shoes. Clogs, sandals, gym shoes.

Are there crisps in the bowl?

Yeah, help yourself.

The atmosphere in the house is happy and unconstrained. The friend later becomes a well-known singer-songwriter. I have brought my sleeping bag along, but I do not stay the night all the same. I have to get home, I say, I have to get back. I never go round there again. Even though it bears a resemblance. The house resembles home. I am taken aback by the feeling of fellowship. That it exists but I cannot partake. I cannot identify myself, even though it should be the easiest thing in the world here, where everything is so alike. I take the train home.

Come on, come back. I have a recollection of my friend, shouting this to me, her head out the window as I make my way down the road. I also remember never finding my way there, never making it to the house, even though I was invited. I couldn't find it, I tell her later over the phone. Who was disappointed, me or my friend? She who could have become a friend, but did not? I who could have been like her, but was not? She who could play guitar. I who could write. We were on equal terms, and yet were not.

The living room in that house resembled the one in the

house Granny and Granddad built. Not the wood panelling but the layout. The door to the garden. The sliding doors between the dining and living rooms. The fireplace to the left, a dark hole. That was how it was when we lived there too, when I was small.

One family like this, another like that. One life in dark readiness, another in enthusiasm. The similarity, and the hair's breadth of margin between.

23

She likes the month of June. Has done ever since she was small, because her birthday is on the fifteenth. Most of the time that falls in the middle of flowering season, unless May has been extraordinarily warm, which has happened in the past. But usually the lilac and fruit trees are in full bloom right on her birthday, they emit fragrances, quiver in all their white, pink and violet, like in a painting, as she goes out through the gate. The evenings are bright, they can also be warm, and she likes walking the streets then. Joy is to be found somewhere, and she needs to get out of the apartment, because joy is a terrible thing to feel when she is indoors, it makes her almost want to take her life. Of course, meaning is not found out of doors either, but she can feel its echo, the brush of it, and outside she can still believe she is a part of everything. That her age is not obvious, because they do not know, nobody who sees her is aware of what she conceals within. She walks between people and enjoys the sight, many of them already tanned and lightly clothed, there is laughter and subdued voices. She can believe she is like them, the beautiful people. The lilac hangs over picket and wrought-iron fences, strewing leaves on the pavements, she steps on them in her light shoes and thinks that despite everything, none of them, not the children, not Mama, not Hartvig, knows who she is and where she is going. She thinks about *the lost erotic escapade.* She does not know where she got that term from, but it is apt, it is gone. She only remembers the briefest flashes of how it was. Like when she is walking along now lost in her own thoughts, she can suddenly become aware of a person nearby, one who is real and waiting, a man who is her equivalent. Just as shameless and forthright, equally daring, equally greedy. Marked by danger. What they call lascivious. She is not quite sure how she came up with the word, or if it is the right one. It is just like a stirring in the streets. And a certainty. Of something beyond. Like that husky laughter she hears over there. Like the gaze of the man on the bench by Frogner church. Yes, not that he is looking at her, God forbid, she is well over sixty, but he is past his prime himself, and it is unmistakable, how he is staring at the women walking past as he sits there on a bench in Bygdøy allé smoking his pipe. His eyes know, his body knows, sitting quite still, he is a mature, experienced animal and she walks by unseen, she is no sight to behold. At home, the warm floors await. The stuffy apartment which the evening sun has heated up to breaking point. The night will not end, she will not be free from it until the heat eases off, which will be late, and God willing it rains tomorrow, so she can get some rest and forget her sorrows. But tonight, tonight. She is still here.

The man remains seated on the bench, and she turns and walks back, passing in front of him. He looks at her this time, but with indifference, complete indifference. How strange things are. If it were twenty years ago and she was still Hartvig's wife, in the midst of life with all its hustle and bustle and the pain and the nerves, then he would no doubt have given her a look. It was not uncommon then for men to do that. And she returned their looks, pretended to drop her handbag or her cigarette packet, oh dear, she might say, and it had happened, not very often, but certainly a few times, that a man had run over to help. Once, God help her, why had she not seized the chance that one time she had it? It was this very area she had been strolling around back then, spring was in the air and she had been to the theatre with Alice. She accompanied Alice to the bus afterwards, but decided to take a walk in Frognerparken before catching the tram home herself. To Hartvig, the house and her responsibilities. It was fine thinking about what was at home as long as she was away from it, but she knew how it would be as soon as she crossed the threshold. As though in a trap. And once home she would not be able to think of life beyond the four walls of the house, the roaring and the racket and her extraordinarily boring day-to-day life with Hartvig, she was a prisoner. So she dragged out her night for as long as she could, thinking she was not so old yet, there were still opportunities to be free. Oh yes, she would be free, but she did not know that then, the tragedy that was in store. It struck her now, how that might not have happened if she had seized her chance that evening.

She had made her way towards the Monolith, that tall granite structure rising towards the sky, among all the other people who had been enticed outside by the fine weather, had walked up the steps and, standing on the platform below it, she had looked out, the light was as though in Paris, she thought, exotic, dim and glimmering. Then someone had stopped and stood near her, a tall man in a light coat, he looked at her, and without a second thought, she took the cigarette packet from her handbag and made a show of searching for a lighter. He took it as the invitation it was and asked if she needed a light.

We must have both seen the same film, she said and laughed. He was no dimwit, because he took the hint and bent forward in an affected manner to light up her cigarette, and said, in English:

Can I help you, miss?

Oh, he was quick on the uptake and easy on the eye as well. She laughed again: *Yes, Mr Gable.*

Oh, he said, oh, I'm not sure which film we're in, do you know?

They continued speaking English for a while, it was such fun, she completely forgot herself.

Your English is really terrific, he said eventually, so much so I am beginning to wonder where I am. Shall we walk a little in order to find our bearings? And he offered her his arm. Fortunately she was wearing gloves so her wedding ring was not visible. I must still look like a housewife, she thought, or even worse, an old spinster. Alice said she had a lively face, but what good was that, she was over forty after all, and it was almost unbelievable that such a handsome man would walk here alongside her. Perhaps he wanted to swindle some money from her, was that what this was about?

She pushed the thought from her mind, because the chat flowed so freely, the laughter too, no, they did not speak of serious things, but neither of foolish matters, he was in point of fact no simple-minded man. His sense of humour was neither embarrassing nor boring like Hartvig's, his remarks were intelligent and sarcastic, his observations about people very apt. They strolled slowly around the park, it was growing dark now, they kept bumping into each other, walking arm in arm, and he no longer laughed all the time, and she was so aware of his proximity, of something dark coming from him, that pulled and was no laughing matter. Just before they reached the main gate he came to a halt and looked her right in the eye. Now it is going to happen, she thought, now it is going to happen.

May I invite you to accompany me home, *miss*? *May I?*

Then she ruined it. She has gone through it in her mind, and spoken to Alice, countless times over the years: did she ruin the best experience she could have had, or was she actually about to be duped?

She thought so, as she stood there, that he was a swindler. No, not at first, at the beginning she was filled with great happiness: she was worth something after all, she was not just mean and angry and ugly, and if she was, it was only because everyone at home had made her so. Because here was somebody who saw her for how she really was. But the next moment realisation washed over her, how easily fooled she was, how ridiculous, she had heard of his sort, what were they called, gigolos? It was probably written across her face, her yearning, and besides she was middle-aged, easy prey.

Are you trying to fool me, *mister*? *Are you?*

She tried to maintain the same jocular tone, but it was no good, he could undoubtedly see by looking at her that she meant it.

Well, I mean really, Alice would later say, one cannot suddenly invite a strange lady home and not expect her to be suspicious?

But Cessi knew it could be done, was possible for them, there and then, because they had hit it off, there was a rapport, she told Alice.

A rapport, Alice said, he might have been taking you in, if he was that type of professional, then he could probably make any woman believe that he and she were birds of a feather.

But be that as it may. Cessi would have put up with him being a professional too, just to experience something else for once in her life. It could not therefore under any circumstances have been rape if she had gone with him. Christ, why had she not just gone with him?

He could have killed you, Alice said.

Be that as it may. Anyway, that was not how it was, and she knew it, even though she agreed that Alice was right. But she only did so in order to be able to live with it. For allowing the opportunity to pass her by. They had stood there, and she could still have saved the situation, steered it in the right direction, because now he was quite serious and she could rest assured, he was not trying to deceive her in any way, because this, he said, was something quite special, surely she had also noticed that?

I'm married, she said, and his face closed.

It may well be the case, he said, that you are married, but I have already considered that, and it is neither here nor there. It does not matter. Surely we can enjoy ourselves for a short while.

Well, I never, Alice said, one cannot simply stick one's head in the sand like that, no, just be happy you saw sense, you would have had problems with him, he didn't respect you. After all, you did say you were married . . .

Yes, it was the fact that she *said* it, not the fact that she was, she realised that afterwards, that was why his face closed, because he saw the way things were heading.

She had stood there thinking you have to do the right thing, Cecilie, because the images flew through her mind, and that horrid feeling swept through her body. Do not behave like the harlot you were, the hussy, the one the boys laughed at, you little whore. They lifted up her skirt and held her arms behind her back while they took turns rubbing her breasts and sticking their hands between her legs. She would never go there again, nowhere near it, never. She could not, was not able.

No, I mean really, she said. It was very nice to meet you.

She put out her hand, but he just bowed, wrapped his coat around himself and walked off.

Nothing would have been horrid or nasty with him.

Perhaps she did the right thing all the same, because no situation should be so abruptly either or, now or never.

Maybe it was both things, Alice said, to console her. Maybe he really was an opportunist, you know, but at the same time was particularly taken by you.

But in those kinds of cases it cannot be both. She knows that. It has to be one or the other, true or untrue.

24

Her skin is sore, her mouth is sore. They stay up at night, sleeping long into the day. Yesterday they did not get up at all, but remained in bed, talking, making love, nodding off and waking again. It was not until nine in the evening that they grew so hungry they got out of bed. They went to town to eat a kebab and afterwards walked back to the student halls in Kringsjå, through the Palace Park, up Bogstadveien, past Marienlyst and through the university area over to Sognsveien. At Café Abel they stopped for a beer. They drank and could not stop, they laughed the entire time, at what she does not know, everything. Erik's stories about growing up in the suburb of Jar, with three brothers, football, ice hockey, skiing and the kindest mother in the world. As kind as hers. Maybe they should start a Facebook group, Erik said, they could call it *the Kindest Mothers' Association*. Yes, instead of talking about someone behind their back, talking them up in front of everyone, I've seen something like that on Facebook. We can *good-mouth* our mothers instead of bad-mouthing them. And then they laughed, it was completely stupid, just nonsense, nothing really.

But what is a kind mother, imagine if she actually is not so kind? Erik said.

That made Beate uneasy. Why did he have to mess around like that, she did not like it, did not want to speak badly of her mother, that was where she drew the line. My mum is *everything* to me, she said, imagine how horrible it must be to have a mother who isn't kind. The thought made her cry, and then Erik's eyes watered up. Out of sympathy, he said, they're tears of sympathy, and again they began to laugh.

But now she is crying from her very depths. Erik is still asleep. There will be no lectures today either, it is way too late and she is much too tired. The tears will not let up, because she feels things are coming undone, that she is losing her grip, the days are going by and how is she to pass the exam? She is nauseous or hungry, dizzy when she stands up. All the same, she does not say no to Erik when he wakes up, not to kissing, not to sex, not to his suggestion of going to the swimming pool.

Erik makes porridge, but she cannot face eating, just drinks a little coffee instead. Her fingers look fat. Maybe Erik thinks they are ugly. Everything about him is so perfect. His back, shoulders, upper arms beneath his T-shirt, his hips and bum in his jeans. Large, strong hands, with long fingers and wide fingertips. He takes hold of everything with such assurance, but is gentle when he needs to be, when her hair has caught on the catch of her necklace, but takes a solid grip when he is lifting something heavy, unscrewing something, holding her tightly. He can do everything and he does not cry. She can only do girlie things with her fingers, and today they cannot do anything, but lie like white sausages on the table, and tears roll down her face. He becomes worried, thinks he has said something wrong. She does not know what it is, she says, there are just so many feelings.

She is daft and girlish. *So many feelings*, my arse. And he is so nice all the time. It is too much, all this, all too much.

What is she going to make of herself, Jesus, what is she going to make of herself in this world, nothing?

She stands at the edge of the pool, freezing, cannot face jumping in, the water is only eighteen degrees. Erik comes out of the changing room, sees her, smiles, dives in and swims the front crawl back and forth once, before swimming over to her, taking hold of the edge and looking up:

You coming in?

But she cannot get in. It is not possible. She starts to cry and says she needs to be alone. Can we talk on the phone tomorrow instead? she asks. Erik gets a sad look in his eyes, but she begins to walk towards the changing room. The floor is slippery and cold. Dear God, he must not let her leave this way.

He does not. He comes after her, puts his arms around her shoulders. It is unpleasant, he is wet and cold, yet at the same time it feels too warm to stand like that, his skin sticks to hers, she wants to break free. He asks if she does not like him any more. Of course I do, she answers, of course, and rests her cheek against his, even though her body does not want to. She just needs to get some sleep, she says, be by herself for a bit. He says he understands, that it is probably a good idea. But she does not know. Is it a good thing that he is all right with it? That he says, okay, fine, then he can read a bit in the meantime, he cannot put his studies on the back burner either, after all. Not a word about her studies. And afterwards he just dives right back in. He is going to swim 1,500 metres before he starts studying, he says.

The tears continue to flow in the changing room. She cannot see what she is doing, attempts to put the key into the padlock on the locker door, but cannot make out the keyhole through her tears, does not notice the puddle on the floor and slips, puts her hands out but loses her balance, banging her knee on the bench.

He manages everything. Being together with her, sleeping, eating, swimming, laughing. And studying. While she is just falling apart. Studying is the last thing in the world she could face right now. She does not want to do anything. The shampoo bottle is wet and slips out of her hand, falling to the floor. She cries about that too, about everything.

Going home on the underground she calms down. Things seem more normal. Men look at her as usual, so she has not become ugly all of a sudden. She can have anyone she wants, if she wants. But she does not. She wants to go home. She wants to go home, but she goes to Bea Britt's.

She is cold from being outside with wet hair, from all the crying, from a lack of sleep. She asks if she can have a bath to warm up. Stands on the warm floor tiles and undresses, lies down in the bathtub, dozes. Her pubic hair sways in the water. It is her hair, her privates. Or are they Erik's? Do our genitals always belong to someone else? Mum and Dad took responsibility for her entire body while she was growing up, and now someone else has taken over.

She had love. That is what she remembers. Mum and Dad's hands. Warm bodies. The feeling of her arm around a neck, of hair between her fingers, of her lips when she rubbed them against Mum's cheek.

Compared to that, Erik is unfamiliar, a stranger, will always be a stranger. But she misses him, and is suddenly afraid because of what she has done.

Erik. The way he walks. His eyes. His voice. His smell. As though he is her. How could she go from him? How can she lie here calmly? She has to get up, right now, has to get a move on. Imagine he does not want her any more? Her heart beats hard and fast. She needs to see him right away, to make sure everything is all right, tell him she did not mean it, whatever it was, she did not mean it, it was a mistake and she needs to put it right as quickly as possible.

How can he have been with other girls? To think that he has. His penis inside someone else. His arms, smell, skin – with another. It could happen again, why would it not? Why should she be a better choice than anybody else? She is not. But now, right now, she has been chosen, and she must not let go, how could she have been so stupid?

She does not have the time to dry off properly and her clothes stick to her skin, wet hair dripping onto her blouse. Imagine he dumps her. She has shown how weak she is. He could not be bothered with that kind of crap, not Erik. After all, he can have anyone he wants. How could she take such a chance? She is spoilt. They have been waiting on her hand and foot constantly, her mother, her father, Bea Britt. Her, the only child. Beautiful and gifted. But they have not noticed her failings, no, how immature she is, governed by a need to be taken care of. Needs that surface when she least expects them.

No missed calls. Will she seem nagging if she rings? She does not know, simply does not. No matter what she does it will be wrong. It was wrong of her to leave. But wanting too much is also wrong. She calls him up all the same. He does not answer the phone. Bea Britt comes into the hall. Her arm brushes against the key hanging on a string from the wall lamp, making it dingle back and forth. The light shines through the sheer material of her blouse, Beate can make out the contours of Bea Britt's arms inside.

That was a quick bath, she says, looking at the mobile in Beate's hand.

He's not answering, Beate says, and starts to cry.

Beate sits at Bea Britt's kitchen table. How is she able to eat? The tears flow but the jam fills her mouth. Strong and sweet, with big clumps of strawberry that Bea Britt bought at the pick-your-own farm last summer. She makes all kinds of buns. These ones are wholemeal, with pumpkin seeds on top and wholegrain inside. With the different tastes and consistency as she chews, Beate finds herself not thinking of anything other than what is in her mouth. Soft yeast, leavened bread, chewy seeds, sweet runny red taste, salted butter sliding over her tongue. She eats four halves, all with jam. As she gets up from the table to place the plate on the worktop, she starts sobbing once more. It was only while she was sitting eating that she was able to keep her anxiety in check.

Bea Britt walks into the kitchen with Beate's mobile in her hand. It is ringing, Erik and the heart symbol she has saved beside his name is glowing on the display.

I was asleep when you called earlier, he says. I cried myself to sleep. I thought you didn't want me any more. Do you think I'm childish? That I don't take anything seriously enough?

No, no, no, she says, but is that a warning sign, she thinks at the same time, something I need to watch out for? Is that maybe how he is, laddish and superficial? Seeing as he asks?

Can I come round? she asks, I'll come over now if that's okay.

But I'm on my way to you, he says, I've just hopped off the number twenty bus in Thomas Heftyes gate.

She asks him to wait for her in the park by the block of flats, at the top of the hill, there is a bench there, and she will get a taxi.

She does not want him to come to Bea Britt's and meet her yet, does not want Bea Britt to see who she is having sex with, does not even want Bea Britt to imagine that she has sex with anyone. Things should be just as usual at Bea Britt's. And they are. Bea Britt walks her to the door as normal, stands in the doorway and waits until Beate has closed the gate behind her. They wave to each other. But Bea Britt looks sad, and Beate feels she is doing something wrong by leaving. What is it that is so wrong all the time? Nothing is how it used to be.

She sees his back as she walks up the hill. It is almost like looking at herself. He does not turn around until she draws very close. That childish look on his face. Maybe it is something that will begin to annoy her. No, no, do not think like that. Do not think, just kiss. Hair, fingers, nose against neck, lips, teeth, bone. Chest, ribs, hips. Tears, spit.

I love you, she says. And she means it. For ever. No matter what happens. Right now she means it. Love is the word that fits the feeling. Erik is the opposite of a stranger, the opposite of unfamiliar. He is like her. Or else they are both just as unfamiliar.

25

His name is Lars Erik Berg. I found him on the Red Cross website, standing in the centre of a group photograph of volunteers on a training exercise in the forest. They were wearing yellow vests and holding long sticks. The accompanying text said that their task had been to search for a missing child. He was smiling in the picture. It was after all only an exercise and they found the child 'alive', it said. The doll was about the size of a four-year-old and had blonde hair and a red woollen hat. She had 'fallen asleep' at the foot of a tree, in high grass. The volunteers' names were not underneath, but as I moved the cursor across the picture to rest on his face, a yellow box with his name in it popped up. Lars Erik Berg. There were only three results for Lars Erik Berg in the telephone directory online, and after checking old tax registers against addresses, I found him. In an apartment building on Jacob Aalls gate. Born in 1960. I studied the photograph of the building on Google Maps and worked out that there could not be more than six households at the address. Several of the residents had the same surname, but no others were called Berg. He might live alone. But there were also the names of other ostensibly single men listed at the address. Maybe he was a homosexual and had a male cohabitant. That was also a possibility. But only one of the men at the address was the same age as him, the other two were more than twenty years younger. And he looked at my breasts. My collarbone, my lips and eyes. Or was I wrong? Perhaps he liked me because I was a writer, not a woman, not because I struck him as attractive. I had experienced that before. I thought there was something there, a connection, only for it to turn out to be nothing, other than in my head. A look that meant less than I imagined. A friendly person whose friendliness extended to everyone, not just me in particular. I was not special, nor could I be, not to anyone other than the children, because the children had no choice, I was the only mother they had. Lars Erik would not have anything to do with me. His slender body, long arms, deft hands. I pictured his hands while he was speaking. Gesturing, animated.

I put his name into the search box of a different directory enquiries service and found the same mobile number, but also the number to a landline, at the University of Oslo.

Lars Erik Berg, fellow of the university, Department of Mathematics.

I looked at the photograph and email address beside his name. Just a double click and some taps on the keyboard and I could make contact. If he replied. I saved his telephone numbers to my phone. Sending a text was also a possibility. I searched for more images of him. The urge to feel love had overwhelmed me. You are the man in my life, I thought. Because that was the face. The receding hairline, greying at the temples. A man who bowed and could blush. The cursor moving gently back and forth over his face. I thought *you, I love every bone in your body.*

In one of the pictures he was sitting beside a beautiful woman, younger than me, and I became distraught: is it her he loves? Not me but her. Of course there had to be a woman in his life, what was I thinking. But the cursor saved me. The name of the woman appeared in a yellow box, she was a student advisor at the department. I was relieved, then felt sick, because the student advisor was only ten years younger than him, they could be a couple all the same. Or he could be together with someone else in the department. A beautiful, successful woman. A woman at the same *level*. Lars Erik was too attractive for me. The leg he threw over the saddle of his bike. The checked shirt. The shirt collar. His throat. One button open. Every bone in his body. A complete person.

I could put my name down as a Red Cross volunteer? No. That would be too obvious. Pushy. Besides, I was a murder suspect, or just had been, I was involved. I was better off walking past the Red Cross building, plan a route past Hausmanns gate 7, a few times a week maybe, or as often as I dared. It would certainly increase the chances of running into him by accident. In which case I could say that I had been at the city archives in Maridalsveien. If I should run into him. Say I was checking out some addresses, carrying out research for a novel and was now on my way to buy some fruit and vegetables in Grønland, at the immigrant shops. After all, I had been to the city archives on many occasions, it would not just be a cover story. Last autumn, for instance, I attended a course in genealogy. I learnt to search the digital archives and found Granny's ancestors. Where they lived and where they came from. I did not discover anything I had not known beforehand. There was not much there. However, the names did reveal secrets to me: that these people still took up space in the world, albeit no larger than a column on a digital register. They existed, the stories of the dead were alive but hidden away. The scanned handwriting from church registers showed me that, the succinct information in the census forms, the records of who lived at the different addresses. Robert Brodtkorb, engineer, born 1867. Granny's uncle. Emigrated to America in 1898. He had an address in Kristiania in the last census before he left: Skippergaten 12A. Naturally the building was divided up into several flats, and Robert rented a room in one. That was the small amount of space he took up. Nobody heard from him after that.

I went down to the City Archives the following morning, but was too restless to go in and sit down. Neither was there any reason for me to do so, there was no one I needed to look up. I remained standing on the pavement outside, mulling over what to do. It was so difficult to think of anything, it always was. Lars Erik would probably not be in the Red Cross building until the afternoon. If he was there at all. Because maybe I had been wrong, maybe he only went there now and again, or hardly ever did, not to the head office, no, he would not go there, he would of course go to meetings at his local branch. Or to a dedicated department for search parties, with an office somewhere else. The head office was probably just for those employed by the Red Cross, and Lars Erik was not employed, he was a volunteer.

Why did he volunteer? Was it out of love? Had he too much of it, a surplus he needed to expend somewhere? Or was it the other way around, maybe he yearned and was attracted to words like *charity, humanism, care,* because he was lacking in something? Did he not believe in God, but was looking for a serious love, as I was?

I had to go through with my plan, whether he turned up

or not. Now that I had come so far, yes, who could have pictured it, that I would one day be standing at the bottom of Maridalsveien and be madly in love. Besides, he might call in by chance. Perhaps he had meetings with someone in administration now and again, and there was as much chance of it being today as any other. In which case he would likely arrive after lectures were finished, but before people went home from work, perhaps around half past three, and that was still a few hours off. I walked along Thors gate to the Oslo public library to give myself a purpose, but could not face going in once I got there. What did I want with books now? This was the litmus test. Was I anything at all without books? Almost nothing, as I walked the streets, down Akersgata, to the right through Citypassasjen, past Det Norske Teatret, to the left on Universitetsgata and across to Karl Johans gate in the direction of Egertorget before again turning onto Akersgata and walking the same streets back towards the Red Cross. I had a pain in my stomach the entire time, an aching knot, and I realised I might be facing a case of the runs at any moment. The more I thought about it, the worse the pressure, so I went into a coffee bar in Hausmanns gate to use the facilities.

By the time I had emptied my bowels it was still only half past two. I decided to stay put in the coffee bar while I waited, and bought a chai latte. All the high chairs at the window were taken, so I had to sit down at a table in the middle of the premises. I did not know where to fix my gaze, everything in there seemed so chaotic. People and movement, the hissing of the steamer, the sound of tables being bumped, the scraping of chair legs, I do not have the head space for it. I closed my eyes and took small sips of the chai latte. The milk and sugar made me queasy and thirsty, so I opened my eyes again and began perusing a newspaper that lay there. It was impossible to read properly without glasses, I was not twenty-five any more, still I could not remember how I had become twice as old, had that really happened? Anyway, I was too nervous to concentrate on reading, because it was getting close to the time I could walk past the Red Cross building.

Was it perhaps spirituality that I lacked? Was that what Lars Erik Berg was also seeking, a spiritual communality? Not love necessarily, because not everything is about love. But then neither is love merely spiritual. Or how is it, can they really be separated from one another? So confusing, so much confusion in so short a life.

To prevent and alleviate human suffering it said in the preamble to the founding statute of the Red Cross. *Compassion.* Yes, maybe that was it: Lars Erik believed in compassion. A human communality. If not he would surely have sought out religion instead?

I needed to pee from all the tea and went into the ladies, but as I pulled down my trousers and knickers I broke into a fit of tears so intense that I could not hold on until I was sitting on the toilet, and most of it ended up on the seat, over the floor, on the waistband of my knickers and the backs of my legs. I dried it up as well as I could while continuing to cry. He was everything I wanted. But I could not have it, could not, not me! His leg over the crossbar. His long back. Defined biceps, smooth skin. He bowed to me.

I had no right to walk here, I was acting under false pretences, I was, he would realise as much. If he saw me. My heart was beating erratically and I had a tingling in my calves and the backs of my knees, it was blood flowing too quickly, dark and keen. I stood at the intersection of Storgata and Hausmanns gate waiting for the green man. I was still on safe ground, there were many people passing to and fro, anybody could have a reason for being around here, including me. On the other side of the traffic lights and along the pavement on Hausmanns gate it was worse. It was unlikely I should happen to be walking down here, just two days after running into him last. Nevertheless, I walked slowly down towards the Red Cross building. A pennant bearing their logo flew on the roof. I looked at the entrance with its high doors, hoping.

A man was standing outside the entrance, smoking. A familiar body and I gave a start, as if some part of me thought it was Lars Erik, even though I had immediately recognised Vegard Hagen, my old neighbour from Torshov. I was actually aware that he had a high-up position in the Red Cross, so it was not so strange to see him standing there, and far more likely than seeing Lars Erik, but all the same it took me a few seconds to readjust.

Vegard nodded at me, but it would probably be unnatural for me to stop, it had been so long since we lived in the same apartment building, and even then we scarcely spoke, exchanged no more than a few words at annual meetings and voluntary clean-ups.

I will do it anyway, I thought, so I did: went over to him. Long time no see, I said.

Yeah, it is, all right, he said, and looked out at the road, but turned halfway as a woman exited the building, smiled and called out something after her about not forgetting Friday. She responded by raising her arm above her head and waving as she hurried off along the pavement in high heels.

Vegard watched her go, I did too, looked at her backside in the tight jeans, how it moved. Then Vegard brought out a mobile, took a drag of his cigarette, looked at his watch and began texting. Do you still write? he asked, while looking at the display. I did not have time to reply before he looked up, put the phone in his pocket and said he had read about me in the papers recently. Yeah, the Emilie case, awful business. His gaze was fixed on an imaginary point in the air to the side of my temple while he spoke.

Oh, that. I'm not a suspect really. The police are just being very thorough. They don't want to spook the kidnapper. Or *murderer*, as the case may be.

Vegard coughed and glanced at his watch again, and I realised I had expressed myself in a clumsy manner, almost puerile, but truth be told, he did not exactly do much to make the conversation flow naturally. And there was me thinking everyone in the Red Cross was empathic and inclusive. But not Vegard, maybe that was asking too much, he was only human after all. In any case, he passed no comment on it, and I began to sweat, felt a throbbing in my temples, what was I to do now, what was I supposed to say to get out of it?

So, what's it like working here, I asked, do you enjoy it, are your colleagues nice?

Jesus Christ, how stupid. You do not work for the Red Cross for the enjoyment factor, this was going from bad to worse, I could see that by his face, how awkward I was making everything. Why was I so far from grown-up, me, who was at the centre of the Emilie inquiry and everything?

Vegard put out the half-finished cigarette with his heel, picked it up and placed it in a bin especially for cigarette ends, which had a grid top to prevent anyone throwing paper or anything else flammable into it. I need to get going, he said.

I stood for a few seconds looking through the glass doors, but all I saw was Vegard by the lift talking to a woman, and then they both laughed. I turned towards the street but no tall man on a bicycle pulled up in front of me on the pavement and smiled. Still, I had to see my plan through, and go to Grønland to buy fruit and vegetables. Not everything could be pretence and deception.

The following day I took the underground down to Vinderen and walked up Rasmus Winderens vei to the university. It would be better to meet him here, more natural for a writer, because writers sit in university libraries working, reading books about philosophy and astronomy and what have you. So I had every reason and just as much right to frequent these environs as him. Or as Anita, for that matter. I wondered what she would say if she caught sight of me in the library, what kind of expression she would have on her face. Happy? Hardly. Embarrassed more like, not dissimilar from Vegard, something along those lines. There had to be something wrong with me. I make for an unpleasant atmosphere. It was so obvious that even I noticed it, the unease I felt within, for existing. Ugh. I did not quite know why it was like that. Anita was avoiding me in any case. Imagine if I ran into her today and she did not suggest we grab a coffee. That would be the final blow, then our friendship would cease to exist.

The first thing I did was go to the toilets and cry. I stood in a cubicle down in the basement of the library building feeling ugly and crying, because it was too late, everything was too late, the race was run, it was hopeless. He was not interested and I was not interesting. We would never be a couple. I would not be able to find him either, among all these people, in all the wide-open spaces between the large buildings.

But I did, as soon as I came up the stairs. He was on his way out of the library with some books under his arm and a green apple in his hand. He happened to turn his head in my direction and caught sight of me. He nodded, raised the hand holding the apple in greeting, but did not stop, was busy, in a hurry. I was too far away and did not think I could call out, could not run after him, no, if we were to meet it had to happen naturally. Pausing briefly outside, he spoke to a group of students, young girls, Beate's age. He smiled and laughed, but then he was off again, raised his hand to them also, a friendly gesture from a friendly man. So close and yet unobtainable.

By the third day of going there I was worn out by the tension of being on his territory, and made up my mind to call upon him. It would be make or break.

His office was in room 820 on the seventh floor of the Niels Henrik Abel building, but I did not dare take the lift. Then everything might happen too quickly. The lift was too fast. I risked standing face to face with him when it reached the floor and the doors opened, he might be standing there, ready to go in. No, that would be too sudden. I had to meet him in a gradual way, so that we could draw to a halt, begin to speak. I was not going to be able to explain what I was doing there, on the staircase up to his department, or in the corridor outside his office, but that went without saying, and was therefore hardly very clever, no, it was intrusive, I was an idiot, turn, I said to myself, do not ruin this, turn around, but I did not.

The office doors were dark green. I found the right number. His name was also on the door, but I could not manage to knock, could not raise my arm, my heart was pounding, I did not dare remain standing still, but neither would I turn, so I took a few steps further. At the end of the corridor there was an extra room built in, a sort of glass cage with white blinds that could be drawn. They were open at the moment. There were two photocopiers and a couple of printers inside, a PC, some cabinets, and a table with a paper cutter, a hole punch and a stapler. And Lars Erik Berg. I saw him in profile, leaning over the photocopier, his long, thin figure. He squinted at the display, pushed his glasses higher up his forehead and tapped something in. The machine set to work, delivering sheet after sheet. He drank from a thermo mug while waiting, placing it on the table beside him before taking out the sheaf of copies, looking through them before laying them on the table. I felt an ache at the sight of his back in the checked shirt. His muscles in motion, causing the material to ripple. He photocopied several pages of a book, cut something out of the copies, taped it to a blank sheet, placed the sheet on top of the machine and made a new pile of copies. He was wearing a wide black belt on his jeans, and shiny black leather shoes. If he had turned and moved towards the door he would have spotted me, but he did not, he was busy with his mobile phone.

Someone came walking down the corridor. A man with green corduroy trousers and curly hair, who looked at me as he passed, I hoped he would not ask if I was looking for someone or needed help, but he went on without saying anything.

I hurriedly retreated a few steps before he opened the door to the copying room. As he entered, I heard Lars Erik's voice and laughter.

I still had time to leave, but hesitated, should I be giving up, now that I had come so far, and was just a few metres from Lars Erik's life? I could just make out the reflections of the two men in the glass window, not who was who, but that there was movement in there, he was in there, all I had to do was tap lightly on the window and he would turn. Instead I left. Once I was in the lift, I took out my mobile and deleted Lars Erik Berg's numbers. We each lived in our own separate worlds, and that was nothing to cry about. In any case, I was a writer, I needed unattainable worlds, I could probably use this story in some way. If nothing else, then in writing. Except I did not write any longer.

26

She did not even want to have that house. Or rather, she did, of course. They had plans, she and Hartvig, and she was a practical person. They were together on the house, for a time at least. He had money and connections, she could put things straight. Moreover, she could speak when Hartvig was at a loss for words, which he was, constantly. You truly have the gift of the gab, he told her admiringly, but later on he would use that against her. You certainly have a devilish way with words, and with that evil laughter of yours it's not too hard to believe you come from hell.

The wife from hell, that was her. Things went swimmingly as long as they were busy establishing their home, furnishing the rooms, planning and sowing the lawn outside. God only knows how many hours she put in decorating and sewing. She was good at it, that was the truth, she was quite simply good at that sort of thing. But she did not *actually* want the house. When it became a reality. She did not want the type of life she and Hartvig gradually came to have, did not want Hartvig. He did not truly see her. He saw nothing other than the fits of rage. She realised that now. That every time she lost her temper she had to be the most docile and endearing wife one could imagine for at least a week. Only in so doing could she offset the balance. One sin required payment by seven good deeds. But she did not want to. Could not. It was abhorrent to her, because Hartvig vexed her. She did not love him sufficiently. But how was it actually, did he love her as deeply as he said he did? When perhaps he did not need to, not as much as her, seeing as he had his work, seeing as he was also capable of switching off his feelings. How did he do that? Oh, she does not know if she even knew him, or just grew accustomed to him, his risibly servile behaviour upon meeting men he admired, for instance. How that annoyed her. And his idiotic jokes, which he made with those he ventured to socialise with as friends. In general, they were so-so, the friends, but always slightly below standard, being with them bored her, those awful bridge evenings were a case in point. But Hartvig was on top form then, in his element, because if there was one thing he was not, it was stupid. Neither was she. She was certain of that. Certain she was meant for something else. She said it to Mama once, but Mama had met her with a sharp look and told her she did not want to hear that kind of talk. So lacking in humility, she said. No, Cessi, you have to play the cards you are dealt.

But which cards did Mama mean exactly? Surely it was not that all the world saw in her was her practical turn of mind, testiness and *sarcasm* (you and your sarcasm) – was that supposed to be the sum total of all she was?

She, who was meant for something else.

What could that be?

Might it not simply be what she had dreamt of? Running her own sewing atelier? Employing girls to make dresses according to the patterns she had created. She herself would only sew selected models. Only the most beautiful and difficult-to-make dresses would come from her hands. She pictured the atelier being located in New York, but after the children were born, she realised it would have to be in Oslo. Perhaps it was even the better location. In America it could be hard to break through and get ahead, while in little Oslo there were few who could sew to such a level, few of class. So she could be the one who occupied that position, why not? If others could become famed and fabled then why not her? She could then earn enough money to pay for trips to America, travel over from time to time to gather inspiration. Was that so impossible, she could not see how a dream like that could be viewed as conceited, and it had an element of realism to it? So why did it not come to pass?

Because everyone demanded so much of her, and had always done so. Oh, her life had been ruined, out of consideration for everyone else, and what did she get in return? Aches and pains everywhere, aches in her joints, pain in her hands, in her soul.

She could still sew. She stared at the sewing machine, knowing there was no one and nothing to prevent her, she had all the time in the world. But she was just not able. It was too late. She no longer had the desire. Now that she could have sewn the clothes she had seen in her mind's eye, it was too late. Well, not that she remembered how she had envisaged the individual garments, but she recalled the feeling she experienced thinking them up. Ideas like that did not come to her any more. No, she was too weary. Better to have a cigarette, a rest, watch a little television. Carry out some chores in between, because she was still good at taking care of practical matters. She polished the floors herself, gave everything a thorough clean, was even able to replace the washers on the taps, Finn had taught her how. All that in spite of her being over seventy years old and nobody expecting great things of her. They never had, but when the children were small, they demanded such intense love from her. She *had* loved them too, but they had crowded her, were always around, she did not have the energy for it, found it hard to breathe, became angry.

As a matter of fact she did sew, she made clothes for her daughters and grandchildren, it was no bother to her, on the contrary, she found it relaxing, joyful almost, forgot all about herself. Bought Burda patterns and fabrics, silk sewing thread and corduroy, velvet ribbons and flowery cotton material, it was terrific fun, she told Alice on the telephone. And they would come, and try on the clothes as she was in the process of making them, the grown-up children, and the little grandchildren. Standing there so sweetly and patiently while she took measurements and pinned seams. Afterwards she prepared open sandwiches and made hot chocolate and they went into the living room to chat, all sitting together cheerful and cordial. She opened the balcony door and windows, because it was almost the height of summer outside, and the chestnut trees were in bloom. When they had left, she sat by the open windows sewing long into the evening. She loved the summertime, there was so much hidden hope in the warm smells, the low voices of the passers-by.

But it was too late for the other thing. Or too difficult. That was just how it was. Twenty years had passed since the divorce, it was nothing, the sand in an hourglass, the years had gone before she knew it, and what had she done? Lots of small things, nothing big, nothing of importance, she scarcely remembered. Enjoyed herself with friends, that was true.

Visited her children and grandchildren. Taken care of Mama. Run errands. Strolled the streets. Cried her eyes out.

No, she did not want the house. But that time Finn came round and told her that Hartvig and his fancy woman were going to build a new house beside the old one, then she felt the old pain again. It was not that woman's plot of land, and the new house had been intended for Cessi from the start. She and Hartvig had talked about it for many years, a new house, one which was easier to clean. The costs would not be too high as they could rent out the old one, because that had to stay within the family, Hartvig said. Property was the safest investment one could make, it had perpetual value.

That Finn got to live in the house was of some small comfort. On the day he moved in with his wife and their little girl she felt such a strong sense of relief she could hardly stand, and had to lie down on the bed for a while. Finally some of her kin were returning to the house. Not that she could visit them very often, that is to say, she probably could, but it did not turn out that way. Finn's moods were so changeable, she simply did not have the energy for him suddenly berating her over something or other. If she then told him her nerves were weak and he needed to take her age into consideration, he grew even angrier, it was like waving a red rag. Besides, she had the distinct impression that Linda thought badly of her. And God knows what Finn said. They no doubt talked ill of her. Dreaded her coming to visit, only felt obliged to invite her. One notices that sort of thing. She was certain it was down to Linda at the end of the day. Even though Linda was in no way suited to the house, not to it, the neighbourhood, nor Hartvig's family. Neither had Cessi been, back when she had moved in, but then she had known how to behave, she had conquered her place. Nobody rode rough-shod over her. And the house was hers, she had worked on it from the ground up. Something Linda obviously did not understand.

Oh, by all means, Cessi might say, I am certainly not going to let it bother me, laughing at the same time, so surely Linda could laugh along? But no, Linda looked away and it was impossible to tell what she was thinking. She did not understand that Cessi was speaking in jest, and she wanted everything done her way, the house, the garden and the manner in which the children were brought up. It was impossible to have a natter with her about the Heyerdahls, or gripe about Hartvig's fancy woman, because Linda did not understand these people, did not know how to have a heart-to-heart, she did not get the *tone* of the conversation.

Nevertheless, she was surprised when Finn came and told her that he and Linda were to be divorced. After all, he had been so happy with her and the child. All of a sudden he was standing in her living room telling her it was all decided. But that was not all, no, his mother was to be upbraided for all the woes of the world that day. Firstly, there was the matter of the house, the fact that he was not to live there any more, his eldest sister was. So Hartvig had decided.

After all, he could not occupy the house now he was alone, he agreed with that, nor did he want to. Fucking shit-hole, he said, but they were words spoken in anger, the same as she had uttered on many occasions, except she had been addressing Hartvig. Even so, he was furious. You don't get it, Mum, he spat, I'm being thrown out of my own home.

And after being allowed to live there for so many years, it

was preposterous. She told him as much, what about your sister, she said, is it not her turn soon?

It's always her turn, Finn roared, always this poor her, so sweet, so kind and good and talented, so fragile, go stick it up your arse, Mum.

But Finn was not going to dent the joy she felt. She and her eldest daughter enjoyed one another's company, the conversation flowed when they were together, about everything under the sun, family, the neighbours, Hartvig. A proper beauty she was too, the most prepossessing of all the children, more beautiful than her mother, truly the one she could be proud of and was happy to show off. That she was to live there was too good to be true. It served to put everything back in its place, after so many years. She would be able to return home, and to her own home this time, not to Hartvig's house and regime, not to Finn and his erratic behaviour.

Not that she took pleasure at the expense of Finn's problems, no, but really, were they not just typical of him, nothing lasted when it came to him. No sooner had he got started on something than he took a fresh tack. He was just as he had always been, she had been right all along, he was difficult, a proper troublemaker. No doubt he had let his anger get the better of him with Linda, or his moodiness had become too much for her.

No, Finn's ill temper would not overshadow her happiness. Her daughter should never have had to leave her home, and neither should she. Now finally they were to return, finally they could live as they ought to have done all these years. Lost time could of course never be regained, but the damage could be put right to a certain extent, and in what better way, by her coming and going in the house, by being there and taking care of things for her daughter, son-in-law and their little ones.

The terrible burden of losing everything, of having to run the gauntlet with the ruin that was her life for everyone to see, the disgrace, all that would fade, melt away, become easier to bear. While at the same time old responsibilities would be lifted from her shoulders, because she would not be looking after work-shy, impertinent maids, or taking care of other practical nuisances, that unruly boy was all grown up and no longer there, the children's bickering a closed chapter, they were now adults. Not that they did not quarrel any more, but she was spared having to hear it. She did, on the other hand, hear all *about* it, but she did not have anything against that, truth be told it was entertaining, something she could share with her eldest daughter, a topic for long conversations.

It is just how it ought to be, don't you think, she said to Alice on the telephone, that life runs its course, she was a grandmother now, and could contribute however she was able, she could help out her daughter who had quite naturally taken over her childhood home. The two others would find a place in the fullness of time. In the meantime it was only right and proper that the one who needed the house most took precedence, the one who managed best and had a good head on her shoulders when it came to money. Moreover, she understood her mother.

Yes, she would perhaps have answered Finn differently if he had not chosen that particular day to ask his questions. There she was, just after getting the rights to her own home back to a greater degree than she could ever have hoped. In a sense she had anyway, because neither Hartvig nor his foolish wife could prevent her from being there. What is more she would offer to do the gardening for her daughter and son-in-law, pick berries, rake the lawn and those kinds of things. In full view of those stupid people. But at the same time she would have to look at Hartvig and his wife in the new house every time she visited, that was a beastly thought, stupid, stupid Hartvig. She turned to Finn.

Well, don't lay the blame for this on me, she said, *I* am not the one who owns the house, your father does.

That was the spark that set it all off. There were suddenly no limits to what Finn accused her of, and what he wanted answers to, once and for all. Things she had forgotten, or hardly offered any thought.

Finn always blamed other people when something was amiss. The divorce from Father was her fault, he shouted. Your bloody scenes ruined everything, me especially. How could I hope to be normal, growing up with you as my mother? You and your damned nerves, you like to think you can always just hide behind that.

He was in the habit of saying he had his nervous tension from her, and God knows, possibly there was some truth in it, he had perhaps inherited her mental frailty. But she became so incensed when he said things like that, and on that particular day she was not able to control herself.

It was no doubt your father who put that in your head, she screamed, and you're forgetting something very important. Let me tell you, and this is a fact, if you had not been so difficult, then I would not have suffered half the problems I did with my nerves, we would have managed fine up there in the house, and divorce would never have been necessary.

She should not say such things, she was aware of that, but could not hold back. It was just as much his fault as her own, when he had been so foolish as to speak to her in that way. Besides, it was true. Not that he understood a word of it, standing there in the middle of her living room with that facial expression she knew only too well, looking all accusatory and hurt, she recognised her little boy then, she certainly did all right.

Could he not just be kind to her! All the times they had faced each other like this, and she knew that all he wanted was to be pampered and cuddled, but she could not, she rebuked him instead, berated him for his behaviour, his manner, his surly retorts, she punished him for all this by being cold, by turning her back, leaving him to himself. Even though she did not want to, did not understand why she did this, when most of all she wanted to lift him up and place him on her lap.

Oh, she felt so alone. She was only human after all, and there were doubtless not many people who would have managed to show their child such patience in the situation she found herself in, very few in fact, she fancied. Alice had often said the same during his upbringing. Dear Cessi, she said, you ought not to judge yourself so harshly, you react in a perfectly natural manner. He *is* a sweet boy, truly he is, but he is also exacting, and you devote more time to him than most other children are granted. One must not demand the impossible of oneself either, dear.

It did her good to hear that, and it was true, it really was. Nonetheless she would be troubled, disheartened, on the verge of tears. But perhaps Alice was right and she did demand too much of herself, perhaps that was the reason she reacted as she did.

Finn never got enough, he was a drain on her, a dark drain, he never let up, followed her around the house, demanding and demanding. Not any longer, needless to say, not in that way. He called on the telephone now instead and was brutish, or came around unannounced, after something, although she did not know what.

I'm drinking too much, he might say. I can't sleep at night. Or as is the case now: I'm seeing a psychiatrist. I would hardly have needed to do that, Mum, if everything was as it should have been. If you hadn't been so bloody selfish, he said. He said this. Him! That self-centred, self-absorbed boy, how had he turned out like this, what had she actually done wrong? Spoilt him perhaps, given him too much attention.

Now he and this psychiatrist were of course discussing his childhood and his wicked mother, yes, they are doubtless in complete agreement, that she was wicked and to blame for all Finn's difficulties. That must be the reason why he suddenly wants to talk about all kinds of things, the psychiatrist has put thoughts in his head and got him asking about things he ought to have the sense to hold his tongue about.

Why did you send me away so often when I was little, Mum? Was it because of the war?

She should have seized the opportunity and said, yes, naturally, because of the war, why ever else? We wanted to look after you, you see. She should have told him she became unwell, was worn out from looking after that enormous house, from two childbirths in quick succession, infants screaming at night.

Something along those lines, that was what she should have said, but she did not. Because Finn was standing there with that sullen, accusing face of his, and then there was this pickle about which of the children would get to live in the house, the irritation welled up within her. They just came out, the words she knew she must not say, but she was unable to stop herself, she said what he expected to hear, but what he hoped was not the case.

The war, no. I really do not think you realise the toil you put us through. You were so difficult.

It was true, that was exactly what he was.

Goodness, how nasty she was. That cold feeling all the way through. But he asked for it. He should not have asked, no, he should not, that just made it— she could hardly tell him that she realised it was wrong, a dreadful mistake to send him away. Then it would be her fault, and that she could not accept, was not able to. Because look at him. His life was a shambles. He had always been that way, so it could not be because of her.

Dear God, it could not be, could it?

Why did he go right for her in that way, he should not have, he should have realised that she could only give him one answer to that question. It lay there, ready to use, because she had spoken of it with so many people over the course of the years, including Hartvig, and the conclusion was always the same: she could not have acted any differently. They had a tearaway on their hands, kind and good at heart, but exceedingly, exceedingly demanding. His little sisters had to be protected as well, safeguarded from his eruptions of violent jealousy.

So he had his answer, and at the same time she looked out the window, hoping he had not heard, that the words had just disappeared into the air and everything would go back to how it had been. Because it was old news, that is exactly what it was, he had heard that he was difficult a thousand times before, even though she may not have said it was the reason they sent him away, not in so many words. No, naturally they had not spoken of it, but told him they wished he would become calmer, learn to concentrate and listen to what was being said to him. Become a good, kind, hardier boy, on the whole, without the mischief and disruption. Competent, experienced teachers were required to that end, that is what they had said, in words adapted to a child's level of understanding, naturally, she thinks they said that in any case.

Are you staying for dinner? she asked, getting up from the chair, I had assumed you would.

He stood there with his stony expression and she made sure to totter a little, then he would see that she was getting old, no longer so steady on her feet, he had to be kind to her.

You fucking cow, Finn said, you fucking, selfish bitch.

And she could not help it, she had to laugh, it bubbled up from within, because this corresponded exactly with something she had always felt, a furious urge to shake and destroy.

27

Knut was not the right one for me. Neither was Ketil, nor any of the others. But one of them *might* have been, I could have been lucky, I know people sometimes are. They say so themselves, in magazine interviews, to friends, at parties. Love at first sight, they say, bull's-eye, could not live without him, that kind of thing. Before I got to know Ketil I thought he had what it took. That I could be myself together with him. Afterwards I started to believe maybe that would not be possible with anyone at all.

Because is that not how it is, when you become close enough to a person, you forget you ever wanted to get so near, forget how you imagined loving a man, that the mere sight of his hands would turn you on and make you happy? That he was like your brother, your best friend, yes, you yourself almost.

But why?

How close is too close?

Every time I attempt to answer I am wrong. But what then is right? Provided something is wrong, does that necessarily mean that something else exists which is right? I am not so sure.

The thoughts are banal. But the mystery is deep.

Beate was sitting on the sofa. Her white blouse was buttoned wrong, her hair gathered in a loose bun, moist strands of hair sticking out on the nape of her neck, she was not wearing any make-up, had come from the swimming pool, was beside herself over something to do with Erik. She cried and said she did not know the reason, did not know why nothing was right with her. Things were not like before, just a few weeks ago she could succeed in everything, could have whomever she wanted, felt strong. Is Erik bad for me, she asked, *is he like poison*, is he? Are you meant to feel this way?

You're just in love, I said. When you are not on your own any more. Then you have moments like this.

I heard what I said, but did I believe it? Even though I recognised it. Because was that really how it was supposed to be? Every time I met a man I felt I lost myself. And I was not even really in love. It was just my imagination. When I returned to my senses, I saw that the man concerned lacked judgement, backbone or something else. It just could not work out.

But Beate was different. She did not make wrong choices. That would not be possible, I told myself, Beate is healthy.

You just need a rest, I said. A hot bath, something to eat, some sleep. A night spent watching TV or chatting to a friend.

Female advice. Some mothering. Was that all that was needed?

I was not even her mother. Perhaps that was the point. Love had to have certain boundaries, everything could not merge together, she could not go to Anita with this.

Beate wanted to be loved the way she was loved as a child.

Me too.

The impossibility of it grew stronger for every day I lived.

Imagine being ninety years old. And all you want is

warmth, affection. Talk about the wrong way around, because who is going to give you that then?

One summer morning right after my divorce from Knut, Anita and Beate came to visit. We borrowed the house while Dad was on holiday. Beate was about three years old.

Anita and I sat in the dining room drinking tea while we looked at the children playing in the garden. It was chilly inside the house, the dark house with the big stone cellar. We both had cold feet and goose bumps on our arms, we laughed, because it was the warmest day of the summer so far. Anita was wearing a red singlet and her skin was already tanned. Fair hair and radiant eyes, she was beautiful, of course. Now and again we listened out to what the children were up to outside. Tuva was a few years older than Beate and Georg, she wanted to play mummy, especially to Beate, place her on the swing and lift her down, take her in and out of the sand-pit, until it all got too much for Beate and she cried for her mother. Anita went out and lifted her up, brought her in and sat with her on her lap, sang to her and kept her amused. I have never seen Anita so happy.

Isn't summer the best? she said. Shall we go for a swim?

Beate came with me to pack the swimming gear. I had a big basket I used to take along to the beach, when Beate saw it she wanted to crawl inside, and I let her. Once inside, only her head was visible and she looked at me and laughed. I carried her down the stairs in the basket. There is nothing special about this memory. Apart from it being a happy one.

A happy memory: the joy of being with the children, all the flowers in the garden. The air shimmering hot above the tarmac, the hot bus ride. Cooling off in the water afterwards and the afternoon turning to evening. The lights of the boats out at sea, the feeling of the water becoming soft, smooth as the blankets we were sitting on, but moist, moving like an animal.

Beate slept on the blanket while the others took one last dip. I lay beside her and nodded off too.

On the way home on the bus, Tuva was bad-tempered and difficult, would not help carry the things, would not sit next to us, hit my hand away. I spoke sharply to her and she began to cry: did I love her? Did I love her more than Georg? Just as much, I replied, I love both of you more than anything in the world. But that was not the problem. What she was really wondering about was Beate: did I love Beate more than all the people in the world? I knew that was what she feared. She was wrong, of course. Not all love is alike. But the love I have for my own children is unlike anything else.

What Anita thought, I do not know. She sat with Beate asleep on her lap looking at us without smiling, then turned her face to the window.

When I think of this memory, the core of it is to be found outside the frame, as it were. It was the moment I opened the door. Right after Anita and Beate had rung the bell. I opened the door and there they stood, Anita at the foot of the steps, Beate one step from the top. Some rays of sunshine were stealing through the fir trees, shining on her chubby knees, her hair and eyes, while the rest of her body lay in shadow. What was it I saw in Beate's eyes? My own love. It flowed so freely in her. The child is the scene of the crime, that is what it meant.

Happiness is not boring. But it is manifest for the most part when it is lost. As hope, an ideal, a flag in the distance. Knut ceased to interest me. Or did he begin to annoy me, was it more that? How peevish he was. He always had to have the last word. That kind of thing. There was suddenly no forbearance any longer. His body did not appeal to me. On the rare occasions we made love, I closed my eyes and pictured someone else. I always chose a specific man, yet never someone I actually knew. But most nights I slept alone, huddled up imagining I was nestled against a safe body, my best friend. I considered these fantasies a terrible secret, almost infidelity. I knew Knut would regard them as such, I could not say anything to him about them. But after the divorce everything dissolved, the secrets became nothing, my fantasies seemed insignificant.

Perhaps it is true what people say, that feelings are fleeting, changeable, but I do not believe that, no, I do not, because ABSOLUTE love does exist, it is UNYIELDING, that means we must yield to it, it is the LAW.

Yes, I sound like a commandment hewn in stone, and it is probably no coincidence, that culture speaks in me, even when it is natural law I am trying to put into words. It is true I cannot see it from outside, but I know that if it disintegrates I can also fall to pieces, I have a mental image of it, how 'tree' is torn from 'river' is torn from 'sky' and is levelled off and blown up, and it is the meaning that disappears, a death of sorts, like Alzheimer's, or an actual death, to die from grief. What I am trying to get to is that transitoriness has limits. My God, have you forsaken me? I understand now what it means, *My God, have you forsaken me?* it means: my love, why are you not here, why can I not feel what I need to feel in order to be human enough?

*

There are so many ways to depict reality. But I have never liked to create an illusion. Why should I act as if I do not exist, me, the narrator, why should I hide? It is completely obvious that I am not to be found anywhere but here. *I* am the illusion. I turn on the wrought-iron lamp above my head and shed tears into the ceramic mug of red wine.

After my failed attempt in the winter to give up being a writer, I decided to move out of the house. The prospect paralysed me. I bought fifty flat-packed moving boxes at Clas Ohlson, but could not face assembling them. It had snowed and the light from outside flooded harshly through the windows high up on the wall. I was standing in my Pantheon, even though there was no aperture in the ceiling, no cupola, only flat ceiling, with a circular stucco, devoid of decoration. My mobile lay on the windowsill and played its 'Hey Jude' ringtone. Tuva had chosen it for me. You do date from the sixties, don't you? she said and laughed, I've heard that it's good for old people to see and hear things that remind them of when they were young, she said, laughing even more, you need to have an age-appropriate sound, Mum.

It was Anita who rang. Just called, as though nothing had happened, after such a long time. She was wondering if she could borrow the Persian rug I had on the first floor, she said.

Borrow, I asked, can you borrow a rug someone else is using?

Yes, because Anita was planning to buy one herself, in the same colours, if she could find it. But they were so expensive, she had to be sure she liked it, that a Persian rug would fit into her home office and, not least, she had to convince Ståle.

You'll probably just end up hanging on to it, I said, that is what will happen. I won't be able to bring myself to ask for it back.

No, Anita said, of course you'll get it back, it's only a month we're talking about.

They came round the following day, stood in the kitchen all busy and energetic, not bothering to take off their coats. Anita did not even have the time to remove her shoes, and I understood why: she had new boots, red Ilse Jacobsen wellington boots, her black trousers were skin-tight, her jacket only waist-length and everyone could see she had a flat stomach. Anita was, quite simply, sexy, as attractive as her young daughter, yes, I assumed men who saw them together would think that, and it was how Anita wanted me to see her. She wanted to outdo me, but Jesus, I was an empty vessel and did not try to hide it, I hardly made any noise never mind the most noise, I could not conceive what she thought I had. And Anita was not the only one. What was it they thought I had within me, all those who circled around: the man in the baseball cap, Beate, Anita, what was it they wanted so badly, I had nothing, only darkness, and what did they want with that?

We have to be going, Anita said, we have a lot of things to do. We're heading to Smart Club cash-and-carry to buy in food for the weekend, and Beate really wants to go to Ikea, which is fine, I can pick up some new plants and flowerpots at the same time. They're pretty much okay, plants from Ikea, don't you think?

She wanted me to come along, eat in the café, like we used to, when the children were small and we went there to eat Swedish meatballs. That was so nice, wasn't it, Bea Britt? she said. As though nothing at all. But it was not nothing. It was jealousy, I was sure. Talk about back to front. Anita wanted for nothing, on the contrary, she had everything I myself dreamt of, and still she was jealous.

Give me a hand, Ståle, Anita said. They lifted the table off the rug, and Ståle rolled it up. The parquet floor was visible. The varnish was worn in several places, the wood greying.

Thanks, Bea Britt, this is really kind of you. Anita hugged me. Do you want to come along . . . ?

She stood there in her black, expensive clothes and for a moment she looked like she did when the children were small and we were still best friends.

Of course I went along. Even though something was amiss, I did not know what, but I wanted to go, like in the old days, to eat meatballs at Ikea together with Anita, Beate and Ståle. I was going to pull myself together, find my way back to my old self, become who I once was.

So there I sat, in the back seat, with the Persian rug I had inherited from Granny. There was not enough room in the boot, so Ståle had to place the rolled-up carpet sideways in the car over the seats both front and back. I looked at the back of Ståle's neck. I would have liked to put my hand around it, it was slender, with a pronounced cleft between the sinews, strong. Why could Anita not just be content?

She was the one driving. I looked down at my hands and thought they looked chunky, clumsy like the hands of a child, but old all the same, the skin had become coarse and wrinkled in the last few years, the veins prominent. Now they lay idle in my lap, limp. I had the same feeling in my body as when I was a child. When I was tired or wet and it had been a long time since anybody had touched or spoken to me. And I could not say it, because I did not know. I just waited. Anita was a two-faced cunt.

We picked up Beate outside the SATS gym in Solli plass.

Ikea in Furuset or Slependen? Ståle turned as she got into the back seat, trying to see her over the top of the carpet.

What's it matter? Ikea is Ikea.

It most certainly is not, Anita said. It has to be Slependen, where we used to go, don't you remember, Beate? You and me and Bea Britt. Tuva and Georg. How the three of you used to run riot in the ball playground. There is a difference between Slependen and Furuset and it has to do with the feeling, they *are* two different places.

Why did Anita have to be so beautiful? Being with her was far too pleasant, I lost all power to resist, went along with everything. Beate smiled and looked out the window beside her, did not say anything to me. Was it because the carpet was lying in the way? Or did she not want to speak to me, was something wrong? Perhaps it was visible. That I had become a child. That I was old and obsolete. Passive and indistinct in the corner of the back seat, with Anita and Ståle sitting in front, as if they were my parents. Jesus, I remembered when I was the one who drove them here and there, helping them move, collecting them at the airport. It was a hassle, Tuva and Georg were small and had to come along. They wailed in the back seat, I was sweating, and neither Anita nor Ståle had a clue. They had no idea how to pack properly, how to strap things onto the roof rack, fill up with petrol or mollify difficult toddlers. I hardly knew myself, but I did it.

I moved at a slow tempo at Ikea. I stood for ages looking around for the water. The tray in my hands. The plate of meatballs on the tray. When I eventually caught sight of the tap, it took time to find somewhere to put down the tray while I got the water. There was a long queue and a lot of people, I was jostled around, the water sloshed about in the glass which sailed back and forth on the tray. I made it to the table where Beate, Anita and Ståle were already eating, put down my tray, but discovered I had forgotten cutlery. I fetched a serviette, a knife and fork and filled a glass of juice from the dispenser that I had not paid for. As if it were Ikea's fault I was on the verge of tears.

It was Ikea's fault. Or their profit, all depending on how you looked at it, yes, because they made good money from our emotional fluctuations as we manoeuvred our way between the sets of shelves, it was unbearable, this urge to amass, our demand to consume, that was what they exploited, the all-round pressure which forced us to the very limits of our endurance. We searched for things but could not find them, tried to choose, but could not manage, and yet we had to, we had to take something home with us. When we were close to collapsing we went to the café, and that was when it could happen, when we sat across from one another at the table and met our most fundamental needs for food, drink and rest. That was when we could feel. That emotions welled up, that they gave rise to tears, was due to the pressure within, the fact that we could finally express ourselves, suddenly came to the fore for one another, almost complete, or at least surprisingly multi-dimensional.

I was unable to take part in the conversation, had enough to do with cutting up my food and chewing. As though I had just learnt how. Beate looked at me. I thought that I was perilously close now to sinking in her estimation. Puncturing her admiration. Was she disappointed in me? Horrified at seeing things were not as she believed? But it *was* as she believed, *really*. I was the strongest of them all. I had the answers she needed, except that they had taken on the wrong colour along the way, no, not colour, they had darkened, become black.

Anita related some gossip from work and everyone laughed. I sat there with my false laughter, without my children beside me. Tuva, Georg. I let them down by appearing so pathetic. Bereft of my Persian rug, my own car, without a man, without an authorship, without an exterior. And Anita did not talk to me, only at me.

Oh, how I longed for this to be over, I wanted to get back to the house, into the living room, onto the sofa, open a bottle of wine and turn on the TV.

There was nobody there who could see me, nobody who knew.

I had to hold out.

It was best not to say anything.

No matter what I said Anita would absorb it, make it into something else, something impossible to contradict.

That's the strangest thing I've ever heard, she would say, *I just don't get it*. Words came easily to Anita and she was used to talking, she talked rings around people with unflagging energy, set things straight, categorised and stated her opinion, you could not fault how she phrased things. *So good to get this out into the open*, she would say, *to clear up this misunderstanding, because I*, and here she would place her hands on her chest, *had the feeling that you were rejecting me*. What did I think, that she was trying to, like, *push* me away or something? No, that was ridiculous, she honestly had no clue what I meant, it was artfully done. Push me away from what exactly, and why in the world would she, no, where was I getting all this?

So I could not say anything.

I could outdo her of course.

I could carry on the same as her. Laugh loudly and at length, speak in a lively way, but only to Beate and Ståle. I could avoid making eye contact with her. Pretend I did not hear what she said. Forget to get her coffee when I fetched a cup for everyone else. I could adopt all her techniques, I could call her next week and say I wanted my rug back, I could invite Beate along on a holiday, oh, there was so much I could do to make me and Anita more alike, to bring us onto the same level, two rivals, evenly matched. I realised that was the price to be paid in order to win back my friendship with Anita. But was it even a friendship any longer? Ugh, I was not interested one way or the other, I had no desire, absolutely none, I was devoid of desire.

The black dog was here. So there was not much I could do. On the contrary, I had to do as little as possible, keep my movements to a minimum so as not to aggravate the pain. I could not face more pain. The sight of the dog was my only hope. It was so beautiful. So smooth, so warm. Mine. I had to give in to it, I thought. Not move. Stay put within the house, drink wine. I thought of my plants, almost bursting their pots, the stalks resembling branches down at their roots, the dust settling upon them, how I usually spray the green leaves with water, *when my hand was very small, Mum used to guide it to help me get clumps of potato on my spoon.* I could peel tomatoes, bake bread, grind coffee beans and grow herbs. I could make my life resemble the pictures in art books, the paintings of French kitchens; pheasants, chickens and vegetables. The pictures gave off no smell, but I knew what chaos it must have been, the sound of voices and scuttling feet, the aroma of blood and boiling soup, *the white light, the colours, shadows, something glimmering, something warm against my ear, small twitches, white and gold, as I lay on my back in the pram.*

That is how it could have been, aesthetic, a compensation for everything, an adult life adapted, cut back, not great, but not bad either. Then Emilie came along with her dog.

28

He has rung a number of times and I see him bring his finger once again to the doorbell. I watch him from the window. He must have been at it for a few minutes. He managed to stir me from the sofa and I have had time to make it down into the dark cellar. The light from the lamp outside falls diagonally across his face, casting dark, shifting shadows beneath his eyes, beside the bridge of his nose and around his mouth. His cap is pushed back. Those white brows and glaring pale blue eyes, like a husky. He is wearing black gloves, I see them when he takes hold of the door handle, pulling and shaking it. I hear his voice but not what he is saying. Then he lets go of the door and stands motionless, thinking perhaps, or listening, before taking a step back and looking up at the front of the house and the darkened windows. I have not put any lights on. The neck of a bottle is sticking up sideways from his pocket. He brings it out and takes a mouthful. It is vodka, Smirnoff, I recognise the red and white label from the shelves of the Vinmonopolet. He suddenly looks in the direction of the cellar window. I back up, duck down. Thirty seconds or so pass, followed by the tinkling of breaking glass, I piss myself. I guess it is the bottle, he has either dropped or thrown it on the flagstones, he has not broken the window, my thighs are soaking wet all the same. I have a build-up of saliva in my mouth. I want to groan to relieve the pounding of my heart, but do not in case he might hear me. He shouts something, fury in his voice. In between the shouting and the mumbling I make out individual words: *you, fuck. Emilie. Cunt.*

I have sat down on the floor. *Do you want to see Emilie,* is that what he is yelling, do you want to see Emilie? The wet denim stings my skin, the odour of piss fills my nostrils. It goes quiet, but I know he has not left, I have not heard any movement, no gravel crunching underfoot. I know the garden and the drive and can work out the approximate whereabouts of someone by the sound: down by the gate. By the pine trees. At the front door. Or I recognise the muffled sound of footsteps when someone walks across the lawn and around the house, the scraping of soles against the flagstones if they go up the steps to the veranda, as Tuva often does when she has forgotten her keys.

Finally I hear the sound of feet on the gravel, can work out roughly when he is passing beneath the heavily dripping pine trees, hear the gate squeak on the hinges as it is opened, scraping the gravel beneath. No sound of it being closed. That does not necessarily mean he is still here but I stay sitting motionless all the same, try to locate hiding places in the cellar without moving my head. One of Granny's Persian rugs lies rolled up under Tuva's old Ikea bed. I put it down here because it was so worn the pattern was indistinct. I can hide there, under the bed, between the carpet and the wall. As I creep under, I get the feeling he has his face pressed against the window looking in at me, watching my legs scramble on the floor and stick out before I draw them up. My heart is hammering, I am out of breath. But nothing happens, I do not hear anyone outside, no clawing at the window pane, no tinkling of broken glass, do not notice any tug on the door from the draught coming from a window or door being opened elsewhere in the house.

I lie there for a long time, feeling tired and drowsy, but am suddenly seized by panic, because I am trapped under here, I cannot lift my head, cannot breathe properly, the underside of the bed is pressing my face against the floor, the back of my head is right against it, I moan, scream almost, yes, maybe I do scream as I struggle to get out from under it and free.

The driveway is empty. It is beginning to get light. If he was outside now he would easily have seen my face in the cellar window. But he is not here. On the flagstones in front of the hall door lies the broken glass from the smashed Smirnoff bottle.

I step out of the wet jeans and knickers and leave them lying in a heap on the floor. Cold and naked from the waist down I walk up the stairs. It reminds me of something, but what is a memory worth? Wandering lonely before it disappears. Perhaps I am remembering how it was to be small and to run around naked. It is precious little help now, on the contrary, it only increases my confusion, because I am mixing up childhood and adulthood, dream and memory.

My toes are ice cold, making the wooden floor in the kitchen feel strangely soft and warm beneath my feet. I leave the lights off. Look out at the road from the kitchen window. Rain-soaked, glistening, deserted. I consider whether to shower before or after I call the police. The deciduous trees, divested of foliage, bend in the wind.

It is difficult to make them understand. I explain everything once. State my name, address and national identity number.

Tell them about the man in the baseball cap. The Emilie case, I say, the Emilie case. To judge by the voice of the policewoman on duty, she does not appear to have heard of it at all, but everyone has, anything else is impossible. She says I need to hold the line while she talks to a colleague. Can you not just ring Eriksen, I ask, please, he knows me, but he isn't answering his mobile. Listen, we'll decide on that, she says and leaves me on hold for five minutes. I am still naked from the waist down, but am sitting on a chair in the kitchen, it feels cold and clammy.

They're sending a patrol car, she says, and asks me to stay close to the phone. Don't go anywhere. They'll come when they come, and it's no use pestering, she says to me, ringing again is not going to help, unless the person concerned returns, in which case I should ring the emergency number.

I take a walk around the house. Look out all the windows. The dark piles with Dad's things on the lawn. The ridge of the neighbour's roof between the trees. Daybreak is pale and wet. It has stopped raining. The sun comes out, making the raindrops shine, colouring the sky red. The wind does not let up. The police car glides into view.

I have put on Tuva's grey jogging pants, and look down upon the policemen as they make their way up the drive. I do not think I have spoken to either of them before, do not recognise their faces. They stand by the door a moment, look down at the pieces of glass, exchange a few words. One of them brings a mobile phone to his ear, while the other looks towards the garden, before taking a step back and glancing upwards. I wave to him but do not think he spots me because he does not return my wave, but lifts his arm and rings the doorbell instead. I go down and open the door. One of them looks at his notebook. You rang, he says, made a report of someone trying to get into the house.

I try to explain but it is too much for them all at once, both Emilie and the smashing of the bottle, as though it were impossible that the two things had anything to do with one another. I can hear that my voice is high-pitched and reedy, because they seem suspicious, I need to make them understand, I am aware that I am repeating myself, almost crying.

I've told you about this man before, I say, someone must have made a note of it somewhere. It's not supposed to be like this, not with the police, don't you make records of important witness statements? Don't you read reports, or whatever the hell you call them? Surely you ought to know about this kind of thing, a psychopath on the loose, a murderer, do you understand, a murderer.

I think we'll go in, the one with the notebook says, let's go inside and calm down. Try not to shout, it'll only make you more agitated.

They make their way slowly and tentatively up the stairs. I follow behind looking at their black boots.

We sit at the kitchen table. I have to go through everything from the beginning, you would think they had not heard of the case, do they not get what I am saying, or understand the terrible significance? The black gloves. The smashed bottle. I say it over and over. How he shouted: *Do you want to see?*

Did I want to see Emilie. That was what he meant, I say. Okay, says the one taking notes, okay, all right, but afterwards when he is speaking to the duty officer, or whoever is on the phone, he recounts things wrongly, does not stress the most important part: that the man in the baseball cap has something to do with Emilie, that he is not just a drunken idiot. He has Emilie. He does not fully understand. No, he talks about me as the aggrieved party. That according to the aggrieved party, an intoxicated man attempted to gain entry into the property at three in the morning. She is very preoccupied about a pair of gloves the man concerned was wearing, and believes he shouted something about Emilie. Yes, she is a witness in the Emilie case, he says. Correct. She maintains that we are aware of the identity of the intruder, or rather the department is, that she has reported it previously, but that is a little unclear, disjointed, yes, she may be in shock, I don't know, there may be a psychiatric element to take into account as well. That is how he speaks.

Yes, that is right, I do have a ringing and a whistling in my ears, specks in my vision, I am feeling sicker than I can stand; he is right that it is shock, I cannot come out of it and sink sideways towards the other policeman, land on his lap, pass out.

When I come to on the sofa the nausea is gone. One of them is sitting on the edge of the seat taking my pulse, his thumb warm against the inside of my wrist.

Are you very fit? he asks. Your pulse is already low, even though you were hyperventilating.

But I have a tingling in my arms, I say.

That's normal, he says, just breathe deeply, but not too deeply.

He lets go of my wrist and gets to his feet. I do not want him to leave and ask for a glass of water. His footfall across the floor is reassuring, the sound of the cupboard being opened and closed almost everyday, as though it were Knut padding around and I was just resting. Finally there is someone here who can look after me. The ringing in my head takes over and I am not able to lift my arms. The policeman has to hold up the back of my head with one hand while helping me to drink with the other, bringing the glass to my mouth. After which he leaves me to lie in peace on the sofa and goes into the kitchen, where I hear him talk to his colleague but cannot make out what they are saying. A few minutes pass, and then the two of them are suddenly standing beside me again.

I cannot lie here any longer, I think, this is far from over. I want to tell them that, but it is hard to move my lips, I do not know if they hear what I am saying, so I tell them over and over that they have to call Eriksen. It has to do with the Emilie case, I say, to do with the Emilie case. Yes, yes, they say, but I do not see them ring. Maybe they already have.

They tell me I cannot stay in the house. I am given help to swing my legs off the sofa and sit up. Are you dizzy? asks the one who checked my pulse. His hair is soft and brown, he is probably no more than a couple of years older than Georg. No, I say. But I want to sleep. Can you drive me to a hotel where I can sleep?

Titanic in Skippergata is the only hotel I can think of that might be cheap. Located in that area, with all the drug addicts and prostitutes around, it cannot cost much. Not that it matters, I could afford an expensive hotel. But it would not be fitting, would not be in keeping with the incident. I need to leave my home out of *necessity*, not because I need spa treatments and relaxation, and necessities are not supposed to cost a lot, they are *evil*. I need to go to a hotel, it is a necessary evil, a burden. They ask if I would not rather stay with someone in the family, or a friend, perhaps. I have no friends

I could ask such a thing of, but I do not say that. Anyway, I am not going to a hotel to seek out company. I want to sleep for a hundred years.

It turns out I am still dizzy all the same, I stumble getting out of the car and the dark-haired one has to hold me under the arm on the way in, I know he can feel my tit against the back of his hand. He and his colleague lean over the counter talking to the receptionist while I sit in a leather chair in the foyer gazing at their backs, their behinds, black trousers with reflective strips bunching up at the tops of their boots.

The brown-haired one accompanies me in the lift and sees me to the room.

Are you okay? he asks.

Yes, I say, I'm fine now.

And I am, because I have everything I want, a bed, a room and a door I can lock.

Remember to lock the door, he says, look, you just pull up the handle.

I nod. I never forget to lock.

So I lie down, flat out on my back, and doze. Now and again I hear the shushing sound of the ventilation system. The traffic outside. The footsteps of someone passing the door. There is no man in a baseball cap here. No one talking and asking questions, nothing to disturb me, except the mobile phone. It suddenly rings. It is Eriksen. His voice is low and confidential. I have to repeat everything all over again. I see, he says. Okay. At times he asks me to specify or repeat something. We go through the course of events. The words I heard. The gloved hands. I start to cry. It's all right, Eriksen says, it's all right. We'll be in touch. Don't go home before I say so.

Not that I want to go home. I do not want any home. I want to sleep.

I am awoken by an intense feeling of anticipation. I am looking forward to something but do not know what. I get out of bed, go into the bathroom and wash my face with cold water. There is a tray with a kettle, cups, instant coffee, tea bags and sugar lumps on the desk by the window. I boil water and make a cup of coffee. While drinking it, I look through the pages of a thick brown information folder. Inside is a restaurant menu in laminated plastic. There is a photograph of each dish. Spaghetti bolognese, pizza margherita, paella, fruit salad and that sort of thing. It feels safe. But nothing is safe. I picture hands placing the food on the plates, holding the camera and taking photographs of the meals, fingers punching in letters and numbers, moving the cursor to the send button in the display and clicking, sending the order off for printed and laminated menus. Every single planned action is carried out by a person who exists. Not only is time transitory, it is fleeting. I sometimes see a similar image of myself, but am unable to hold on to the image, it is cinematic. I see myself perform a series of rapid movements while I rush forward in time and disappear.

The few traces I leave are from an existence governed by rules. I must, for example, perform specific tasks in order to obtain food. Do what I am asked. As is expected. I am not the one who has made the rules, but I need to follow them just the same, because no others exist. That is what is so difficult, not to mention impossible, to understand. That thoughts and ideas can originate from people, but once put into practice in life they are no longer human, what is done is just done.

Either I have not stirred the coffee sufficiently or the water was not hot enough, because the last mouthful I take is strong and bitter and feels syrupy on my tongue, tiny granules of undissolved coffee powder.

It starts to rain, streak after streak of water down the window pane. Drowsiness suddenly fills my head, I just about manage to get to my feet, stand and sway on the wall-to-wall carpet. Maybe I can lie down for a little, just rest for a few minutes before going down to reception, because I need to, I need to get a move on, there is something I have forgotten. Something that needs taking care of, what was it? There is something I need to clear up, straighten out, take responsibility for. Probably something to do with the children. To do with Lars Erik.

Who said that death is final? I will just lie down here for a while, close my eyes, such a lovely shushing sound in my head, I almost disappear into the grainy sleep, the grains are shadows, sediment, a blurry precursor to the brain adjusting and the images beginning, the dreams, to be drawn down into the only place there is freedom, the only place I do not need love, because sleep takes care of me, envelops me, promises more, promises I will be spared re-emergence, a return to loneliness.

But I do not make it all the way down, sleep does not take me. Something disturbs it. It is the key. I cannot remember having been given a key to the hotel room. But I must have, so where is it? I need to get out of bed and look. So I cannot fall asleep, I lie there thinking I will soon get up. Maybe the policeman forgot. Perhaps he put the key in his pocket. He might come in when I least expect it. It is because I am so tired. I am getting mixed up. That is why I fail to remember that keys are not used any more. You are no longer handed a key attached to a metal fob or a wooden tag, you are given a keycard which you insert into an electronic holder by the door when you enter, to turn on the lights. It also activates the TV, and mine is on. The screen display has been the same since I came in: *Welcome, Bea Britt Viker.*

I take the card out of the holder, stick it in my back pocket, shut the door behind me and take the lift down to reception. There is no one there. Only yucca palms in huge, red pots on the floor. The pots double as lights and are illuminated. I stand by the counter, placing my elbows on the polished wood, or is it fake, laminated to resemble solid wood? The receptionist is seated at her desk behind the counter, with a PC, three telephones, a bottle of water and Post-it Notes. She does not take her eyes from the screen until I ask if they have a computer for guests to use.

No, unfortunately, she says in Swedish. We only have Wi-Fi.

She is called Annika. It says so on the brass name badge she has pinned to her white blouse. She is dark-haired, with a prominent cleavage, push-up bra, I think, and her hair is probably dyed.

Would you like the code?

Oh, she is so *angenäm*, as they say in Swedish, so pleasant. It makes me want to be around her. Just sit here in the foyer being filled by that comforting, subdued tone of voice she uses to guests as they come and go. And as Annika's friendly attention trickles over me, I will become part of it, I will become like her: pure, pretty and simple. I regard her shiny dark hair cut in a Cleopatra style. What is wrong with getting dressed up, taking trouble with your appearance, playing a part, pleasing others? Probably nothing.

I don't have my iPhone or my laptop, I say.

Oh. That's a shame. She directs a beaming smile at me before turning back to the screen.

I remain standing there. She is not going to help me if I do not ask, but I do not like to ask for anything. It makes it so obvious that I am needy. Why can she not work that out herself?

I want to go to Lars Erik. He is the light, I think. If only I had not deleted his numbers. I could just forget about calling? It would be just as natural for him to get in touch with me as the other way around, why do I have to play the active part? Can he not just turn up? Maybe I will go to Jacob Aalls gate instead. Walk up and down his street a little. He has to come out sooner or later and then he will catch sight of me. Or he might be on his way home. Imagine he is on his way in with his girlfriend. He probably has one. And I am standing there. By coincidence as it were. Of course he will understand it is not a chance encounter. He will be forced to face the fact that I want something from him and feel aversion to that. That is the way it goes when you cling on too closely and are the wrong person. Thoughts of me will pop into his mind and he will think *ugh, no,* and try to shake them, try to think of something else. He will know that I have misunderstood and think it strange I could believe him to be interested. Or maybe he is used to it. Women like him and I am no exception. This is so lacking in originality. I am not the sort of woman he is attracted to *and I should have realised that*. He will wonder why I think I am, because that is the kind of thing you notice after a couple of seconds, at first sight in fact, so why did I not notice it? Women like Annika are probably more his type. He would assess my appearance and feel disgusted perhaps, because he has no wish to think of my body in that way. As under consideration. As the one.

I ask Annika if she can look up a telephone number for me.

Yes, but of course, sure.

Lars Erik Berg, I say. In Jacob Aalls gate. She looks back at the screen, her fingers darting quickly across the keyboard. She has green eyes and a small shapely nose that wrinkles when she smiles. She is most certainly his type. Striking, congenial. Too young of course, but men rarely mind that. On the contrary, they think it's nice having so much firm, smooth flesh beneath their hands. Hands that run over naked young bodies at night. And my body? It cannot be compared. After all, it is mine, and that shows all over, it is a wound to the world at large. My breasts are like two flabby, anxious eyes, withdrawn. Not very come hither. And I am not the kind to lead someone on to somewhere not worth going.

Will I write it down for you?

I nod and am handed a sheet of paper with the logo of the Titanic hotel. Annika has written his name in capital letters, LARS ERIK BERG, followed by the address, which I know, and two telephone numbers.

Is that all right? Annika smiles and I say thank you, but it will never be all right. She has nice, smooth, closed walls within. Not like me, with doors that open and shut when I least expect it. Letting in forests of darkness. Keeping out quite ordinary daylight. I go back up to my room.

29

It was the sea. She sat in the chair and felt the sun warm on her face through the window pane, it was spring now. The windows should have been cleaned. But she closed her eyes and pictured the sea, it seemed warm. She saw it from above, as it were, stood on deck peering down while the ship moved astern, the water foaming and churning far below, a dizzying pull. Mama's back at the railing, in a white blouse, some strands of hair had come loose from under her hat and stretched out straight in the wind. The sunlight was so harsh she had to squeeze her eyes closed.

A draught was coming from the half-open veranda door and she struggled up from the chair to shut it, she wanted only warmth now, to sit inside this cocoon of light. When she closed her eyes once more it was dark, the waves moving slower, the ocean a warm little animal. She was not on the ship now, no, they were in the rowing boat, her and some friends, home on the south coast of Norway, in Sørlandet. Alice was there too.

She felt her long plait dangle against her back. How they laughed. Rowed and laughed, each with an oar, but they were unable to move in a straight line like that, and that made them laugh even more.

How foolish they all were, they thought she was old, but look, she was not, she was sitting in the boat, they rowed slowly alongside the large sea-smoothed rocks that disappeared down into the sea, crabbing with light, Alice holding the lamp. *That* is me, she thought. Cecilie, fifteen years old. They were free to think she was ninety, and nag about all the things she had to remember, first and foremost to eat. And she opened her eyes and looked around the room, the pictures on the walls were hers, yes, pictures from all periods of life. There was the portrait of her. She was four years old and placed in a chair in front of a burgundy drape. A little girl with a white ribbon in her hair, dear me, of course she could see it, she remembered it too, how bored she was, sitting and sitting in that chair, not being allowed to turn her head and ending up with such pain in her back. Now it was only a picture. But there it hung, beside the photographs of the children and grandchildren, the painting of Mama and Mama's childhood home, she saw it all plainly and clearly. But what was even clearer was the white light penetrating the room, an extremely cold, harsh light, it told her what those nagging people did not know, that the room was on loan. Utterly random the lot of it. All the trouble that went into keeping everyday life and events in place, but something else seeped through, the vivid moments, every single one, just as detailed and intense, for ever. Mama on the deck of the ship. The warm sea. The straw hat with the cord that chafed her under the chin.

I will soon die. I am returning. To myself. It is only me, you see, I am the only one who is me, and am for always.

The sea could roar. It filled her head, foamed, bubbled and boomed, the beating of the waves, the rippling sound of shells and pebbles being sucked out, and hurled in.

There was a lot about the sea.

Mama loved the sea.

Her and Mama and Finn. Her beloved brother. His eyes, only kindness to be found in them. They collected shells at low tide, at Granny's and Granddad's. One day it rained and she slipped and fell on some stones, cutting her knee. It was not deep. She was placed on a chair in the living room. Mama bent her head down to bandage her knee. Cessi looked down at Mama's dark hair. A bun, curls and clips. The lilac outside, rain falling on them, their smell carrying through the open window, the pane covered in raindrops. Oh no, she is not old. After all, she is where it all started, she is always there, at the beginning.

Do you want coffee, Mum? A voice from the kitchen. She does not drink coffee. Blackcurrant juice is what she wants. Not coffee either now, someone beside her chair mumbles, she hears them, the children, even though she is unable to make out a word. They cannot get over her not smoking any more. She may well have smoked at one time, but not really, not at all, in which case it was a mistake. There were many mistakes.

Those resentful children.

Do they not understand they have their mother to thank for life? Without her they would never have existed. What is it they say? Love and praise. Honour thy mother and father.

But life has been hard. She is resentful herself.

Dearest Mama, bring me home.

The way the images get mixed up. Did she have children or was she a child? Naturally she remembers being in the family way. But was that actually her? She begins to doubt more and more. The grown-up children do not smell like her children, they smell of salt, privates and sweat, yes, and perfume and deodorant, naturally.

This warm, warm feeling. So marvellous and tender. It is called love, is it not. But was it actually directed anywhere? Was it not just being filled to the brim by the children? By being a child. Did it really make any difference if she was the child or the child was hers, did the emotions not stick together so closely that no one could separate them, selfish love here, motherly love there?

Mean. She was mean and ungrateful a lot of the time.

Because there is nothing meaner than being self-centred, is there? Knock that out of her, Papa said, knock that right out. Egotistical and quarrelsome, we do not want any of that. So he said, he, who was not much more besides.

A storm at sea. She never saw that, but she had experienced strong winds, on the open sea, on the voyage to Norway, waves steep and deep, grey mountains the ship rolled between, was thrown about, she was scared to death, and the sea must have been like that when it took Finn, only worse, darker, fiercer, and the explosions and flames on top of it, God grant he did not know he was drowning, that he disappeared the same moment it hit, blown to pieces, gone. That was the Germans, that was. And they might not know that out there in the kitchen, but after that nothing was as it had been before. Jesus Christ does not help anyone, no help is given for that kind of loss. Lose Finn. He was good as gold. They made up their own alloy, she and him, the Cessi-Finn-alloy. Against Papa.

It was only on loan.

It was only on loan.

It was only on loan.

But it was mine.

30

I am lying naked under the duvet. I have placed my mobile and the sheet with the telephone numbers on the made bed beside me. The ventilation system is running but the air in the room is stuffy all the same, damp after my shower. My hair is wet at the tips.

I will, I won't.

Outside the windows, rain is falling again, bucketing down in Skippergata, car tyres hiss on the wet street, sticking to the tarmac. I will. I have made up my mind.

But still I cannot do it. Because now I do not know whether to text or call.

No, I need to wait. I am too hungry and thirsty to do anything, and I have no food. There is chocolate, nuts and wine in the minibar but I cannot face eating at the moment. I do not want to either.

Yes, I do. I want soup. I can picture it. Dipping a spoon into cream of cauliflower soup, I can see it, I am there: aboard a boat, a ferry. I am with Lars Erik. A creamy coloured light over the fjord. It is drizzling. Fine droplets move diagonally across the windows, there is a sound of voices in the carpeted space, we are in the passenger room, below deck.

The sight of all the people gets my hormones racing, a tingling in my breasts. His voice. The water, the side of the boat. The foam, drone of the engine. The glass, droplets. The sun behind the white cloud bank. The cauliflower soup, the cream. The tablespoon, worn. The head of the cauliflower, bumpy. Steam. Chair legs. Shoes, men's feet. Black leather. Chest. Cutlery, crew, service. Plastic flowers, white tablecloths. His hand. First lying on the table, then crooked around the knife handle. Plaice, raw vegetables, white sauce, cabbage and carrot. White, plump. Cream, foam. The nail, the strong middle finger. What do I know about love? The rolling, swelling. Tottering on the wet deck outside. Older people in light clothing. Outside, not in here. Billowing clouds. From out of nowhere I love him.

I fell asleep again, outside it is no longer bright. But it continues to rain. I look out the window. The car headlamps are shining on the dark tarmac. The street is filled with people on their way home from work. I pick the mobile up from the bed. No messages, no missed calls. Nothing is happening. Do I have to just sit here? Will everything be like before, unreal? The world far off, irrelevant. I switch on the TV. Stand naked on the carpeted floor looking at it. Nothing new in the Emilie case. There will be a press conference with any updates tomorrow morning at ten.

The telephone rings while I am on the toilet. I have brought it with me and placed it on the edge of the sink. The display lights up: No Caller ID. I am certain it is Eriksen, ringing from a police mobile with a concealed number, but no one answers when I say hello. I can hear breathing. Is it him, I think, the man in the cap? It must be him. Who else could it be?

Hello, I say again, but still he does not reply.

You piece of shit, I say. You little shit.

I do not make a sound, and then I am aware of him. His

presence, the faint sound of his breathing. It cannot be anyone else. Lars Erik Berg would never resort to this to get in touch. He would have introduced himself. Remember me, he would have asked, would you like to meet, have a coffee?

You know what? I say. I am going to kill you. And if I don't, I'll get someone else to do it. Cut your prick off. You're nothing, you hear me? You're a piece of shit.

He is still there. But I do not say anything more. About a minute goes by. Then I hear a child call out. Not right in the telephone, a little way off. In the same room. Not a small child. An older one, like Emilie. Is it *no* she cries out, or *I*, or maybe *help*, or some other words I cannot make out?

Hello, I shout, Emilie, hello, are you there, it's me, Bea Britt, I'm coming. But he has hung up. She could not have heard me shouting into someone else's ear anyway. If it was her. I cannot be sure. I know nothing about him. I do not understand this. The road to violence.

I try to dress as quickly as I can, but my fingers are shaking too much. When I finally get hold of the right end of my knickers I am so worked up I rip the material along the seam, leaving the elastic on my hip. I have not dried off properly either, and both my knickers and trousers are damp at the crotch, I roar in anger.

What have I done, I think, what have I done, exactly what I was not supposed to, done exactly as everyone else, precisely what he was waiting for. I have not understood the fifth commandment: Thou shalt not kill.

You should not threaten to kill either, because that sort of thing activates violence, brings it to life.

Violence is alive but Emilie is not.

It cannot have been Emilie I heard because Emilie is

already dead, and that is through no fault of mine. He has fooled me, fooled me twice over, he has already killed her and he was manipulating children's voices, my emotions, this is what he wanted, my attention, my distress, my dependence.

I grab the mobile to ring Eriksen but it slips from my grasp, falls to the floor, popping the cover off and sending the battery sliding across the tiles. I cannot believe it. I wail, I cry, I curse and have to talk myself around. Okay, right, I say, okay, okay, it's fine, it's fine, don't buy it, no, no, he's fooled you, okay, okay.

That must be what it is. A hoax. It was not Emilie calling out.

The battery is smooth and my hands are shaking, but the sound of my own voice fills my head, and that helps, my fingers relax, I put the battery in place, click the cover back on and tap in the PIN code.

Eriksen does not pick up. He must be going out of his mind. Why is he not listening out for his phone to ring? I call three times without getting through.

Bloody idiot, I shout out, while pressing one digit after another as hard as I can, bloody arrogant police fucker.

I sit down on the side of the bed. I could just as well lie down and sleep. It would not change anything. It is all out of my hands. The police will sort it out. They are on top of things, know what they are going to do, they know best. They told me to stay put. I do not need to lift a finger. And nor do I have the energy. My feet are ice cold. But I am safe here, everything is being taken care of.

Snot is running from my nose down into my mouth. I consider getting up to fetch some toilet paper. Wiping my face.

Ringing. I remove it with the duvet cover instead. The things in the room do not know what is happening. The bed, fridge, desk. Nothing of the outside exists in here.

Everything will pass, disappear, if I just stay here long enough.

And she got to her feet, I think, she got to her feet, picked up the mobile and, fingers moving frantically, typed in the emergency number.

At the same time as thinking this I am doing it. My heart is beating erratically or too quickly.

Something dramatic occurred in her life, I think, while waiting for them to pick up, and she was forced to take matters into her own hands.

I could not remember afterwards if it was a man or woman I spoke to, I got the feeling it was both, that they were two.

They asked me to lower my voice. Take a calm, deep breath. Is anyone injured? they asked. Does this concern a fatality or a life-threatening situation? They said the same things many times, asked me to repeat my name and where I was calling from. I calmed down, managed to explain.

Okay, they said, all the details have been taken down. Take it easy, we'll look after this. Stay where you are.

I remain sitting on the edge of the bed. My body suddenly feels tired, the mobile heavy in my hand. A few minutes pass. I cannot recall ever having been so sleepy. I wonder if I am actually asleep. A strange buzzing in my head. I realise I need to shake myself loose. Raise my arm.

I raise my arm, move my fingers. Tap in the number for Lars Erik, but hesitate to press OK. I can still let it be.

I let it be. The display goes dark after a few seconds, but

lights up again right before an incoming message makes a beeping sound. It is an MMS, a picture, sent from an unknown number. It takes a few moments before I understand what I am looking at. Just white, and something red. A sheet or tablecloth, with a large bloodstain that has soaked into the material, dark red, uneven round the edges.

Sinking in. It took such a long time to understand. That it was not about me. What I think or who I am. The man in the cap does what he does. He could be prompted by impulse or following a plan, either way he is at work, and action will follow action.

Nausea. How can I know he will not harm Tuva or Georg, or that he has not already? I do not know. I do not know if it is their blood, if it is Emilie's, or Beate's, his own, if it is real or just an image he found on the Net.

My God, I do not understand when it really matters. I am not there when I am really needed, I arrive too late, let go too soon, do not think my actions matter. Otherwise I would have taken better care of my children. All these years and now I am going to let something happen to them?

I forward the MMS to Eriksen and tap in Tuva's number as fast as I can, but suddenly cannot recall the last two digits and have to go back and scroll through my list of contacts.

Why am I so dense? Why did I not think of the children first?

No, I have been thinking of myself, just myself, as though this was a matter between the man in the cap and me, between him, Emilie and me. It has been a square and I am inside, trapped, but also one of the corners. The man in the cap, Emilie, me and Lars Erik. I am within the square. Lars

Erik, I have been thinking, he is the one who will save me, he is the way out, yes, but of what exactly?

I still have time.

I ask Tuva to make sure that Georg goes to her place. He needs to take a taxi over, I say, and then the two of you need to stay in the apartment. Don't go out and don't answer the intercom if anyone buzzes.

Mum, honestly, Tuva says, is this really necessary? You can't even be sure it's the guy in the cap, maybe he's just a common-or-garden nutcase. Can't we just head up to Dad's instead? It's so boring here, and I've hardly any food.

No, I say, your father's house isn't safe. It's too easy to break into. Think of all the cellar windows, and the shoddy lock on the veranda door. You have neighbours all round at your place.

Beate does not take her phone so I am obliged to ring Anita even though I do not want to.

Okay, she says, okay, her voice a few notches deeper than usual, like a man's, I would never have recognised it as hers. Then she calls out to Ståle. I hear him say something or other in response before I am cut off.

She did not say anything to me, did not ask about Tuva or Georg, did not say goodbye, had nothing to give. No, she was not my friend any more, she was looking after herself, she was anti-solidarity.

I get up to fetch a glass of water from the bathroom, but stop and remain standing in front of the mirror by the door. This reflection makes people smaller, I think, I am not so little and thin in reality.

Damn Anita. I want to hear Beate's voice with my own

ears. I try her number again but she does not answer. I move closer to the mirror while keeping the phone pressed to my ear. My complexion looks soft and smooth, it is due to the dim light, in reality my skin is wrinkled and rough.

The photo he sent might have been Photoshopped, I suddenly think, opening the message anew to check if there was something I missed, anything that can tell me who or what I am looking at. I still think it looks like blood on a sheet but the picture is slightly grainy, I cannot tell for sure. And is the stain really as large as it seems? Perhaps the camera has zoomed in on a tiny area, I have no way of knowing as there are no other objects in the frame to compare it with, everything apart from the stain is white.

My mobile vibrates in my hand, rings, giving me a start, making me think it is him, since I am standing looking at the photograph he sent. But it is Beate. Ståle has already managed to collect her from Observatorie Terrasse and she is now sitting in the passenger seat beside him, surrounded by the warm hum of the car engine, with low music coming from the speakers. I picture the windscreen wipers, calmly sweeping aside the raindrops and strips of water that blur the lights of the oncoming cars, the traffic lights shifting from red to green.

Beate's voice is clear and free of concern. She has a father and he likes cars, he earns money, he is strong. Ståle, Beate and Anita, a model Norwegian family. They are as they should be, make use of material wealth but do not splurge, at least not very often. They are well-intentioned, decent and humane. It is true they drive the latest model Volvo XC 60, with large alloy wheels, black and polluting, seated high up, shielded, encased in a metal cocoon of safety. But why not.

Life is short and a body needs pleasure, a body does not last for long, so why not buy security if you can, I believe you should, I think, and picture Beate when she is studying, when she is sitting at my kitchen table reading, crying and falling into a darkness she cannot control, at the thought, at the mere thought of the violence, the unjust treatment of the children she is reading about, Beate, who almost goes under at the hint of rejection, does not know what to do when the chill wells up in her, the chill from out of nowhere, when pain appears without any reason. What shame. What shame Beate feels then. Safe, unhappy and ashamed. Beate, a child of affluence. But nothing lasts for ever, Beate my girl.

There is an incessant beeping on the line, someone trying to get through, and I hope it is Eriksen.

I have to hang up, I say, take good care of yourself.

It is Eriksen. He sounds like he usually does, calm. But what he says indicates otherwise.

You mustn't go anywhere, don't leave the room at all, I'm on my way.

There has been a clear change in circumstances, I am no longer a suspect, but more of a witness, I am a possible victim, I need protection.

Innocent and vulnerable, I notice that corresponds better to how I feel, and my thoughts soon turn to Lars Erik, I get a tingling in my stomach.

Eriksen is probably no different from anyone else, I think, his knowledge comes from personal experience. What difference does it make what I say, if he has not first thought it himself, if it does not fit with the rest of it. What the rest of it is, I do not know, he keeps it well hidden, the police give nothing away. Perhaps there is no coherent rest, just a patchwork of bureaucratic routines, investigative theory and tactics, people on duty at different times, reports and sick leave.

I call Tuva once more to hear if Georg has arrived. When she picks up the phone I hear his voice in the background and a dog barking. Whose dog is that? I ask. It's Georg's, Tuva says laughing, he got it from the dogs' home, and who do you think is going to end up looking after it?

Sudden rage.

Jesus, how braindead are you, I scream. We can't sit here talking about dogs now, don't you get that?

Yeah, no shit, Tuva says angrily, and hangs up.

This is all Anita's fault, bloody traitor, if it had not been for the telephone call with her I would not have screamed at Tuva.

Anita the cunt, I yell, fucking selfish cunt, you're not the only one with a daughter.

Neither am I.

Selfish cunt.

Eriksen rings from reception. I hear Annika's mellow *hej* first, followed by the terse, macho tone of Eriksen's voice, no doubt attractive to some, it depends on who is listening, but I am unresponsive, everything within me is oriented towards Lars Erik, in his voice lies the Promised Land.

I'm coming up, okay?

Oh, he is handsome, I can see that, a powerful cranium and a broad chest, hairy hands, but it is mostly in the way he moves, calmly and self-assured: here comes a man with his strengths in check, he has control and it makes my knickers wet, even though he is not my cup of tea.

Old and frightened.

We're searching for him at several potential sites. Eriksen is standing in the middle of the room, examining my mobile while he speaks.

There are psychiatric issues, you see.

Yes, I say. I told you as much.

True, true, Eriksen replies, you did. But at that stage we were already aware of him. He has been regarded as a person of interest in our investigation for some time.

I reckon he's in the woods, I say.

Could be, Eriksen answers, but, like I say, there are several possibilities.

He pockets my mobile. I'm going to hang on to this, in case he tries to get in touch again, he says. If there is anything, you can ring me from the phone in this room.

He takes a sheet of stationery from the hotel welcome pack and writes down two mobile numbers. You can call either of these, or the emergency number if you can't get through. But it's very unlikely you'll have any need to, as long as you stay here. He is dangerous, you know.

Eriksen smells good, I do not know if it is aftershave or deodorant but I take a step closer to him.

Can you give me a hug? I ask.

Eriksen does not budge.

We can arrange for you to see a psychologist if you'd like, he says, I can request a patrol car to take you to A&E.

No, I say, no. It's just, I don't know, a bit of a strain.

Well, imagine what it's like for her parents, Eriksen says, just imagine.

I hear my mobile ring as he goes out the door, but it is no longer my concern, I think that I put up with too much, just to avoid responsibility, and that Eriksen is a cheeky bastard.

I lift the receiver of the room telephone, tap zero for an outside line, followed by Lars Erik's number. When he answers I am no longer nervous.

Hi, I say. It's the writer.

It takes a moment before he says anything and I do not know what to make of that, whether he is nervous, surprised or does not like the sudden intrusion, the unexpected sound of my voice in his ear. I cannot quite decipher the tone of his voice when he does say hello. It might be pleasure or scepticism, or it might not denote anything in particular. Perhaps he is with his lover, perhaps she, or he, is looking at him with an expectant expression while he is talking.

He must not hear that I need him.

You have to be able to take care of yourself. I have never been able to take care of myself. What can I say so as not to give that away? That I have never really stood on my own two feet, I do not know why.

Yes, sorry for calling, I say, but I just wanted to, well, I don't know, this is maybe slightly abrupt, but, I don't mean to be pushy.

But but but, every time I said *but* I was giving myself away, revealing false humility, *excuse me for existing*, letting slip an inability to keep desire restrained, not managing to hold back, because I so want, I want so desperately to be close to Lars Erik. To look at his body. His collarbone. Those angular shoulders beneath his shirt. His penis beneath the material of his trousers, flaccid in the darkness. How can I arrest that urge? The train is moving and I am on it, thundering forward. I am the train. What is this desire, why does it exist, what am I supposed to do with it? Keep myself alive? Hardly. The children keep me alive because I need to keep them alive. That is the cornerstone of the pyramid, the bottom level, the base, *the foundation*. The question of hope shows up on the next level: is there any hope, *can something soon break through, blow up, pulverise the wall closing out paradise to such an extent that I do not know what paradise holds, but it is not fruit trees and tropical heat.*

So what is love? Caring in perfect equilibrium, to hold and be held? No, that is too small, too vague, an indifferent statement with no rejoinder in the world of the corporeal. Arms sweeping glasses and pots off a kitchen worktop in rage, flinging plates through the air, humiliation ticking and pounding, people throwing themselves on the floor in despair, screaming the most terrible things, and still that does not qualify as hate. It is merely insufficient love. But when is it enough? Is it when I am enthralled by another person, want to take in every centimetre of them with my gaze *and love every bone in their body*?

I ask and ask, but bang against a barrier in my mind, no answer appears, I come no further, blurry images of village squares and arid fields appear, a church, a graveyard, stone walls, sheep grazing. Either they are irrelevant or incomprehensible, apart from showing limited areas. Does that imply that love operates in sectors? One for a child. One for a dog. One for a friend. One for mother and father and sister and brother. For lover and grandmother. For God.

Yes, because some say that love is for God and from God, a pervasion of spirit, that spirituality makes you love the world and all in the world as yourself, and the world spirit is the highest. Or God, in other words. I have no sense of that. Have no sense of God. No sense of anything. Oh, why can I not access the spiritual too, why has my hope of all-encompassing love taken form in this one body, this man, this person, this wonderful being? As the only possible key to, yes, to what? I do not know, but it is a paradise.

I tell Lars Erik about the police and the hotel. The man in the baseball cap. The photograph on the mobile.

It doesn't sound good, he says, and I nod at the sound of his voice. What is it I hear? A deeper tone of voice or is he holding the telephone closer to his mouth? Is it empathy?

Something reminiscent of Mum's bookshelves on clear, white winter days.

The shelves went from floor to ceiling. Row upon row of book spines. It was the weekend perhaps, or else I had finished school early and was lying on the sofa. Mum was airing the room. The smell of snow came in puffs through the open window. The covers of the books were cool and smooth, one book after the other closed and put back on the shelf, in place. The cushions were plumped up, the coffee table cleaned. Framed pictures behind glass hung between the shelves, shiny and still. Nothing disquieting was to be found in the room, no despair, nothing that could topple, or fall, nobody screaming or crying.

Lars Erik's voice.

Do you want to come over?

31

Emilie should not have been walking alone on the road at that precise time. I imagine that is what he thinks. Not in words, of course, more something he feels. That it was not so much his fault, as it were. He could not help it. But it is over now. She is gone. Swallowed by the air. Only her body remains, and in a while neither will that, everything will have disappeared, as though nothing had been, nothing mattered.

No, I do not know.

I have no access to the inner workings of his mind. Flickerings, a lot of light, vague images.

When something that is gone recurs.

In the head. In the hands. In the soul, the heart, the genes. That is inheritance.

In direct descent.

But what is genetic inheritance and what is merely Freudian repetition compulsion?

I think about the process in relation to Granny's death. Her last days. But life is no simple process. All the threads. The path of rage for example. From one generation to the next. The fierce urge to expend energy. The need for intoxication. And the darkness. A will that digs, gnaws, is distraught, at a loss.

I wonder if Granny had images of the sea in her head, if that was why she went there. Did she picture the waves? Did the sea fill her mind because her forebears were from the coast, worked on the sea and were sometimes taken by it? Like her beloved brother Finn.

No, what she saw and what she thought? I do not know, I am fantasising. She probably saw something quite different than I did, but just as confusing.

Was she perhaps just filled with restlessness that night? She went to bed but got back up, put something on and walked out through the brightly lit doors of the nursing home without anybody noticing. Maybe her feet just moved of their own accord along the roads she knew so well, out there in Blommenholm, and that was how she ended up on the nearby beach, by chance. Maybe she was not following any plan nor was guided unconsciously by inner images, but it still seems oddly loaded with meaning that she should go there, to the sea. She stripped off nearly all her clothes, lay down on the cool sand and fell asleep. Even though it was June she was freezing when they found her, but if that was the reason she fell into a coma from which she did not come out, I do not know. Nobody said anything about it and neither did I ask. She died within a week, ninety-four years old. I was there with Dad on the last day. They had rung from the hospital and said she would no longer eat, neither solids nor liquids.

Her lips were pale blue and cracked, but she managed to press them hard together when the nurse attempted to moisten her mouth with a cotton bud soaked with liquid. To alleviate the discomfort, she said, this is like dying of thirst.

Granny's eyes were closed and she did not answer when we spoke to her.

Mum, Dad said, Mum. She lay quite still. Cecilie, he said, Cecilie.

Yes, she said then, out loud, yes.

Dad stroked her across the cheek with one finger. Back and forth. I do not think it was a caress. He was looking for a reaction. Look, he said, look, she is smacking her lips. It's because I provoked the sucking reflex.

I nodded.

Shall we go? Dad asked. And then we left.

32

Dr Vold going and dying at such an early age. Oh, how typical, life had always been like this to her, she had endured a harsh, brutal existence, everything was taken from her.

It was many years ago, but she still cannot think of that day when she found out without crying, she can still sense the smells around her at that very moment, the heat of the apartment, the light in the room, it was early evening, in June, shortly after her seventieth birthday, an exceptionally hot day.

It was all so sudden, she was utterly unprepared. Because she had often thought of him, in both one way and the other. As company in lonely, heated hours at night, alone in her bed, and yet not so very lonely, not when she could fetch *him* from within. Or as somebody to converse with on bad days, when someone had been angry with her. If one of the children had rung up and given her a ticking off over the telephone, or a shop girl had been impertinent, and thus brought her to the verge of tears. Then she would, as it were, turn to him and they would discuss the matter. Her thoughts brimmed over on occasion also, on long rainy mornings, or in the winter, when it was cold and dark, then she could become so clear-headed, solve one important question after another, and Dr Vold was almost certainly the only person who would understand. Then she made up conversations between them.

But she particularly needed him when difficulties piled up and she could not take any more, when being herself simply became too much and she realised that now, now she needed to telephone or send him a letter. But then nothing came of it. She spoke to him in her head and the worst of it blew over, after a few days' wait. It was impossible to understand, considering how easy it would have been for her to make an appointment with him. He had started his own clinic. She knew that much, because he wrote articles for the newspaper and it was there in black and white: by psychiatrist and senior consultant Harald Vold. He writes kind words, about consideration, fidelity and benevolence. She had heard him giving a talk on the radio too. That precious voice. Not that he had any marital difficulties. Seeing as *she* was so blasted demure and meek and perfect. That wife. Otherwise Dr Vold would hardly be married to her, oh, no. Never a harsh word between them. Nor did they raise their voices in front of the children. Imagine, they had four children. And the housework was no doubt a lark in *that* home. Ugh.

That was probably it, that she could not come into *his* life. So what would it give her, to converse with him in reality? Just jealousy and despair. She could not have him, so who should she turn to, she did not know anybody similar. She was not good, pretty and kind, like *his wife* was. No, she was angry, selfish and self-indulgent. Vulgar, into the bargain. She had no hope. No, why torture herself by pretending any different, rubbing it in like salt in the wound, and him sitting there all good and kind and noble, while she, oh, she could not face finishing the thought. Because it was precisely his kind-heartedness that made him believe that she was also that way, that she was like him. His thoughts were pure. But she knew better. She was aware of the nastiness inside her while he had likely just seen it in others, heard them speak, seen them weep, he could not know how an inner darkness *really* took shape. Like an infection, doctor, an ugly, malignant infection, for which *there is no cure*. Nevertheless, beneath it all she had perhaps harboured the tiniest hope, something she herself had not been aware had kept her up.

Because that evening she had fallen. As sure as if she had been standing on something.

It had been insufferably hot, perhaps close to thirty degrees, and she had hardly had the energy to do anything all day, but had lain in bed for the most part, listening to gramophone records and reading some articles in *Reader's Digest*. When the sun finally shifted from the windows she got up, opened the balcony door wide and all the windows in the other rooms. That caused a nice draught and made the living room bearable. She fetched a bottle of beer from the refrigerator, picked up the newspaper from the floor in the hall, but did not see what was on the front page before she spread it out on the coffee table. A jolt in her chest, several, she read the sentences in a staccato:

Dr Harald Vold unexpected death. Much too soon. An authority. A pioneer. Founder of the clinic. Highly respected. Loved by his patients. Colleagues and family.

Loved.

So it was too late. She would never make an appointment at the clinic, never see him again. Never enter his office. Sit on the chair he always had at an angle to his desk.

Their talks in his office.

That time. The emotions from back then swept through her. How strong. How in the midst of everything she was.

The children, she thought. The house. Oh, God, Finn. The warmth in Dr Vold's eyes. His brown office. It was in Kristian Augusts gate. You could hear the trams passing on the street below, and their sound had made her so expectant, she suddenly recalled. It was probably the freedom of being in town. Of thinking that she could hop on a tram at any moment. Hold on to the strap and look out the windows. At each stop new houses, different streets, unfamiliar faces. Well, she *had* made it into town eventually, but there was hardly any freedom to speak of. Not like she had dreamt.

When it all came down to it she had hardly been so bad a person that *he* could not bear her, no, that was suddenly clear to her now, that he must have even liked her, she was only human after all, and the doctor thought well of people.

He never sank down in them.

Now it was too late. She was out of time. She had not settled it, now it was final. Disconsolate, because so much had happened to her in life, and that was after all why they, her and Dr Vold, had agreed that she would go back to him when the divorce was well and truly over, then they would continue their conversations. But she did not go, and therefore nothing was properly cleared up, but remained vague, deadened, the apartment became her little mouse hole, as though she were packed in duvets and left in peace. But the peace was not *in* her, only surrounding her, like the fact that nobody came to visit if she did not want them to, she was in charge of herself and her own affairs. And in time she had got a television and her own pension. No, but she had made a big mistake, she understood that now, sitting there sobbing in her living room, while at the same time she noticed that the draught was a bit much, her neck was becoming stiff, she ought to shut some of the windows but could not get to her feet due to all the tears flowing from her.

Oh, Dr Vold, do you know what my biggest mistake was? No, do not mention what I did to Finn and the terrible consequences that had, I really cannot take the blame for that.

No, it was the brooch.

She now knows what she should have done all that time it was lying in the hollow of the desk lamp. Week after week she had gone to the doctor's office and the enamel pin with the curved tulip leaves still lay there.

She should have talked to him about it. *They* should have talked about it, together. She should have asked to hold it in her hand and he should have let her. She should have described to him what she saw and told him why she wanted so much to have it. He should have asked and she should have answered. Because it is so beautiful, was the first thing she should have said, the green colour is so clear and deep, and the curved leaves, yes, they look both willing and determined, they are opening and striving at the same time. In one direction, do you understand what I mean? And look at that gilded edge, the areas of gold, so clearly defined, each colour in its place, no doubt whatsoever. If I could wear this, I would have felt quite different. Like the Cecilie Viker I want to be.

Dr Vold would have smiled and delighted in such beautiful speech. Naturally he could not give her the brooch as a gift. She was well aware of that. It belonged to another woman, who had lost it, or thrown it in despair and now it lay at the doctor's awaiting its owner. No, it was not Cessi's, but they could talk about it. He would allow her to pin it to her blouse so she could feel how she was about to become. Describe it to me, he would say, who are you now?

That was how they would have talked, about the pin, and he would also have held it in his own hand, studied it closely in order to understand why it was so important.

Yes, it is beautiful, he would say, stylish, the work of an artist.

That would have transformed her. There would be no way back from her words, their conversation would have led her over to the right side of everything. She would have known that Dr Vold knew. About her. It would have been the first step.

Oh, Dr Vold, time ran out, she wailed into the sofa cushions that Mama had embroidered when young, but then she had to get up and go out, she ran out the door, out into the evening sun in Bygdøy allé. No, she will never forget that day. He was dead and as she came out of the shadow of the tall, dark facades of the buildings, for a moment the sun shone between the branches of the chestnut trees and hit her face: the green flickering on the leaves, the dense golden light.

33

I put my finger on the buzzer beside his name. I hear his voice immediately afterwards through the crackly intercom. The sight of the wire-mesh glass in the entrance door. It seems familiar. The motion of the door as I push it open. The smell in the stairwell. As though we have already slept together.

I leave wet marks on the linoleum-covered stairs. He lives on the third floor. The windows on each landing are on the latch, probably due to how muggy it is out, the insides of the panes are misted up and I notice the smell of wet earth from the lawn in the back garden. The wind brings the rain in gusts, the treetops bend, the undersides of the leaves turning towards the sky.

He is standing in the doorway waiting. A long body dressed in a white T-shirt and jeans. His upper arms are smooth, I want to run my tongue over them, or, I do not feel the difference between my tongue and the flats of my hands, do not know if I want my tongue or my palms to suck him in.

Hi, he says, hi, and bows slightly, he bows to me and steps aside, invites me in, places his hand on my back as I pass, an inclusive gesture. The hallway smells of lilac and coffee. The kitchen door is open and I can see a candle and two cups on the table. I ask if he has company, but he does not, only you, he says.

I remove my shoes, I must have got wet, I say, it's really bucketing down.

He asks if I would like to borrow a jumper and I nod, yes please, I say, gladly, and I wonder if he thinks I am pretty, or does not think about it at all, I wonder how I look, I wish my gaze could speak for me.

I stand watching him from behind as he walks down the hall and opens a door at the far end. His left hip gives slightly with each step he takes, I think it is beautiful, but maybe it is due to a slight misalignment in his back, that long, slender back. I wonder why he is so thin, I suspect you can see his hipbones protrude when he is naked. A slightly rounded stomach, I can imagine, a narrow strip of hair going from his privates up to his navel, I can feel my hand on his stomach, between his hipbones.

The door closes almost completely behind him, I hear the click of a switch, see a stream of light in the chink of the doorway, the bedroom most likely, and he is now standing in front of his wardrobe looking through the shelves for a jumper for me.

The jumper is blue and soft. He looks down over my body as he hands it to me, blushes and says he probably does not have any trousers that would fit. I look at his mouth and think how it has been like that since he was born, and all the same we have not known about each other until now.

I go into the bathroom to change. The tiles are warm beneath my feet. I see no signs of a woman, no trace of more than one person. The glass on the sink has one toothbrush in it and the deodorant in the mirror cabinet smells of man. The same smell as the blue jumper. I am soaked to the skin and take everything off, including my bra, before pulling on the jumper. I leave my blouse to dry on the grey and white floor tiles. There is a dark blue toilet bag on top of the washing machine, which is on a cycle, everything is neat and tidy in the room. The basin is clean and the soap is new, it is black, slightly translucent, some sort of natural soap, ecological.

If only this could begin. If only it were possible.

A heavy blue dressing gown hangs from a hook on the door. I wonder if the days and nights have been lonely, if he has put on the dressing gown and walked to the kitchen with heavy steps? Has he sat face down on folded arms crying into its soft material? Has he felt sad and looked out the window, uncomprehendingly, as children do not comprehend when they feel unloved? Or am I the one who has done that, yes, it is me, who has lived so many years in the belly of unhappiness, curled up, sloshing around in lethargy, shapelessness and self-pity. Not him. Or, what do I know, precious little. When I come into the kitchen he puts his arms around me and holds me. It lasts for maybe a minute. We breathe evenly.

Lars Erik fetches the coffee cups and switches on the TV. We come straight into extended coverage of a news item, just as the newsreader says they are going over to their colleague on the scene. The picture changes and we see a reporter standing with a microphone in front of the gates to a house. It seems so familiar, I think confusedly, am I not actually well aware of where this is? Perhaps thoughts are always slower on the uptake than senses, or is it just the camera lens rendering my house unfamiliar? Because of course it is my house and I understood that immediately: the gate, gateposts, trees along the drive, the many windows, the front door; it is home.

That's my place! I cry.

Shush, Lars Erik says, hang on, they're saying something.

I see all the policemen being filmed in the garden. They are moving so slowly, I think, and it seems oddly pointless, I can see no meaning to their movements.

They have pinpointed someone's location in the house and the police are aware of their identity but cannot give any more information at the present time, the reporter says. This is repeated in the studio before the news presenter asks the same questions again, and the reporter gives similar answers, only in different words.

It's the man in the baseball cap, I say, it's him, I'm sure!

Lars Erik looks at me but does not say anything and that is not so strange. He does not know any more about the man in the cap than what I have told him and that was not much. Perhaps he thinks he is a figment of my imagination and that I am not all there, perhaps he is just going along with everything I say.

Oh God, this pressure inside!

Emilie. When he took her. Long and thin. Soft. Only a child. I picture her. *She does not understand.* Her eyes. *Straining to understand.* Frightened. She used to hum when she was out walking. Took photos of herself with her mobile. Or of the trees, the dog. When she saw me she lit up. I was someone she could talk to. She always had something she wanted to discuss. How dogs thought. Why the leaves of some trees 'piddled', as she put it, dripped sticky goo onto the tarmac, onto her hair. Why I was always at home. What she would do with my garden if she were me.

I do not think she is alive.

It is over.

The parents.

Jesus.

He must have broken in after I left. By way of the veranda door, I guess. It was not locked in any case. I turned the key and left it open before going out to sit in the police car, I could not face any more. I was completely exhausted. The house could not protect me. He could just enter. I was never going back anyway.

I do not understand how the TV stations found out about the police operation so quickly. It must have been the neighbours. Some of them telephoned. They have stood out in their gardens, behind windows, out on the road and filmed what was happening with mobile phones and then sent the film clips off to the news desks. Not that it bothers me, as long as someone puts things right they can do what they want, as long as I am spared doing it.

Lift this from on top of me!

The cameras zoom in on the garden, showing Dad's unsightly stacks, the police have taken them apart, placed things all over the grass. Plastic drums, a washing machine, car tyres, planks, corrugated sheeting. Georg's old kick-sledge. We often used it on days with snowfall. Started up at the Montessori school and went downhill, kicked across the tramlines, past the house and down to Slemdal. How he laughed.

They film the darkened windows and one of the cameras catches movement, something pale, a face. Look, I shout, and the reporter shouts as well. The cameraman must break into a run because the picture shakes, but we see that the police react, looking first towards the house, before running quickly away, as simultaneously we hear shots. He's shooting, the reporter shouts and the camera shakes again, filming suddenly the tops of the pine trees in the garden, black sky, I recognise the crunching of the gravel in the drive, we hear breathing and swearing and rain trickles across the camera lens, the TV screen.

Nobody is injured, but we aren't allowed to stay here, the reporter shouts, his voice mingling with the shouts of the police in the background: move back, we need everyone to move back.

The presenters in the studio do not appear to know they are on air. They are not looking towards the camera and their expressions show concern, their features slack. A panel of experts composed of a psychiatrist, an expert on criminal violence and a police investigator begin discussing among themselves, they sip water from their glasses, look pale. The camera gradually zooms in on one of the presenters. She must have been given an update, I do not know how, maybe on a screen we cannot see. She tries to gather herself, searches for words to smooth things over, frame the situation, render it safe and understandable, but she makes several slips of the tongue.

A man has taken up residence in the house of a previous suspect in the case, she says, pardon me, has taken refuge in the residence of a previous, no, excuse me, sorry, the residence in question belongs to an individual with the status of witness. The individual concerned is under police protection and is not currently at home. We do not know if there are any others in the house.

Then a summing up of the case, using past footage. Of the house. My face. A search party moving in a line. Emilie's face.

Lars Erik switches off the TV. It's not certain he has

Emilie with him, he says, placing the remote control on the table.

I look at his hand and think how soon it will be touching me, and I must be sick in the head to entertain that thought right now. But it is not thought. It is everything at once, I am being thrown back and forth, am in all places at all times, it is chaos. I need to make this stop, I think, but the next moment my body is filled with anticipation, tingling all over because I know something is going to happen. Even though I do not know what, it will come, yes, it has happened already, something with Lars Erik and me. Sweet and good. The next moment I see Emilie and the dog, how they walk down the road, on dry tarmac, they have turned the familiar corner and are approaching my house. I feel the dog's fur under my hand and perceive the scent of Emilie's hair as she crouches down beside me. At the same time I breathe in the smell of the garden after rain and picture Granny as she walked across the floor of her apartment, slightly bow-legged and unsteady, slow-moving. And I see Dad. He is driving the car with Granny sitting beside him, I am in the back seat, Dad jams on the brakes, we are not driving very fast but we all lurch forward, and Granny turns to him and says, Fuck, Finn. And then they laugh. I see the empty garden, dense and dark, and become so sad I nearly fall, because I recognise this darkness, it pulls downward and downward, like a plumb, or it is rooted.

Isn't there anything we can do? I ask.

His type, Lars Erik says, they don't go far. He uses places nearby to build his sick fantasies around, I'm sure of it. To provide them with, like, a charge. She's probably hidden close by. In the woods maybe, but not far in.

I see the man in the baseball cap in my mind's eye, and nod, because that is exactly what I would imagine he is like.

Residential areas, gardens, there weren't many places to search, Lars Erik continues, and we combed that area, along the train line too. But, of course, that was several days ago.

There are also spinneys and thicket in the area, I say, behind Slemdal School, for instance, and if you follow Stasjonsveien you come to Holmendammen lake and the patch of woodland by the kindergarten, the stream, the trail leading further up.

Sure, but there're always people there, hikers, kids, people walking their dogs, difficult to hide someone, don't you think?

I have put my blouse back on, it is synthetic and dries quickly. The material is white and smooth, my nipples protrude beneath when I am cold, becoming stiff, but I am not cold now, it is warm in the apartment, they stiffen all the same, and they ought not to, not now we are talking about where Emilie could be.

I don't know, I say, I just have the feeling you're right, that she isn't far away but somewhere in or around Slemdal.

Then that's where we'll go, he says. Don't you think that would be best? That we search?

I nod, and put his blue jumper on over the blouse.

We walk to Majorstua station. It is raining heavily and umbrellas are useless in the strong wind. The water runs down our faces and our clothes are soon soaked through and cold against the skin. I sit close beside Lars Erik on the underground on the way up. The damp material of our jeans warms up where our thighs are touching.

Going to search feels like the right thing to do, I say,

hoping with that I can choose a good version of myself, that the will to act is the way to go, because that is how I want to be: strong-willed and able to act. Together with Lars Erik.

He nods but does not say anything and straight away I realise I should not have either. We cannot sit here talking loudly about Emilie where anyone could hear. And it is not me I should be thinking of but her, she is only a child and needs to go home now, whether she is alive or dead. Yet my self-contemplation continues: I must have a hole in my personality, I think, where compassion leaks out and Lars Erik has probably noticed it by now, he must have heard it in my tone of voice, what a paltry person I am, my humanity is a skin to be shed. Now all of me is visible, exposed.

But Lars Erik takes my hand as we stand up to get off at Slemdal. As though we were a couple. That must be what it looks like as we walk closely along the platform in the rain. If people only knew how it all was.

We cross the train line and take a left onto Stasjonsveien. A police car passes, followed by an ambulance, but neither are sounding the sirens or going at speed. They drive up Gulleråsveien, probably on the way to my house.

We'll take a look around the school grounds, Lars Erik suggests, she went here after all. He must have had his eye on the school. Watched all the children. Picked her out. I just don't understand what it's got to do with you.

I didn't tell the police, I say. But she stopped to talk to me a few times. With the dog. I didn't dare mention it. I mean, they suspected me.

You should have told them all the same. Better than keeping quiet.

We walk past the bronze statue of the wild boar on the way into the school playground, the one I used to pat when I was a child.

My dad went to this school too, I say.

What did you say? Lars Erik asks, glancing at his watch, he is pale.

Nothing, I reply.

It makes no difference to Emilie.

We both catch sight of something white lying against the wall of the lean-to at the same time. Lars Erik immediately breaks into a run, reaching it before I do.

A sheet or tablecloth covers the face and body, the arms lying right out to either side, it is easy to see that the hands and fingers belong to a girl, that they may be those of a twelve-year-old. We see the contours of a head, shoulders, hips and knees. The bloodstain that has soaked into the material between the hipbones.

Is she supposed to be laid out like a cross, is that it? Does that mean something, is it some sort of message, something I should understand? My brain struggles but everything comes to a halt at the boundaries: the dead body, the tarmac, the grass, sky, cars passing on Risalleen. There is no other meaning.

Jesus. Mum.

How will I manage this?

Just be glad it is not Tuva or Georg lying there, you be glad, I whisper to myself, be glad, be glad.

Lars Erik is on his knees. What is he doing, is he crawling? Yes, he is moving towards the white sheet on all fours, but is it happening quickly or slowly?

There is something about my knees too, the ground is coming closer.

Her hands sticking out. Lars Erik crouches beside her. He places two fingers on the inside of the closest wrist. The muscles in his back move beneath the wet shirt.

No pulse, he says, but you can be mistaken, it may be so weak that I can't feel it. He lifts the sheet away from her face. She is blue, or yellow, I can hardly tell, maybe both, it looks as though she is smiling, the corners of her mouth are turned up, the skin has puckered, stiffened. There's no doubt really, Lars Erik says, but still feels for a pulse before replacing the sheet.

Don't look at her any more now, it's not necessary to see everything all the time.

He takes me under the elbow and leads me a few steps away, the white sheet disappears from my field of vision and at first my salivary glands begin to work, then vomit fills my mouth, it streams out, I bend over, place my hand on the wall of the mini football pitch and let it flow, it drips onto the ground and I cry. Lars Erik cries too.

It's not good for you to see too much either, I say, but that's different, he replies. It's my duty, I'm in the Red Cross. I'm in the Red Cross, he repeats, and that protects me, so that I can protect you. You're not supposed to be alone, you see, it's no good being one person, when you're faced with something like this.

It goes black, and I lurch forward, the ground coming to meet me as I call out something, try to call out. When I come round I am lying with my head in Lars Erik's lap and he is holding his mobile to his ear, I hear him say yes, hear that he is talking to someone. Yes, he says again, we're at the school playground.

It's under control, he says to me, putting the mobile down on the ground beside him. They're on their way.

Yes, I say, I can hear the sirens.

It's the police, he says. I've called them. The ambulance. The police. They're coming to take care of things. To look after all this. Tidy up, drive her away, wash everything down, speak to the journalists. Get the formalities in order. That's why they're here. It can be too much for one person.

But we can't go yet, I say, don't go, we can't leave her here alone.

No, we're not going anywhere, Lars Erik says, we're here now.